THE MAGIC OF
TREE FARM

ERIN GREEN was born and raised in Warwickshire, where she resides with her husband. She writes contemporary novels focusing on love, life and laughter. An ideal day for Erin involves writing, people watching and copious amounts of tea. Erin was delighted to be awarded The Katie Fforde Bursary in 2017 and previously, Love Stories 'New Talent Award' in 2015. For more about Erin, visit her website or follow her on Twitter.

THE MAGIC OF CHRISTMAS TREE FARM

Erin Green

First published in the United Kingdom in 2018 by Aria, an imprint of
Head of Zeus Ltd

9 7 5 3 1 2 4 6 8

A CIP catalogue record for this book is available from the British
Library.

ISBN 9781786697974

Aria
an imprint of Head of Zeus
First Floor East
5–8 Hardwick Street
London EC1R 4RG

About *The Magic of Christmas Tree Farm*

The scent of pine fills the crisp air as local villagers select their perfect tree. Picking the tree is the easy bit, creating a perfect Christmas is a bit trickier…

Nina has the most magical job in the world, matching customers with their perfect Christmas tree. Working at Christmas Tree Farm is always fun and full of laughter but the weight of past tragedy bears down on her. Her admirer is a great distraction, but is he the right man for her?

Holly is just trying to be a normal teenager, having to deal with the mean girls in her class. But then the most handsome boy at school takes an interest in her. Have all her Christmases come at once?

Angie is trying to bring her family together and save her broken marriage. It's not something she can force, but it's the only gift she craves. Will her Christmas wish come true?

It's the season of goodwill, and at Christmas Tree Farm anything could happen…

Also by Erin Green

Single Girl's Calendar

A Christmas Wish

Dedicated: to that precious moment when your stomach flips

One

Nina

Saturday, 8 December

The Christmas trees loom overhead dominating the morning's inky skyline, as I trudge along the farm's muddy driveway towards a busy eleven-hour shift.

The dawn chorus hasn't started yet; there's nothing around at this hour, apart from a stray fox on his morning prowl, as the birds prepare their opening notes. Despite the serenity, my heart feels like a lump of coal wedged behind my ribs.

My torch bumps against my leg as I walk the lonely track even though I don't use it. It's purely for emergencies, as I know the route like the back of my hand. The farm dominates the local area providing a green and pleasant boundary to our tiny village of Baxterley.

The air is thick with the fragrant smell of the Norway spruce planted each side of the dirt track. Mature trees planted decades ago resemble giants; their outstretched branches hang low as if greeting my early arrival to work.

A flash of red catches my eye: there he is, my fat robin bouncing on a spruce bough, his head twitching and his beady eye watching me, before taking flight. I say 'my' – he's one of many living amongst the Christmas trees, but I pretend there's only one, *mine*.

'Welcome to the Christmas Tree Farm,' I whisper to him as he perches on the farm gate. The farm's wooden five-barred gate bears a decorative sign overhead proudly declaring 'Grower of the Year – Champion Tree', which we won at the British Christmas Tree Growers' Association's annual competition – the equivalent of a five-star accolade for any restaurant or hotel, an award my boss is eager to promote to the public.

'Our Christmas trees are categorised by species and cut to size. Please ask if you can't find the spruce you require.' After nine years, I don't need to practise my selling spiel but do purely through habit.

I release the metal latch and tether the gate open, and enter in preparation for a busy day. It'll save someone having to run down later to unlatch it.

I'm permanent all year round. There are not many of us – Boss Fielding hires and lays off a crowd of casual workers each year. Thankfully, I proved myself to be a hard worker long ago, so get to enjoy the beauty of this farm all year round.

I sat my exams in June 2009, left school and a week later started work here – who'd have thought Christmas trees needed nurturing in July? That was nine years ago; couldn't say how many trees I've sold in that time.

An icy wind blows. The forecasters have been threatening snowfall across Warwickshire – such a prediction is guaranteed to make my boss happy. Snowfall increases Christmas tree sales as a sunny day increases ice-cream sales. Though, for us farm workers it means working in snow drifts and blizzards. It's one thing breaking your back to sell spruces to the general public, but another game clearing tonnes of snow prior to a shift to make the farm safe for public access.

I continue along the rutted but lengthy track, wide enough for tractors, which can be dark and gloomy at this time of year, yet I'm never lonely here. How can anyone ever be lonely whilst surrounded by nature, and her ever-changing beauty? Each season delivers its own delights – winter is simply the pinnacle of our year.

I've learnt that if my hands are busy, my mind is occupied too. That's the magic of Christmas Tree Farm – there's always a warmth and excitement which helps me to forget… A lengthy shift filled with chaotic families browsing, selecting and, sadly for some, arguing over their choice of Christmas tree is what I need. You wouldn't believe the time taken by some families to choose their tree and we only sell four species: Blue spruce, Nordman fir, Norway spruce or a Fraser fir.

Even when the type of tree is selected, some argue about the height: a teeny weeny, a standard or the ultimate jolly green giant. Most families buy just one so I understand their desire for perfection. *Their* perfect spruce can equal their perfect Christmas. Occasionally, some families purchase multiple trees: one for the lounge, another for their hallway and a tree with roots that can be planted in the front garden. We charge by the foot, so it can be an expensive purchase and cost can be the deciding factor. At some point today, I'm bound to hear the age-old remark, 'Or should we leave it and dust off the old plastic one from the loft?' I'll smile, pretend I didn't hear and hope they don't ignore our range of beautiful spruces. In my opinion, you can't beat a real Christmas tree – guaranteeing seasonal cheer *and* a gorgeous fragrance. If push comes to shove and they are still contemplating the dusty artificial one in preference to our beauties, I'll swiftly move the family towards a Norway spruce and accidentally charge the wrong price. Call it what you will, Christmas spirit or seasonal kindness, the boss will never know. Let's face it; life's too short to worry about money. Our spruces will be bare, brown and beside the dustbin come 6 January, so you need to enjoy them while you can.

Today is the opening day of the season, 8 December. If it's anything like the last nine Christmas seasons, I'll dash between families, trying my very best to fetch, carry and answer every plausible question thanks to my extensive knowledge of each species. I'll smile sweetly, serve mulled wine and warmed mince pies and greet everyone as they arrive at the farm.

*

The farm's yard spreads before me. Lit by overhead floodlights, it's a vast open space dedicated to spruce sales. Already 'Little Drummer Boy' is festively par-rum-pum-pum-pumming through the tinny speakers conveniently positioned out of reach of disgruntled staff. I haven't heard the tracks for an entire year, but I can recall the sequence of twenty songs from previous years.

'Nina!' cries Bram, dressed in his thermal coat and steel-toe-capped boots, as I turn the corner of the first log cabin, affectionately known as the cashier's cabin. 'Have I got a treat for you!'

I smile as his deep voice greets me. Bram, the eldest of the boss's identical twins, thinks that every time he asks me out on a date it will be the time I accept. What he fails to remember is that we are close friends. We've been best friends for life since our year seven maths class. A tight friendship, which includes his younger twin Zach. Their characters are like chalk and cheese, or rather a Blue spruce compared to a Norway spruce. Both

13

are strong, sturdy specimens, well nurtured and in their prime.

The transition towards dating either of them feels a bit icky; the anomaly of mixing business with pleasure doesn't feel right. The twins have grown up on the farm, amongst the vast fields located on the north, south and east side of their sturdy farmhouse.

'Morning, Bram, let's hear it!' I drag my beanie off my head, ruffle my mousy-brown locks and watch as his animated features deliver yet another exaggerated plan, probably concocted last night after four pints of Stella in The Rose, the village's only pub.

'Nina... don't give me *that* look... I was thinking we could...'

I don't hear his suggestion. His grey eyes dance with excitement, long blond lashes flutter like butterfly wings and his mouth, well, it doesn't stop moving. His dad, Boss Fielding, calls him Motor-mouth behind his back and the work force laugh at the age-old joke. Abraham loves being the noisy, over-the-top, competitive twin. 'It's better than being Zach!' is his usual comeback.

'So, what do you think?' He falls silent and waits, pushing his blond fringe back and into shape. My answer will be the same as it always is.

'Oh, Bram... what can I say?' I whisper, flattered that he still finds the energy to chase me after many rejections. He's offered me numerous dates: candlelit dinners, hikes up Snowdon, a weekend at V Festival, breaks in Barcelona and even skiing in Austria. Funnily enough the weekend spent fly fishing was an easy 'no'.

I head towards the snug, our designated staffroom, another log cabin positioned alongside the cashier's cabin.

'Come on, Nina.' He strides after me; he knows my routine. 'I promise, I'll be a true gent... treat you like a lady.'

I dash up the wooden steps, push open the heavy door and am greeted by the warmth of the snug's wood-burning stove. An eclectic mix of donated sofas, armchairs and coffee tables make for a cosy room.

'You'll wine and dine me, you say?' I ask, unzipping my jacket.

'I swear, I'll treat you like a lady!'

'Abraham! You amaze me...' I say, a coy smile escaping my pretence. I can't pretend I'm not flattered and I admire his determination.

'So, what's it to be, Nina?' he asks, giving a cheeky wink.

'Bram... we'd ruin what we have.' I cross to the coat racks and remove my jacket. Bram follows me.

'We *won't*. What do you say?'

I hang my jacket on my named peg, decorated with a carved plaque; an honour only bestowed upon permanent staff members. Some staff have already arrived and changed into their work scruffs but Shazza's peg is empty – she'll arrive with seconds to spare. Kitty's quilted mac is already hung up. Beneath each peg sits the owner's plastic box of clothing, personal items brought from home in which to dress and build layers against the cold.

'I say, we've been mates for thirteen years and I value our friendship!'

'I don't. You're the crappiest friend a guy could have... you don't do drinking games, you hate football and you never agree to my plans.'

'Just think what a nightmare I'd be as a girlfriend, then. I'd be complaining all the time, texting around the clock and demanding to know your whereabouts on the hour every hour. There, does that feel better?'

'No! It feels like a sodding rejection *again...*'

Bram shakes his head, leans against the old battered couch, as I grab my designated storage box to dress in my additional layers.

We've been through this same routine a million times since day one. He's not leching – that's not his style. We never feel uncomfortable around each other. Bram and Zach are my best friends, and that's how it's going to stay.

I snap closed the press studs on my red tabard, rummage in the large front pocket to ensure no one has nicked my marker pen, notepad or woollen gloves. Today, I'm in luck.

'Nina Salloway... you'll be the death of me.'

'Let's hope so,' I jibe, grabbing my thermal coat complete with the company logo and my Christian name embroidered across the back, and pull it on. 'Come on, race you to clock on.'

'Nina!'

'Stop it, Bram. The conversation is over.' I head towards the door as Shazza hastily enters like a blonde whirlwind, muttering a greeting plus a brief excuse about younger siblings hogging the bathroom. 'Morning, Shaz. Anyway, Bram, I bet you "White Christmas" starts playing after this track.'

Bram shakes his head, purses his lips and follows me from the snug. 'You love me really.'

'With *all* my heart.'

*

Angie

'Can we talk?' I ask into my mobile phone. Nick's silence lengthens. This doesn't feel promising. Having spent a ten-minute drive thinking, practising and repeating a lengthy speech to forget it all the minute I park at Christmas Tree Farm, I have just one task for this morning: to choose *my* tree. So why am I calling him? 'Nick?'

'What?'

'Did you hear me?'

'Angie, I heard you but... I really don't know what to say.' His voice is monotone, untrusting and sadly, lacking in eagerness to please me. 'What is it you want to discuss?'

'*Us.*' Christ, could the man make it any more difficult? Throw me a line here, *please*.

I can hear his breathing, a series of sporadic sighs laden with uncertainty.

During my solo practice run-through, he jumped at the chance of my suggestion, ended the phone call and was mid-journey heading my way.

This isn't supposed to happen. Aren't I granting him what he's repeatedly asked for throughout the last eleven months? And yet, he's now stalling. I obviously don't know the man as well as I thought I did. *Pity.*

'Look, Angie, what more is there for *us* to discuss?'

'Nick…' My words run dry. My prepared speech has fallen flat and now my own cogs are failing to connect and produce a viable explanation. 'Can we go for a drink? Tonight?' I hastily add, not wanting him to choose something midweek, forcing me to relive this episode morning, noon and night whilst waiting for our prearranged meeting. *'Please?'*

He is thinking, *still*.

What is there to consider? Surely, you jump in with a 'Yes, I'd love to' or an 'Of course, name the place and I'll be there.' Even an unexpected, 'Your place or mine?' would be better than this.

But no, total silence.

'Shall we say eight o'clock outside The Rose at Baxterley?' I say, battling the fear of rejection. Surely neutral territory away from our home town of Atherstone is a reasonable suggestion? I preferred the good old days when mobile lines crackled and broke up – it was better than this humiliation.

'OK. Eight.' The line goes dead from his end.

I look at my screen to confirm: he's gone.

'Bloody hell, Nick. Thanks for nothing,' I screech. I have a good mind to call him straight back and cancel, but fight the urge, knowing I'd be causing hurt to only one person. I fling my mobile into my handbag before I can speed dial.

I undo my seat belt and then sit back. A brief glance in my mirror confirms that my roots need touching up, though my messy bun is forgiving for my age.

Crowds of excited customers bustle past my car bonnet: old, young, couples, families, children holding hands, skipping – all festive and cheery on a Saturday mid-morning. Here I sit alone chastising myself and nursing a bruised ego; only yesterday I vowed to remain single.

Could this be any more depressing.

I sit watching the happy families through a misty windscreen, which is rapidly diminishing my view, waiting for my annoyance to subside. But it's impossible to escape the replay in my head when I asked... or perhaps I begged for a date at The Rose.

How has this happened? Surely, I should be like the passing parade of happy, smiling people, focusing on creating the perfect Christmas. It should be me sauntering along the rows of pre-cut, netted trees, with a beaker of mulled wine in hand, nibbling on a warmed mince pie. In previous years, I have spent more time at this farm than I care to remember – seeking out the perfect spruce. Each year I have wrestled a tree home, decorated and watered it. My tradition repeated on the first day of sales every year since I've owned a house... so, seventeen, no eighteen years! Bloody hell, where has the time gone?

I want to return home. Do I truly deserve to be denied the annual traditions just because this year, my all-important 'fabulous at forty' has been the crappiest year of my life? And now, Nick. Does he have misgivings too?

I wish I hadn't called.

And *now*, I wish I hadn't driven to Christmas Tree Farm either. As I observe the irritating festive spirit surrounding me, I sink deeper into my car seat.

*

Nina

'Nina!' calls Zach, handing out the hot drinks during our tea break. 'Do you fancy sprinkles or marshmallows on your hot chocolate?'

'Neither,' I reply, knowing my answer will spark a reaction from the other ladies.

'Are you serious?' asks Kitty, her delicate features shooting up to view me. 'Are you feeling OK?'

'I need to start cutting down on sugar.'

'Seriously, there's nothing of you...' Kitty gives me a head tilt and a tender look. Her gentle blue eyes are seriously telling me off.

Kitty Pardoe is slightly older and much wiser than us younger folk but she remembers what it's like to be twenty-five. I've known her since my first day when she took me under her wing. Since then, she's been promoted to chief cashier, but today Kitty's been relegated to sales as Jackie, the boss's wife, is holed up in cashier's cabin given that it's the first day of the season. All morning, like me, Kitty has dragged cut spruce around the sales yard.

We've already had three weeks of wholesale deliveries, before the season started in earnest, and if that isn't enough to kill you before starting the commercial sales I don't know what is. Why any family would show up just after eight o'clock to purchase the first commercial tree of the year is beyond me, but, hey, that's the kind of madness that happens around here come Christmas time. If the opening day is like this, I'd hate to predict what the final Saturday before Christmas will be like.

'If Nina's refusing her marshmallows, I'll have her share,' shouts Shazza, sitting at the far end of the snug, her socked feet planted upon the side of the wood burner.

Zach drops the additional marshmallows onto Shazza's drink before delivering mugs into our eager hands.

'Thank you,' I say.

'My pleasure.'

Kitty looks away but keeps a quizzical eye on Zach as he returns to the kitchen counter to collect his drink and swiftly leaves the snug.

'What?' I ask, as she turns to me and sighs.

'He really likes you...' says Kitty, sipping her drink.

'We're just friends, that's all.'

'Seriously, Nina, the bloke's got it bad,' calls Shazza across the room, slurping her oversized drink.

'You've both got the wrong end of the stick *again*.' This is all I ever get nowadays. If it's not Bram chasing for a date, it's others suggesting I date Zach.

'A Christmas romance would be so sweet,' adds Shazza, repositioning her feet on the wood burner. 'It's the perfect season to be loved up and snuggled close.'

'Such a pity that Christmas is cancelled, where I'm concerned. So, fill your boots, Shazza... choose a bloke and enjoy the season!'

I put my drink down and stand. Can't I enjoy a hot drink in peace? It's not as if I don't deserve a break after hours of hard work in the cold.

'I would if I could,' says Shazza, as Kitty flaps her hands in vain to silence her. 'No, Kitty, I won't hush. Christmas is coming whether she likes it or not!'

I hastily leave the snug, traipsing down the steps and across the yard to get away from them, shutting out the blare of 'Mary's Boy Child' and dodging the families as I head for the large equipment barn. The mouth to this barn stands wide open, as always. Inside the farming equipment and tractor are neatly parked in rows, bales of stacked hay fill one corner and along the far end is the makeshift winter pen in which Gertrude, the farm's cranky donkey, and her companion Arthur, the billy goat, reside during the winter. Leaning over the tubular fencing, feeding them carrots is Zach.

'Hey, Zach, how's things?' I say nonchalantly, sussing out his mood. He doesn't look up but continues to stroke Gertrude's muzzle. The donkey is appreciative and nudges his hand, demanding another carrot.

'Fine, thanks, and you?'

I join him leaning against the pen.

The inside of the barn smells warm and safe, away from the car engines and chatter from outside. 'You enjoying that, Gertrude?'

'She loves a good fuss,' he says, his eyes fixed upon the animal. Arthur, the billy goat, gives a sweeping glance at the carrot and returns to eating his hay bale. 'Have you spoken to Bram today?'

'Yes, he's got another brainwave about me and him sharing more adventurous times together... Lord knows where he gets his ideas but...'

Zach turns to stare at me, his large grey eyes dilated and wide. The same flutter of long blond eyelashes frame his gaze, beneath an identical blond fringe.

It's so unfair that males have such long eyelashes – do us girls ruin ours with caked mascara?

'Are you all right?'

'He wants to be more than just friends, Nina. That's what he's getting at.' His words are softly spoken; he scrutinises my features. I look away towards Arthur, with his giant curling horns, as if he were the interesting one.

'I know, but we've been here before. I don't think that we should...'

'So, tell him, then.'

'Zach.'

'Seriously, he honestly believes that one day you and him will be an item – he's thought it for years and yet you never correct him. You never put him straight. It's as if...'

'Hey, don't judge me.'

'All I get twenty-four hours a day is him chatting bubbles about you. You know the score, he's trying his best to impress, and yet you're not going to be honest with him, are you?'

'*Honest?* Look who's talking!' I knew my words would hit home, but, given his hurt expression, he hadn't expected a verbal punch.

Zach bites his lip and turns away.

My voice softens.

'What about you being honest for once, Zach? Oh, no, I forgot – you can't be.'

'I choose not to hurt him. There's a difference.'

'And I choose to ignore him.'

Zach's grey eyes flash a warning look.

'Are you pair trying to skive or can anyone join in?' calls Bram, striding into the barn to view the pair of us suspended in silence.

'We're on our break, so don't come the crap!' calls Zach, his persona instantly changing.

I stare from one to the other, officially their piggy in the middle.

'Skiving more like... anyway, Dad said he needs all hands on deck as a crowd has suddenly descended, so your break needs to be cut short.'

'Bloody great!' mutters Zach.

'Don't shoot the messenger – Dad's decision, not mine. Nina, can you rally the troops from the snug? They won't be happy but...'

I nod, instantly leaving the barn.

*

Holly

I wait at the end of the Costa counter, clutching a spoon in my hand, watching the barista put together my hazelnut latte. All morning I've been dreaming of this latte. It's my treat for working part-time in the chemist, and wearing this awful nylon uniform, which clings to my woollen tights.

'Hazelnut latte!' The barista shouts past me, as if he can't see me waiting by the counter top. I step forward and receive the warm offering, eager to scoop the cream from the top as I walk home.

'*Holly!*' screams a group of teenage girls from the seated area. I turn around, and instantly regret reacting to their outburst. Six smirking faces, with smudged eye-liner and overpainted mouths, creepily smirk back. 'Come and join us!' hollers Paris, one of the mean girls from school. A cackle of laughter bursts from the other five as they try to hide behind each other.

Head down, I dash towards the exit, my blonde ponytail swinging with each step.

They're about as funny as chlamydia, as my best friend, Demi, would say.

Once I make it to Long Street, I stare fixedly ahead and walk past the remainder of the coffee shop's large window where I can undo the lid on my latte to scoop and walk. Scoop and enjoy. Scoop and relax. Scoop and forget.

'Holly!' a male voice calls from behind me. 'Wait!'

I continue to stride along Atherstone's busy street. No one in this world can make me stop and stand, giving those six bitches something to watch or even record on their phones to post on social media. As soon as I reach the safe frontage of the chip shop next door, I stop and turn.

It's Alfie Woodward. My stomach flips and I nearly drop my latte. I quickly plunge my spoon into my coat pocket; it feels babyish to be scooping cream when it's Alfie. Every girl in year eleven, no, scrap that, every girl in our school wants to be *friends* with Alfie Woodward. He's the 'darling of the ladies', as my mum would put it. And, get me, Alfie Woodward, from the back row in chemistry class, actually knows *my* name. Not a reaction that the mean girls would have intended for me.

'Hi. I didn't think you'd heard me,' he says, zipping up his jacket as he nears. His dark hair is shorter than in yesterday's chemistry class – obviously, that has been his Saturday morning task.

'Sorry... I... well.' I shrug, looking up into his smiling face. What am I supposed to call the name-hollering in Costa?

'I was inside with Jordan and Tom. I heard them catcalling you. Anyway, ignore them... I was wondering if you were going to youth club on Tuesday night? I go most weeks. Your mate Demi goes sometimes but you're never there!'

I shrug. What can I say? Err nope, because the mean girls go every week? Or how about, yeah, sure, I'll turn up, get verbally abused for two hours and return home to cry... sure, save me a seat and I'll see you at seven on Tuesday?

'There are others that attend, not just those witches,' he adds, as if he can read my thoughts. 'I could call round for you, if you want?'

Alfie Woodward calling for me!

I blush. I see his blue eyes swirl and scan my features, taking in the subtle change in my pale complexion. Holly Turner, for once in your goddamned life play it cool.

'Well?' A tiny smile frames his top row of perfect teeth.

I purse my lips together to hide the metal train tracks that I begged my parents for, but now wish I'd never had. Right now, I'd much prefer my unsightly teeth buckle.

I give the smallest nod, having lost the ability to communicate in English. In fact, if Alfie stands before me for very much longer, with his new haircut, smart zipped jacket and white trainers there is a chance I may abandon control of my grip and lose this latte to the pavement.

'OK. I'll drop round just before seven on Tuesday.'

Brain, now is the time to function, be it a simple OK. Please don't let me down, not right now.

'Thanks, Alfie, that'd be nice of you. See you.' I turn about quickly. It seems rude, but I can't face him any longer. My smile is going to burst forth and I'm about to do the geekiest grin ever witnessed on Atherstone's Long Street.

'OK, see you in school,' he calls, as I head towards home.

'Yeah, first thing in chemistry.'

'No, you've got history first, then geography...'

I attempt a nonchalant wave. Demi is not going to believe this.

*

Nina

In a matter of hours, several hundred Christmas trees are sold and taken home by happy families. The boss instructs a second wave of spruce cutting, which means the yard staff will be run ragged with netting and pricing labels. This is the busyness I crave. Busy hands, busy mind.

'The farm couldn't have been any busier without snowfall,' boasts the boss as he deploys his instructions.

'Are you all right?' asks Kitty as I peel off my layers of work clothes in the snug when the end of the day finally arrives.

'Nah!' I can't muster a smile, which I know Kitty deserves.

'Want to talk about it? I'm good for a chat. Connor will happily wait in the car for me.'

I shake my head. Connor arrives each night to collect his beloved Kitty; he never complains if it is raining and Kitty asks him to taxi us home to save me from getting soaked. Theirs is a true love match, of mutual respect and commitment – the stuff of fairy tales.

The last thing I need is to start talking. It isn't just the twins; if I start to talk my feelings will overflow. And, after an eleven-hour shift, who wants to get the emotional mop bucket out to clean that messy puddle?

'Thanks, but another night,' I whisper, my eyes beginning to glisten. 'I need to go straight home, have a hot bath, curl up on the sofa in my pjs and watch Saturday night TV.'

'And then return tomorrow for another long shift.' Kitty giggles, trying to lift my spirit.

'Yep, but I'll have rested and I'll be fine.'

I collect my winter jacket, button the front and pull my beanie over my mousy-brown locks.

'Bye.'

'See you tomorrow, Kitty,' I say, heading for the door.

'Nina!'

'Yeah.' I turn, my hand on the door latch.

'I haven't forgotten. I know it's been a year since... the hospital... I just wanted you to know, I have remembered.'

I'd nearly made it to freedom without anyone saying a word.

'Thank you,' I whisper as my eyes prickle with tears. I need to leave. I want to be alone.

The door closes behind me, my heavy boots thud down the steps, and I quickly march towards the farm track and along the lonely lane beyond towards my cottage. Finally, I can release the knot of emotion that I have swallowed every hour since waking and let the tears flow. It feels good to have made it to half six without my barriers coming down. The release comes easy, and swiftly. I don't wipe the tears that hang from my chin; I let them fall. Just as I have every day for the last year. One year ago today, my dad was taken into a hospice, not quite the hospital that Kitty remembered. One year ago today, he left our cottage for the final time.

*

Angie

'Hi.' Same old Nick, man of few words and predictably late.

'Hi,' I reply, reaching up to greet him with a peck on the cheek. Something I haven't done in months. I'm fighting the urge to ask where he has been given that it is ten past and we agreed eight o'clock. At this time of year, the pub's picturesque duck pond is silent and dark, providing little amusement. So I have stared at my phone screen in the entrance doorway, as loved-up couples holding hands navigate around me to enter the bustling pub. Each woman has given me the pity look for being stood up, while the guys have given me the once-over. And now Nick's arrived, my stomach is flipping and I'm not sure if I should nip to the ladies or not. Or will my innards settle once we order our drinks? Food maybe? I remember how nervous I was on our first date. My hands didn't stop shaking for the entire time, which was ridiculous given that we were seated in the student union bar sharing Hooch and a plate of cheesy chips.

'Shall we?' asks Nick, taking the lead and holding the door wide. I smile. No explanation for poor timekeeping but, yeah, manners. Nick has always had good manners; they cost nothing but are worth a fortune.

His greying hair is neatly clipped at the neck. He's made an effort. I've never seen those shoes before so they must be new. I note that he's spending money on himself – that's nice to see. But maybe he's spending money elsewhere too?

'Thank you,' I say, stepping into The Rose, hoping that everyone notices that I am now only preoccupied with my date for the night and my phone is tucked safely away. The pub is decorated in swathes of red and gold, sumptuous garlands and glittering baubles pinned to every aged beam. I exchange a brief smile with a younger woman, a mute yet grateful appreciation of relief: my date has shown up, eventually. Small festive get-togethers fill each inglenook and alcove as the bustle of the bar envelops us, as clinking glasses, quick-stepping waitresses and the constant drone of chatter fill the air, drowning out the festive music.

'Angie?' Nick indicates towards a solitary corner table. I nod in agreement – the quieter the better for this conversation. I know what I wish to say, but given recent events my delivery may fall flat. I watch as he nears the table, flicks a crumb from the surface and pulls out a chair. His hands linger on the back rest as he waits for me to take his offering.

He gently pushes my seat under as I settle. 'Thank you...'

He doesn't cross to the other chair, but sidesteps towards the bar.

'*Nick?*' I call.

He turns; his brow furrows on hearing my voice. I nod towards the other chair. I just want him to be seated, for a moment at least, to allow me the time to speak. If I can get the words out, as they are formed in my head, then we can start our night on the right footing.

'*Drink?*' His thumb indicates the bar. I shake my head. He looks confused and returns to our table.

He settles opposite me. I can see his hackles are up.

This is it. I instantly need to say what I wanted to say this morning, but he'd stalled me, otherwise tonight will start on the wrong foot, if it hasn't already. I take a deep breath. I now hope no one in the bar is watching the woman who was stood up earlier. Because the moment this is out, I can't take it back. *Ever.*

His clear blue eyes search my face. He's waiting and I'm struggling to find the words that I practised in the bathroom mirror. The same ones I practised in the car and again while staring at my mobile screen not five minutes ago in the doorway.

'Nick, I've thought about what you said the other month. I would like us to try again.' I continue, avoiding an interruption. 'It'll be difficult. I know that a lot of things have happened since January… but I want us to make our way back to what we once had.' I pause.

There, I've said it.

He's waited months to hear me agree to his original suggestion.

'My biggest fear is that we slide back into what we had... that isn't what I want. So... I would like us to pretend that we are starting afresh as if *this* is our first date, that we recently met off some website thingy-bob, which people do all the time nowadays. I want us to reconnect and chat as if we are meeting for the very first time... Nick, are you listening?'

He's staring. I can't read if it's a good stare or a bad stare. Can a stare ever be good? Is that a nod of the head, or a nervous twitch?

Nick stands, pushes his chair under and heads to the bar. OK. No reaction. OK.

'Nick?'

He turns; his brow furrows on hearing my voice – it's like Groundhog Day, as he's just re-enacted what he did minutes before.

'Drink?'

'Yeah, but you didn't ask what I wanted...' My voice fades. I had to say it; I had to make a stand so he knows I mean it.

'But, Angie, you always have a large rosé.'

'You don't know what your date wants unless you ask her, Nick.' Am I being pedantic?

His eyebrows shoot into his greying fringe. His shoulders drop and he slowly returns to our table.

'Angie, what can I get you to drink?' he asks, politely.

'A vodka and cranberry, please.'

'But you hate...'

It's my turn to frown. This isn't going to work. He's not even trying and we haven't completed a minute on our first date. If we can't get past the drinks conversation there isn't a hope in hell, after what were our eighteen years of marriage and one hasty divorce.

With a terse OK, he heads back to the bar. He heard my proposal and now I'll have to wait to see what happens when he returns with our drinks.

*

'Do you come here often?'

'Are you seriously going to use that line?' I snort, dabbing spluttered vodka from the table top.

Nick shrugs.

'What? I'm trying, like you asked.'

'OK, maybe I should go first... So, Nick, tell me something about yourself.'

He takes a sip of his Guinness, returns the pint glass to the table and repositions himself in the hardback chair.

'I'm Nick, I'm forty–three years of age... recently divorced. I'm a design engineer by trade – mainly commercial, but I do some freelance work when asked. I work in the city, so most days I commute into Birmingham but some days I work from home.'

I smile. Well done. Now, my turn. Ask me?

The silence lingers. I continue to smile. He'll automatically ask about me, because that's polite conversation and Nick has manners. My smile fades. He continues to smile, his eyes sparkling and alive. He's waited so long to hear me say I'll try again.

Silence. I'm not going to prompt him. He needs to ask now. Now. Now, will do. Shit, pure silence, simply starring at each other... so I'll ask some more and take an interest in his career.

'Have you been a design engineer for long?'

'Nearly twenty years. I left school, went to uni—'

'Which one?'

'Angie... you know which one – the bloody same as you!'

'You don't know that. You haven't asked me anything about me.'

'Christ, Angie!'

I compose myself.

'So, tell me... which university, Nick?'

He sips his Guinness, and eyeballs me above the rim of his glass. Will he play ball or is that it, game over?

'Aston in Birmingham. I lived near campus for three years, shagged around as much as I could and then—'

'Nick!' I grumble.

'What?'

'Why say that? You know I hate it when you talk like that.'

'Because this is bloody ridiculous. Do you seriously want to listen to me drone on about how I met you, my wife… or rather ex-wife… all those years ago?'

'No, but… oh, never mind.'

'What? Am I to carry on or are we ceasing this act?' he asks.

'Carry on.' I swig my drink, wishing I'd asked for a double.

'So, anyway, I met my wife, we married and then this year, after eighteen years of marriage… she walked out on me…'

I wait for him to add anything but he doesn't. I could bite back, but I don't. I leave it. I wouldn't bite back on a first date, would I? And this *is* my very first date with Nick Woodward, a date that I've been waiting for all day. A date that I curled my hair for and dressed for, arriving just shy of eight o'clock to be left waiting in the doorway for ten minutes. If this is our first date, which I am hoping it is, he's lost brownie points for such rudeness.

Continue.

'Have you any children, Nick?'

'One son, he's just turned sixteen… it's been painful to watch him struggle with the divorce…'

'You bastard! That was a cheap shot!'

'What was?'

'That! He hasn't struggled.'

'Yes, he bloody well has... anyway, what would you know? We haven't met before, have we?'

'Funny,' I snap as I try to regain my composure, having had my child brought into my first-date conversation.

'Anyway, as I was saying... he's had it rough. There's been days when he wouldn't open up to me... or his mother. In fact, he's still not speaking to her properly... Which I find quite upsetting as they were so very close before she took off from the marital home.'

I sit back and wait. Under the table, I curl my nails into my palm and squeeze tight. I want to scream. I want to cry. I want Nick to stop, but he's now on a roll and he's playing the game as I asked and I really can't pull the rug from under his feet because I asked for this. This pain. This hurt. This gut-wrenching detail about my own flesh and blood. I asked Nick to pretend and he's in full flow. I didn't think it would be *this* painful hearing about my child's reaction to my decision, but it is. But I can take it. I can. And I will. I. Can. Take. It.

So, go on, Nick. Tell your story because in about five minutes, if you use your beautiful manners, you'll be asking me to do the same. And I've been practising. I've been waiting for this moment all day, since I shot from the farm this morning because I couldn't face buying a Christmas tree for my two-bedroomed rental apartment. As it happens, I couldn't imagine a tree anywhere other than in the three-bedroomed home I spent eighteen years of married life living in.

*

Holly

Have you seen FB?

D x

I don't reply to Demi but log in to Facebook in the darkness of my bedroom. I haven't seen FB nor any other social media all day; sometimes ignorance is bliss. I glance towards my sleeping sister, Hannah. I can't risk disturbing her much-needed beauty sleep. She'd definitely grass on me in pure spite, but that's fourteen years old for you.

The screen reveals all in a split second, a mile-long thread consisting of comments and colourful emojis. Paris's posting reads:

Mirror, mirror on the wall, from Costa's doorstep who did Alfie Woodward call?

The message was written five hours ago.

Great, the world and his wife will have read and responded by now.

I slide the screen and virtually every mean girl that attends our school, regardless of year group, makes a stream of suggestions. Alfie, the top dog in year eleven... Shock horror – who did he chase after in Costa?

I smile. A whole host of names has been suggested and slyly, towards the end, the bitches couldn't hold out any longer for a correct suggestion so relieved everyone's misery by naming me.

> Holly Turner... and she was sucking on a spoon when he shouted her.

Paris had written:

> I love her tacky uniform, wish I had one.

I kill the screen and lie back, pulling the duvet to my chin.

I should be upset, but I'm not. I've received worse treatment from those girls, having known them since primary school. Alfie chased and called me – they'd happily switch places in a heartbeat. History class may prove interesting come Monday, but, first, I have Sunday to survive.

I quickly text Demi.

> Thanks for the heads up. Yep, it's true. Alfie spoke to me on leaving Costa. All good. But hey, mean girls copped a good view H x

I turn off my mobile. The last thing I need is a middle-of-the-night interrogation from Demi about what was said. I need sleep.

I plump my pillow and close my eyes. All I can see is Alfie Woodward, his new hairstyle, his big blue eyes and a pleasing smile. My stomach flips. Falling asleep *isn't* going to be easy, but I wouldn't change this for the world.

Two

Nina

Sunday, 9 December

My alarm rings at six o'clock.

I hate being woken at this time.

The rain hits the windowpane, a rattling sound I love at night whilst falling asleep, but on a morning it suggests that today's shift will be pretty miserable.

Why don't I have a normal job in a warm office or a sweet-smelling salon? I shouldn't complain – after I flunked my GSCEs it was a good job that Boss Fielding took pity on me and gave me a work trial.

Living in a small village like Baxterley, everyone knows your business. The amenities consist of the pub, a beautiful church and acres of surrounding countryside to keep the inhabitants entertained. Dad and I rarely mixed with the locals as we didn't need anything from them. We didn't need their company or the latest gossip. In fact, we probably *were* the local gossip. No one crossed our threshold apart from the Fielding twins.

My cottage is a chocolate-box type, with a low roof, quirky whitewashed walls and a dainty front garden with a privet hedge. I was born in the front bedroom, played tea parties with my dolls upon the summer lawn and, now, can't bear to sell. Some homes creak and breathe, hum or murmur – the cottage has always been silent. I've spent my entire life listening to her silence, and yet this last year, it has become much louder, deafening. Surprising given that I'm the sole occupant.

Friends rarely drop by, or rather they've stopped dropping by. If Bram and Zach did drop round nowadays, apart from being shocked that they'd made it past The Rose, they'd see I've let the place go to pot.

I need to get a grip sooner rather than later, but, hey, who am I pleasing here?

I pull the duvet tight beneath my chin, as a huge tear rolls down my cheek and slides sideways into my hairline.

How did I allow this to happen?

I've left everything as it was the morning he was taken into the hospice, though I knew he wouldn't return home – the kindly staff said as much.

How has a year passed? How has Christmas come around so soon?

And yet, it has.

*

Angie

My head is banging nineteen to the dozen.

What the hell?

I struggle from beneath the duvet, and make my way to the kitchen dressed in an oversized tee shirt, my eyes closed for the entire route for fear that daylight may burn my retinas and cause untold damage. Unlike the half bottle of vodka I drank alone, having arrived home after my first date with Nick.

I struggle to force the paracetamol to pop through the silver foil. I quickly swallow two down and note the time. It's seven o'clock on a Sunday morning, frigging hell! The only day of the week I get to lie in and yet I ruin it by waking early, go figure. But *that* sums up my world.

I flick the switch on the kettle and lean against the counter top, lazily eyeing up the half-bottle and the single glass on the breakfast bar. Not good, Angie, bad habits lead to more bad habits. I turn away, as if that solves anything. It doesn't.

Sunday mornings with Nick were lazy lie-ins, tea and toast on a lap tray and a snuggle under the duvet amongst the discarded newspapers.

I let out a sigh; even that hurts my pounding head.

Right now, I'd give my back teeth to be warm in bed, beside a sleeping male, knowing that I can turn over for another hour's kip or excite him purely by breathing heavily upon his bare back.

I look round the two-bedroom rental apartment. I moved in just eleven months ago, and the best thing about it is that I can do as I please, twenty-four hours a day. But the promise of freedom has faded rapidly in recent weeks. If I had the choice, right now, I'd be wrapped in Nick's arms, beneath his warm body, hoping Alfie was OK making his own way to football practice.

The kettle boils, and I pour the steaming water into a mug drenching the teabag.

The vodka bottle mocks me. An all-seeing, all-knowing buddy, who was once a passing acquaintance but now is my best friend chosen over others any night of the week.

I should have gone straight to bed, but I didn't because, despite my desire to be held in his arms right now, last night, Nick annoyed me.

'So, you're saying your son wouldn't welcome you dating a new woman?' I asked.

Nick frowned.

'What I said, was that my son would be very dubious about me dating the same woman,' he said, eyeing me suspiciously. 'Especially if that same woman hurt both me and him. He's been affected by the split, Angie. You seem to forget that.'

'But surely Alfie would gain security by having two adults return to the marital home?' Did Nick know that

I was talking about us?

'Not necessarily.'

It was my turn to frown.

'It's been tough, I can't stress that enough... the lad's at an impressionable age and to have you, his mother, sorry, I forgot the first-date rule, to have my marriage break down in such a manner... it has left him...' I watched as he searched for the right word.

'*Yes?*' I wanted to hear this little gem.

'Vulnerable.'

'Bollocks, has it! He never knew if I was there or not. He was never in, always out playing football with his mates, off down the skate park with the gang... From the age of ten, he's treated our place like a hotel, coming and going whenever he chose. With me acting as taxi driver every time a distance needed to be covered for collection or delivery to a stadium, pitch or activity further adrift. I'm surprised he's noticed there's only two of you living in the house!'

Nick sipped his pint, and smirked.

'As this is our first date, I'm unsure how you know such details about my home life.'

'Sod off, Nick.' Play it your own way.

And he did. In no time, Nick was in full flow telling me how his teenage son hardly leaves the house after school, rarely goes out at weekends, and as for having his boisterous mates crammed into his bedroom to play computer games, they've faded away to a sporadic door rap on youth-club nights.

'He's angry, he's hurt, but most of all he feels rejected. His confidence has nosedived, Angie.'

I snatched up my vodka, emptying the remains in one gulp. There was nothing *he* could tell me about the child I'd carried, birthed and raised.

I clear the mocking vodka bottle away to underneath the sink, put the dirty glass into the dishwasher and pretend to rewrite events, imagining that I went straight to bed on arriving home.

I glance at the wall clock. I'll give it an hour or so, then I'll give Alfie a call and see if he wants to come and choose a Christmas tree with his mum. I bet he jumps at the chance despite Nick's twisted opinion. I know my boy.

I instantly feel better. That's what I'll do: we'll nip to the farm to buy my tree, purchase new decorations, then return to transform my lounge. Afterwards, have a bite to eat at that posh little deli on Long Street. That'll show Nick, and next time we talk about our children on a date, he'll have to report back differently. If there is another date, that is.

*

Nina

'Nina, can I have a word, please?' asks Boss Fielding as I trudge towards the snug for my eleven-thirty coffee, or the late break, as we call it. Each day staff change breaks so that we're never on coffee all together but everyone gets fair dibs at the biscuit barrel.

'Sure.' I follow his lead towards his office, another log cabin that blends into the woodland theme without causing too much offence. The same can't be said of the Pogues's Irish lilt streaming 'Fairytale of New York' from the overhead speakers.

The boss's boots thump up the wooden steps before he stands aside to let me pass.

'Take a seat, Nina.' He settles behind his desk. He's a huge guy, with a greying beard, outdoorsy kind of fella. I've always imagined Boss Fielding could give Bear Grylls a run for his money, surviving in the open air with just a knife and plastic sheeting.

I can't remember the last time I was invited to take a seat. Boss Fielding didn't invite me in for a chat when I returned to work last January – surely a family bereavement was the right moment for a quiet chat. On my return, several of the farm staff sidestepped me, hid behind log cabins or simply ignored my absence. Strange that. But I suppose it makes it easier for them, when they don't know what to say or, worst still, if they make you cry.

Kitty and Shazza didn't ignore me. And it goes without saying that Bram and Zach were with me every step of the way. That was all that mattered to me, back then.

'Nina, now, I don't want you to take this the wrong way...' The boss stares beyond me as he speaks, his grey eyes not meeting mine.

Never a good opening line for a conversation. Don't take it the wrong way, but you're fired! You're being replaced! You're no longer required on sales but we think you'd be good on wholesale deliveries. You're... I can't predict another line ending so sit and stare.

'Nina?'

'Yeah, I'm listening...'

'Look, pet, we're worried about you. Me and Jackie... we know things have been tough, what with... you know. But, well, what I want to say is... is... that... Should there be anything you need this Christmas... you only have to...'

I burst into tears.

I rummage inside my tabard pocket for a tissue – nothing.

His expression drops. His words falter. From experience I know this is the worst possible thing to do to Boss Fielding. He's raised two rough and ready boys, on a harsh diet of farm life; their upbringing consists of strict orders, hard graft and calloused hands. He's as emotional as a tree trunk, yet here I am snotting and snivelling in his office without the assistance of a female for twenty yards. After nine years of employment, I know that the boss is officially out of his depth.

'Right, so, sorry to have made… you know… but a chat was necessary.'

Have we actually conversed during the time we've been seated? Or have my emotions thrown him that far left from his comfort zone that he is having a male meltdown at the prospect of offering comfort?

The cabin door bursts open.

'Hey, Dad… they've found a bunch of empty cider cans and the remains of a campfire down at…' Zach barges in without care or concern. He glances between us, halts at seeing my tear-stained face and an emergency registers in his brain. 'Hey, Nina, what's up?'

Boss Fielding watches in awe as Zach kneels at my chair, produces a tissue in a heartbeat, and awaits my response.

'Your dad just wanted a quiet word and I… I… I…'

'Shhhh.' His father looks on, baffled by the ease at which his second son gives comfort.

'Zach, would you pull up a chair, lad?' He nods towards the spare office chair, which Zach hastily pulls beside mine.

'As I was saying…'

I dab my eyes and try to focus.

'Yes, well... Jackie and I... we were wondering if there's anything you need... for over the Christmas period... you only have...' He stops talking, shakes his head. 'Zach, help me out here, lad.'

'What he's trying to say, very badly, is... shout if you need anything, yeah?'

'Yeah!' confirms his father, grateful for having his son throw him a line. 'You're welcome to join us for Christmas dinner... if you choose.'

My tears have dried but my voice has turned into hiccups. So I nod instead. I've made a big enough fool of myself this break-time without adding to it.

'So, all done?' asks Zach, as his father hastily shoos us from his office. 'Excellent! Come on, let's get you a hot chocolate and an additional ten-minute break.'

Zach stealthily guides me from the chair, out of the door and down the steps towards the snug without any fuss or further embarrassment.

'Thank you,' I say as he settles a large mug into my hands and I sink into a faded old beanbag.

'My pleasure.'

'He started to talk and I simply burst out crying.'

'Kitty mentioned she'd just seen you following Dad towards his office – I knew it would end in tears. I tried to act blasé on entering, but probably failed.'

'He was trying to be kind and it went wrong... but there's nothing I need.'

'You just need to ask if there is. As he said, you are welcome on Christmas Day if you fancy sharing our turkey,' said Zach. 'I was heading over to tell him that the cutting crew have found a pile of empty cider cans and a burnt-out campfire on the far side of the woods.'

'The kids have scaled the fence again?'

'Mmmm, maybe not scaled it but found a hole or cut their way into the south fields... I might ask Shazza what her brother has been up to lately.'

'Zach, you can't accuse and she would never grass on her brother.'

'Why?'

'*Zach*, they're teenagers, what harm are they doing?'

'Trespassing, Nina... if they have an accident it could be serious. Don't worry, I'll word it carefully, but Shazza needs to mention it at home.'

Most small villages have a specific spot where teenagers choose to hang out. In Baxterley village, some teenagers ignore the park benches favouring the thrill of a midnight cider fest amongst our Christmas trees.

'You know that wasn't his intention, don't you?'

'Your dad? Oh, yeah... but still, I've made a right tit of myself, *again*.'

'It'll give the workers a laugh when he starts twitching in about twenty minutes. Bless him, he gets so jittery when he tries to do anything that's not chopping down Christmas trees.'

We both start to giggle. *This* is why I love Zach so much. He's sensitive, caring... the total opposite to Bram. But, I love Bram *just* as much. It's moments such as this that define how our triangular friendship has developed into such a tight bond. We support and provide for each other like no other friends I have. Even Kitty and Shazza – as kind and as caring as they are – don't compare to the twins.

'What?' asks Zach.

'Nothing.'

'You looked like you were about to say something...'

*

Holly

'Holly!' hollers my mother outside our bedroom door.

It isn't the nicest sound to wake up to on a Sunday morning but, given that I spent most of the night dreaming of Alfie, I willingly accept the yin-yang balance of life.

'Holly, up now, before you make us all late and we have to do battle with the rest of Warwickshire.'

Hannah silently watches me from her bed; her mat of blonde curls framing her face in a cute tousled manner.

'How comes she's not moaning at you?' I ask Hannah.

'You're the eldest, you should know better,' she jokes, adding, 'What's the fuss about you on FB?'

I shake my head.

'Something about Costa and a spoon...' she grins. There are days I love my sisters, all six of them, but right now sharing a room isn't one of the joys. How I long for privacy and a room to call my own.

The bedroom door bursts open, my mother storms in fully dressed in her usual black leggings and big shirt combo, a tea towel in hand, looking as if she's been up for hours. My mother never does anything at a normal pace. Her internal gears are quick march or lightning speed. If we seven girls ever move as fast as my mother when we're older – there'll be no stopping us. We could have the Forth Bridge painted in two days, Buckingham

Palace windows cleaned inside and out in under three hours and Big Ben's tower washed, scrubbed and repaired by lunchtime!

'Up the pair of yah! Your father's screaming blue murder down there having to wait – he wants to get a tree and be back home before the footie starts.'

I don't have time to answer – my brain doesn't function as quickly as my mother's.

*

Angie

I queue behind a family of nine and balk in horror at the sight of such a lively brood. How can one couple produce so many children? I scan the crowd for a male child, but there isn't one. Once they've stopped skipping and bouncing they huddle round the two older girls. I can't help but listen to their babbling conversation, as the parents stand aside talking spruce heights and prices.

I watch the youngest child wave her hands around happily as the sister jiggles her on her hip. A lump lodges in my throat as my innards tighten. I never wanted a girl; Alfie was perfect. But I'm suddenly overcome by the sight of so many young girls. I hate hormones sometimes.

The small freckly sales girl with the mousy hair isn't about. I can't understand why we're queuing. The boss's wife is buzzing about like a mad ass and I can see one of the twins, but the other is nowhere to be seen, which is strange. Maybe this year has brought about change amongst the farm staff too, though Noddy Holder's traditional 'It's Christmas!' yell from the overhead speaker system seems unaffected.

I want a six-foot-tall Blue spruce. In previous years, Nick always said 'no' to one, but this year I can do as I wish. I have it all planned out. I'll purchase brand-new decorations to complement its natural colour; garlands, baubles and the star will be sparkly and fresh. This year, I can please myself.

Except Christmas is not about me. It's about Alfie. My expectant joy disappears for a second as I remember his words on the phone this morning...

'Why now?'

'Alfie, please don't speak to me like that.'

'Seriously, Mum, why now?'

'I just thought it would be great to spend some time together. We could visit Christmas Tree Farm and purchase my tree... then decorate together like we always do.' I was taken aback that my son would question my motive.

'*Did!* Anyway, I'm busy.' His tone was flat.

'Alfie?'

'Mum?' he retorted.

'Is *this* really necessary? I'm trying to make arrangements for a pleasant day with my son and you flatly refuse me, as if I'm the wicked witch of the West.'

'You phone up at the last minute, expecting me to drop my plans for the day in preference for yours, you mean?'

'What's so important that it can't wait?' It was bound to be a teenage thing that could wait until another day. Teenage things usually could. He simply didn't realise yet.

'I could ask you the same, Mum.'

Life was so much easier when he was three years of age and would gladly agree to any of my suggestions in a heartbeat. What had happened to Mummy knows best?

'Look, Mum, the last thing I need right now is to start organising date-night with my mother. I've got mock exams coming up, I've got football trials and...'

'And, what?' What could be more important?

'Well, Dad.'

Shoot me, why don't you? I shouldn't have interrupted him; *that* answer was pure karma... my punishment for not respecting my teenage son's growing independence.

'OK. So, when, Alfie? It's been weeks.'

'Months *actually*, Mum.'

'Yes, OK... longer than I'd planned.'

'I break up from school on the twenty-first, so...'

'Alfie, I was hoping for before then. Tonight perhaps?'

'No can do. Sorry. I have an English essay to write and then I've promised Dad we can do a box set of...'

A bloody box set – was I hearing him correctly? My only son would prefer to sit and waste his life on a sodding box set with his father than see me?

'If that's your attitude, I honestly don't know why I bothered.'

'Probably because I'm your son, Mum. And you should have been bothering about my welfare for the last eleven months but you haven't... you skipped out and—'

'Enough!' My patience broke.

'OK. Enough. Let me know when you're free, Mum, and I'll see what we can arrange, but dropping on me at such short notice really isn't the best.'

'Tuesday night? I could be home early, pick you up from school, cook us a nice meal.'

'Tuesday is youth club, Mum. Thursday would be better for me.'

Thursday? Sod it; I had a late meeting at work. I couldn't imagine my bosses at ASAP Parcel Delivery accepting my apologies; given it was our busiest time of year. Knowing the budget for overtime payments, they'd expect the payroll department to be present...

'Can I help you?' asks the young woman, her eager bright blue eyes staring at me amidst a smattering of freckles. I jump in surprise. What happened to the Von Trapp family of girls?

'Sorry, in a world of my own,' I apologise, before pointing at the Blue spruces a stone's throw away from where we are standing.

'Any particular height? We have three, four, five or six foot.'

There's only one size for me and that's six foot. Six-foot-tall, dark, lean and... Nick would always head for the Nordman fir while I lingered beside the Blue spruce hoping he'd change his mind just one year. He *never* did.

I follow the girl towards the designated spruces and watch as her neat little steps stride ahead. I really shouldn't call her a girl any more – she's obviously grown over the years and I've failed to notice. She is, in fact, a young woman with a pretty smile and sparkling blue eyes. Her mousy-brown hair pokes from beneath her bobble hat, she's clomping about in heavy boots and a padded jacket but she's fresh-faced, willing to please and attractive in a very natural way.

This wisp of a woman is as strong as an ox: she drags, stands upright and presents the spruce to me before lugging it across the busy yard towards the cashier's log cabin. I feel quite embarrassed, as I'd have struggled, but I suppose she's used to it after all these years.

'Thank you,' I say as we reach the cashier's cabin.

'You're very welcome. Do you need an aftercare leaflet?'

I shrug, unsure if we were ever offered such a leaflet when purchasing a Nordman fir.

The young woman dashes to a wooden box, grabs a leaflet and returns, offering it to me.

'Here, follow the instructions and the spruce will retain its needles for a lot longer.' She gives a cheery smile and a nod before darting off to help the next festive customer.

How am I going to carry the spruce back to my car without Nick's assistance? *This* will be a definite first.

*

Holly

Any family outing always ends in an argument. Whether it be a flying visit to McDonald's, a family appointment at the dentist or buying the Christmas tree – Mum and Dad will spend the afternoon in silence having rowed about something, or in some cases nothing at all. Dad wants a six-foot tree that fills the Christmas tree corner spot while Mum wants a table-top-size one so that my youngest sister, Hope, doesn't drag it from its perch now that she is walking, unlike last year when she was a cry-baby in arms.

It is embarrassing to stand watching your parents bicker back and forth as both hold onto their respective tree sizes and the young farm worker stands between them, patiently trying to help them decide. I jiggle Hope about on my hip bone, willing them to hurry up.

'*Shellie!* Come on, babe,' pleads my dad to my mum, lifting his Norway spruce up by its netted, pointy top. 'This is a proper tree.'

'*Steve!* You come on! It's no joke when a toddler pulls it over ten times a day, believe me. I'm the one at home picking up the glass baubles before they get smashed, or eaten, or trod on, or...' says Mum, holding a small Fraser fir, or so the label says.

I sigh. How much longer will they conduct this stand-off? My money is on Dad – he usually wins the arguments despite Mum's silent treatment, which can linger for several days.

Ironically, 'Do They Know It's Christmas?' plays overhead as a gentle reminder that we're supposed to be counting our blessings.

'Shellie, we've always had a Norway spruce... it's a proper Christmas tree.'

'OK, the Norway spruce but a table-top version... three foot, four at the most.'

'Shellie?'

I watch the other families mull around and drift away from my parents.

I know what people think. You can see it in their eyes as they view our clan, count the heads, configure the gender ratio and then look shocked that the two adults have continued to breed – that's what it feels like sometimes. I'm not entirely sure that we seven girls will be the end of nappies. I'm sure my parents, at thirty-four, haven't given up the idea of having a son. Personally, I'd have given up the ghost after Hayley, and definitely by Helen but, no, they continue to dream, and bonk. I used to worry when I was little that if they ever had a boy, we girls might be turfed out to an orphanage and the little prince would be their sole responsibility. Now, I realise that won't happen, but, should they ever produce another 'Y' chromosome for the household, I'm sure my dad will throw a street party bigger than the Queen's Diamond Jubilee.

'Holly, come on!' shouts Mum. Her disgruntled tone confirms that Dad is triumphant, dragging his six-foot Norway spruce towards the cashier's cabin. I vow to hide in my room the first time Hope pulls it over because Mum will scream blue murder until Dad gets home.

I follow my clan, hitching Hope higher onto my hip. Hope waves her arms around and shouts gibberish to the group of families as we walk by. I hear the 'oh' and the 'ah' from females as we pass – Hope's cute, there's no denying it, but it's really not reason enough to keep producing offspring. Dad's dragging his huge tree, Mum is moping after him and a smattering of little girls traipse after as I trail behind.

'Out the way!' a male frantically shouts just as a mass of beige fur charges through the middle of the busy crowd. I step aside and freeze, clutching Hope to my chest, as the massive curly horns of the goat are flung from side to side, instantly clearing a gangway amongst the happy families.

'Arthur!' The cry fills the air as several farm staff come running from all directions, armed with carrots, ropes and a yard broom. Two young men lunge and grab at the animal as it takes centre stage. Both men are identical in looks, uniform and mannerisms as one clasps the ever-moving horns and the other stands astride its back, clutching handfuls of fur. A young woman runs across and ties a rope about the goat's neck as the crowd look on, relieved, before the trio calmly walk the creature towards an open barn.

'Naughty!' shouts Hope, wagging her chubby finger at the disappearing goat.

'Yes, naughty...' That's when I spot her: Paris Williams, with her parents. She's too busy yapping to notice me. She's animated and gesturing to a woman, who I presume is her mother. She looks like a kind lady, warmly smiling as Paris chatters non-stop. A mum like any other, in a puffa jacket body-warmer, tight jeans and with blonde highlights. Her dad looks pretty ordinary too. Short back and sides, nice jumper and loafers. I hoped they were demon parents who treated her badly, which would give her an excuse to be so mean to the likes of me and mine. But they're not. They are Mr and Mrs Pleasant, from Any Street in Normalville. Paris has no excuse to act the way she does; she'll have been raised to have manners. I near, and Paris sees me from the corner of her eye. Paris continues to chatter, casually turning to look over her shoulder and, shock horror, it's me and my clan. Her mouth drops wide. Her mother watches her sudden reaction, follows her gaze and silently deciphers her daughter's expression. I smile as we come shoulder to shoulder. Paris scowls.

'Paris?' Her mother's voice is curious but questioning.

'What?'

'Stop it. Please!' mutters her mother, her brow furrowing before an instant smile is sent in my direction.

I continue to walk, focusing ahead yet straining to hear their conversation.

*

Nina

As soon as Boss Fielding gives permission to leave, the others dash home. I head towards the north gate so that I can walk amongst the Blue spruce along the gravel pathway to the water's edge. It's just a ten-minute walk, but each step removes me from reality; gone are the sales yard, the hustle of co-workers and even the heaviness I drag around each day.

Acres of silent Christmas trees stand in rows behind me as I stare across the farm's natural lake that arcs before me. The water blackens as twilight falls. Ghostly clouds drift above against a darkening sky, throwing strange reflections upon the surface. I breathe deeply, filling my lungs with the sweet moist air. And, slowly exhale.

I love this spot. I've spent all day promising myself that I'll come here for a few minutes to enjoy the solitude and clear my head.

Nothing bad ever happens here. In fact, nothing bad ever happens at Christmas Tree Farm. The funniest moment of today's shift was Arthur's poor attempt to dash for freedom – thankfully we caught him in seconds and no one was injured. The worst thing that ever happened was when Gertrude the donkey escaped for a weekend to roam free amongst the fifty-five acres. Even that ended well when she eventually came home hungry for carrots.

To my right, a flash of red catches my eye. On the nearest Blue spruce sits my fat robin, a fiery redbreast upon spindle legs, his head twitching inquisitively as he watches me.

Instantly, I feel calmer.

'Hello,' I whisper. I'm not one for superstitions or urban folklore but he frequently appears when I'm alone, be it here or in the sales yard. I probably sound stupid talking to a tiny Robin but... I'll do anything to feel better for a few minutes each day.

Slowly, I reach out my hand, my fingers quivering with excitement. Nothing.

Who am I kidding? The robin sits and bobs on his spruce branch, peering at my hand before flying off in the direction of the holiday rentals; six sturdy cabins nestled amongst the mature spruce edging the lake.

In the distance, an embankment creates a secluded landscape, hedged with immature Fraser firs. When the wind is blowing in the right direction their distinct spicy fragrance drifts towards you, but not today. I select a flat stone from those scattered at the water's lapping edge and skim it across the surface, just as my dad taught me as a child. The stone flies ahead and bounces four times before it disappears into the murky depths.

I'm losing my touch. As a youngster I could do at least five, if not six bounces.

A year ago, I stood here and endured a torrent of rain. My face stung with the relentless pelting, Mother Nature masking my sobbing tears for my father.

I can't do that today, despite the rain being imminent. I've clocked off, the boss will be closing the site shortly to return to the farmhouse, and so I need to derobe my layers in the snug before heading home.

Dad's never coming back. I know that. Tuesday sees the start of my two free days from work and I'll make a start by organising his possessions. Tonight, I might remove his boots from the hallway, his mug from the coffee table and even empty his ashtray. *Might.*

*

Arriving home before the rain begins feels like a personal accomplishment for the day – overshadowing the couple of hundred spruces I sold.

The village streets are a blaze of flashing fairy lights and inflatable Santas decorating each cosy home. My cottage looks bare in comparison.

Dragging my jacket from my shoulders, I struggle to find a hook on the full coat rack, so hang it from the newel post. My shoulders ache, my stomach rumbles. I'll eat and have a shower later, if I manage my first task. I step over and around each pair of his boots and with some trepidation head for the lounge.

Buzzing around the lounge, I repeat the winter's night routine from my schooldays, when dad was still at work, and I'd arrive home first. I switch on the standard lamps and switch on the TV; the curtains are already drawn. 'In for the night', was how he'd term it. Just the two of us, cosy at home for the rest of the evening. How I wish I could return to those days of just him and me. Evenings at home spent moaning about the rubbish on TV, our disgust and sometimes tears at viewing the day's news from around the world while we balanced dinner trays on our laps and chomped our evening meal. Who'd have thoughts that our shared irritations of life would be the thing I would want to relive and not the Christmases, the birthdays and milestones of life. Isn't it crazy what the grieving heart desires?

I stand by the hearth staring at *his* coffee table. My aim is to complete my task quickly and efficiently. I won't think about anything or anyone. I won't imagine him seated on the sofa, will ignore his voice replaying in my mind, and his deep throaty laugh. I'll simply pick it up, walk to the kitchen, empty and wash the ashtray. I have a choice regarding drying. I can either wipe with a fresh dry dishcloth or leave it to air dry, bottom side up, on the draining board – a sight that had greeted me most days of my life. Despite my slovenly cleaning habits, I can't bring myself to wipe it dry on a clean tea towel.

My vision blurs as tears cascade over my lashes.

'I can't do this,' I mutter to the empty lounge.

I glance at the end seat of the sofa where his frail body used to rest.

We denied Dad's MS in our daily world, ignored the medical advice, the group sessions and offers of support or help, to ease and rectify the suffering. We got up each day, we went to bed each night and MS stood quietly watching from the corner of the lounge biding her time.

It's now or never, as nothing good ever came from keeping a pile of grey ash.

<u>Three</u>

Nina

Monday, 10 December

From inside the snug, we hear the thump of boots on the wooden steps.

'Quick, look sharp,' whispers Kitty as we run towards the door.

'Ah, Boss...' I swoon, a big smile in place.

'You ladies need to get a wiggle on. There's work to do and you're gassing like old washerwomen. It's all hands on deck up on the south side, tidying up the empty cider cans that those little bastards have left behind.'

Kitty gives me a warning stare, whilst pulling on her gloves, and hastily exits. I attempt to follow suit.

'Given your layers, I'm assuming you haven't read the daily task sheet this morning, Nina?' He points towards the notice board, which we're supposed to read each morning, but don't.

I couldn't lie, so shake my head.

'You're on the interview panel.'

'Interview?' My heart sinks. Put me on the cutting crew, the netting machine, or give me the labelling gun, even the worst job of all, the 'scrub the yard clean' team, but please don't put me on an interview panel.

'Five candidates... first one starts at half eight so best foot forward – you're sitting alongside Jackie and Zach.'

I look down at my clothing layers, which I now don't need.

'Are the interviews for casual workers?'

'Oh, yeah, casual all right.' Boss laughs as he leaves me to de-layer without further details.

*

Angie

My Monday morning alarm ruins a dreamy rerun of a night of passion shared several months ago with an Italian called Fabio. I lazily drop my arm over the side of the bed and cancel the alarm noise, then lie back to enjoy the lingering afterglow of my gymnastics with the fabulous Italian stallion. A flashback comes to mind – it's amazing how taut flesh can sway your willingness to experiment after eighteen years of marriage!

We met during a particularly hectic time in my divorce from Nick. I was trying to organise papers, estimate costings for child maintenance and prove bank balances. When, bingo, Fabio showed up on a dating website that had been lacking in interest and intent for several weeks. It was a gamble, as online dating always is, but boy, oh, boy was he generous with his time, his moves and his carnal knowledge.

I giggle, pull the duvet up to my chin, and grin like a Cheshire cat.

The beautiful Fabio taught me things about my body that even I didn't know. Seriously, it's amazing what knowledge a woman can gain from changing partners, even if it is for just a few weeks.

If the truth be known, Fabio had been entirely false in every detail, apart from his amazing bedroom talents, and soon disappeared when he mistakenly revealed his role as a husband, father, painter and decorator, with a wife and three kids, masquerading as a single stud on the website SinglesFun.com.

'Such a pity,' I mutter, flinging the duvet back to start my day. Fabio could be a decent start to any woman's day. In fact, if payroll queries prove difficult today, I may well have myself a Fabio flashback to help me through the mire that is Monday morning.

I quickly shower, eat breakfast and am dashing for the front door when my mobile pings.

> Sorry to text so early... can we talk tonight... I've been thinking. N

My heart stops on seeing his text. Nick doesn't text. Prior to this he hasn't texted me in the entire eleven months that we've been apart, separated or divorced. Not even when I packed my suitcase and left the marital home without anywhere to go.

What the hell is this supposed to mean?

Shit! Don't think, Nick. Seriously, not now that I've realigned my thinking and am making an effort to reignite our relationship and return to you after the long months spent refusing your request.

How am I supposed to focus on work if I don't know what's happening between me and Nick?

I press speed dial and listen impatiently to the ringing tone.

'Hello?'

'Nick?'

'Angie? Sorry, I didn't want to presume but...'

'What, Nick?'

'I wanted to say that I totally agree with what you said Saturday night. That we probably lost track of each other over the years and that, yes, I can see how things I did might have seemed to you at the time but, seriously... I do want this. I want for us to work.'

I slowly exhale.

'So, if you're willing to forget the other night, because I have a feeling it wasn't what you'd truly wanted, I was wondering if, maybe later this week, or next weekend if you prefer, I don't want to interfere with your work schedule... but anyway, how about we go on a proper first date... again?'

'Nick...' I can't swallow the huge lump that is wedged in my throat.

'Yeah?' He sounds so vulnerable, so open to starting afresh.

'Oh, my God, Nick... This is what I was trying to say to you but... you... oh, never mind. What and when are you thinking?'

'I hadn't got that far... but it's a definite yes, we're officially going to try again and get this, *us* back on track?'

'Yes, Nick.'

'Excellent. Have a good day, and I'll phone you later with details. Bye.'

'Bye.' I press the button and end the call, hugging the mobile to my chest.

Has that just happened? He sounded so positive, so on board. Bloody hell, this might actually be happening for us. Wow, this is going to be a great Christmas after all.

*

Holly

I call round for Demi just before half eight, as I always do on school days.

'Are we supposed to hang around with him from now on, then?' asks Demi, as she slings her bag on her shoulder and pushes her blazer sleeves up to her elbows for our short walk to the school gates.

'No, it isn't that intense. He asked why I'm never at youth club and then offered to call for me next Tuesday.'

'So, you're going out?'

I stare at her.

'Did you not just hear me?'

'Yeah, but Alfie Woodward asked to call for you, in which case – you're going steady and if not yet then defo by Tuesday after youth club especially if he walks you back home... OMG if he buys you a Zube tube drink at the youth tuck bar then you're going out!'

'What is a—?'

'See, you know nothing. Seriously, you need to get with it. They cost a quid, seriously a quid, and most of the lads won't buy you one but if Alfie buys you one this Tuesday, and I think he's gonna buy you one – otherwise what was the point in him asking to call for you? – well, then... he's serious.'

'And if he doesn't?'

'He defo will.'

I stare at my best friend. This 'going out' situation is entirely new to me. To Demi it is old hat. We may be only sixteen, but she's already snogged half our school class. I've snogged no one. Apart from a peck on the cheek in a Wendy house from a five-year-old boy at primary school

'If he wants to snog you are you gonna let him?' asks Demi as we walk past Mr Phillips and Mrs O'Dwyer chatting whilst on gate duty, manning the school entrance.

'Demi!' I snap, glancing between the teachers.

'They don't hear anything. Well, are ya?'

I blush. I totally might, if he is respectful for the rest of the night, but if he starts messing around and pushing his luck then there is no way I'm falling for cheap stuff like Demi has in the past. Simply no way.

'OMG, you are! But don't do tongues, right – it's way gross unless they've brushed their teeth. And if you change your mind about Alfie, you can always dump him at youth club and then come out with me afterwards. We've found somewhere new to go after dark.'

I eye Demi cautiously. She's my best mate but she lacks common sense at times.

If Alfie Woodward smells of Colgate when he picks me up on Tuesday, I may well do tongues; otherwise it's a no-goer!

*

Nina

We sit in a row behind Boss Fielding's desk, each with a pad of lined paper on which to take notes, though I always end up doodling on mine. A single hard-backed chair sits opposite, with a clean glass and water jug for company.

'You could have warned me,' I whisper to Zach, sitting on my right, positioned in the centre seat. Jackie's empty chair is on the far side, but she's nipped to collect the first candidate.

Zach smiles.

'Enjoy it. It's better than a morning spent working in the yard.'

He's right, but only just. Isn't it a bit late to be taking on more casual workers? It's not as if the crews aren't coping; in under three weeks they'll find themselves looking for work again. I never had an interview, simply a work trial.

The cabin door opens.

'If you please…' says Jackie, in her warmest, most posh interview voice, holding the door open for the candidate. Today, she's looking smart and sleek wearing numerous floaty scarves. Usually her alluring feature is her vibrant red hair and large earrings set against our embroidered uniforms.

He fills the doorway immediately, his bright red suit, black boots and magnificent beard making my eyes pop.

Zach gives me a sideways glance.

Is this a joke?

'We're employing our own Santa this year,' mutters Zach. 'That way Dad can give the orders, saving us the embarrassment from last year.' I heard of the incident: the agency Santa was slightly tipsy on Christmas Eve and walloped a child for drooling on his best beard. Boss Fielding had to compensate the parents for the distress caused, for which he wanted to wallop the Santa.

I watch as the Father Christmas clomps his way across to the candidate chair and settles down.

I want to laugh out loud. Boss Fielding was right – you can't get more 'casual' than his role.

Jackie takes her seat, straightens her notepad and introduces the panel. I love the way she bolsters our roles as if we're important – calling me a treasured member of Sales is pushing it a tad too far.

'So, Mr Claus, we'd like to ask a series of questions. Each candidate will receive the same questions and there's time at the end for any additional information that you feel we ought to know prior to selection,' explains Jackie.

I didn't even know I was interviewing; I haven't got a question. I stare at Jackie, hoping to communicate my needs.

'Firstly, can you explain why you wish to be our Father Christmas here at Christmas Tree Farm?'

I watch as the candidate smooths his long white beard before resting his huge hands upon his rotund belly. He definitely looks the part, given his ample size and tiny wire-framed glasses. He gives a decent answer regarding our associations with all things Christmassy. I scribble a note, because I feel I ought. As he draws breath, Zach jumps in with a question.

'Can you tell me about your career as a Father Christmas?'

As I sit back and listen, watching his mouth move beneath the layers of white whiskers, I wonder: would I have been frightened of him as a child?

'Thank you. Over to Nina for the next question.'

I jump in my seat. I didn't hear his answer and now I'm expected to ask an insightful question.

'Santa, nice to meet you... I was wondering... Could I ask...? Have you ever...?' All eyes are on me and I can't think of a single thing to ask. I wouldn't have known my name should Santa have asked me.

Suddenly, I know.

'What's the best thing a child has asked you to deliver on Christmas morning?'

'Lasagne.'

The panel chuckle.

'Seriously, lasagne? I bet their parents were pleased about that request.'

Santa goes on to explain it was her favourite meal, so that was all she wanted. As he talks I'm congratulating myself on such a creative question. But am pulled up when he asks me one.

'And what would you like?'

'*Me?*' I stare along the panel, tears springing to my eyes before I realise. 'I'm not doing Christmas this year,' is all I can muster. I don't wish to elaborate; if he has an ounce of true magical spirit, he'll know why. Surely, it's only Scrooge and the bereaved that avoid or cancel Christmas?

Santa gives a gentle smile. I hastily note: candidate one copes well when faced with an unexpected answer.

'Moving on,' says Jackie, eagerly. 'How many elves will you need to assist you during a shift?'

'Are you allergic to reindeer?' asks Zach, soon afterwards.

All too quickly it is back to me.

Why wasn't I given prior warning regarding the interviews?

'What's your reply when children say they don't believe in Santa?' I ask proudly, sensing the other two are impressed by my questions.

'I ask them to prove that I'm not real. They never can.' His blue eyes twinkle as he gives a deep belly laugh. I like him; this would be my kind of Santa.

'Is there anything else you would like us to know?' asks Jackie, her pen poised for detail.

Santa shakes his head.

Ouch, bad move – you should always give a little additional information even if it's just about your love of the job.

'Could I ask one last question?' I ask, unsure where my sudden confidence springs from. 'Can we hear your best ho, ho, ho?'

Both Jackie and Zach stare at me in disbelief before staring at the candidate.

'Sure,' says Santa, before performing his belly laugh. A deep bellowing roar erupts as his rosy cheeks lift high upon his face, causing his eyes to disappear, and his hands clutch at his jiggling belly.

I'm impressed.

Within no time, Jackie wraps up the interview. Santa says goodbye and is escorted from the log cabin.

Phew, end of interview one.

'This is surreal,' I say, more to myself than Zach. 'What's with the allergy question?'

'Dad's gone the whole hog and booked reindeer to accompany this year's grotto.'

'Are you joking me?'

Zach shakes his head.

'Nope. He's going for it this year. He wants it to be the best Christmas the farm has ever had. It's taken Jackie four days to find a suitable company to supply such livestock.'

Great. More joviality, just what I need.

'I'm really not up for fun and games, Zach.'

'Funny, given that you've got the knack for creative questions. Dad will be pleased.'

'Oh, no, you don't. I don't want more involvement with interview panel stuff.'

The cabin door opens and Jackie introduces candidate number two, dressed in an identical red suit but not filling it with a rotund frame like the first. A whiff of whisky fills the air as he settles himself in the candidate's chair.

Candidate three rudely fails to show up for the interview. Candidate four is as wiry as a telegraph pole so his suit hangs from his bony shoulders and candidate five is a replica of the first candidate – in fact they could have been Santa twins.

'Have you chosen?' is all Boss Fielding asks as we break for lunch, having sent the four interviewed candidates home awaiting a decision.

'It's not easy, but yeah... we've employed a Santa.' Jackie laughs, unsure how to tell her husband what we've actually done.

I'm pleased with the choice; it seems somewhat obvious.

'Nina, did you enjoy it?' asks the boss as I leave his office. 'Put you more into the festive spirit?'

I shake my head no, but realise that I enjoyed it more than I care to admit.

Four

Nina

Tuesday, 11 December

'How are we?' asks Zach, entering the cottage. Bram disappears into the lounge. I notice Zach looks at Dad's boots lining the skirting board and the mountain of coats piled on the coat hooks.

I shrug. What can I say? I texted asking for help with my task and within the hour they came running, as always, despite it being their day off.

'Here… put these on.'

I stare at the blue overalls Zach hands over and start to cry.

'Come here.' Zach's arms wrap around my shoulders. My head rests in the middle of his chest and I'm buried in a tight bear hug.

When did the twins grow so much taller than me?

'Thanks. I've got a feeling I'm in for a day of tears.'

'Plenty of hugs available,' says Zach.

I break from his hug and head towards the lounge.

'What the hell?' exclaims Bram.

'OK, Bram, we suspected it was bad,' mutters Zach.

'Bad? Are you kidding me?' cries Bram, turning to stare at me. 'Nina, you've been living like this?'

'Bram!'

'No, Zach... she needs to wake up and smell the bloody coffee, man. Just look at this place. It's a bloody hovel – your old man would go mental if he saw this... I've never seen anywhere look this uninhabitable, Nina.'

I lower my head and stare at the grit on the carpet. I provide a garbled explanation of wanting to hold onto the past, not wanting to get rid of his belongings, not wanting to face facts, not wanting to admit how I'm living alone.

'OK, so we'll sort it, *today*,' soothes Zach, hushing his brother's tones. 'Go grab the plastic box from the back seat of the truck, I'll grab a load of cloths and Nina...'

I look up to be greeted by his warm smile.

'Go put the kettle on... we need tea.'

I'm glad of an excuse to leave the lounge; Bram's wrath is prickling at my skin. I linger behind the kitchen door and listen to their hushed tones.

'Cut it out. Nina needs our help, not a fecking lecture,' hisses Zach.

'Leave it out... just look at this place. If I knew she'd been living like this Dad and Jackie would have rehomed her at ours.'

I busy myself with the tea making.

'Have you got any black bin liners?' asks Zach entering the kitchen as I put three clean mugs on to the kitchen worktop.

'Yeah, under the sink unit.' I point to the correct cupboard.

I watch as he unravels the roll, pulls free several bags and dumps the roll beside the mugs.

'We'll need them later, but first I'll get rid of the newspapers and stuff – there's nothing you'll want to keep, is there?'

I shake my head. Why would I wish to keep old yellowing newspapers dated from last year, and before?

'Not even a completed crossword or two?' he adds.

My God, he knows us so well.

A smile breaks my morose features.

'That would be nice. He did love his morning crossword.'

'Just one or two, then.'

I pour in the boiling water and mash the tea and acknowledge just how lucky I am.

*

By half four, the twins have cleared the hallway of every item apart from the staircase, the wall-mounted mirror and the row of coat hooks. The lounge receives a similar treatment courtesy of ten black bin liners, a yellow duster and a can of polish. Every surface, be it wood, glass or tufted-carpet shines like a new pin.

'Nina?' calls Bram, staring down at me as I scrub at the skirting boards. 'You OK?'

'I'm fine… just wondering how I'm going to overcome this embarrassment or repay you fellas.'

'Easy. I'll settle for a date on Friday night,' says Bram, a glint sparkling in his grey eyes.

Zach turns about to glance between us as he fills a black bin liner with coats.

I remain schtum. He's got a bloody cheek.

'Come on, what do you say? We'll get a taxi into town and enjoy a nice meal, yeah?'

I don't answer. I'm torn. What's stopping me from saying yes?

Bram gives a nod.

'Well, that's a turn-up for the books – you're usually so vocal about my suggestions. Eight o'clock, it is.'

*

Holly

A knock resounds upon the front door at ten minutes to seven. I didn't want to wait in the hallway so I am on the upstairs landing, dressed and fully prepared to dash from the house. Hannah leans against our bedroom door and smirks. I lean over the upper bannister, and watch my mother open our front door. A task she's done a million times, but this will be a first.

'Hello, is Holly in, please?'

My stomach flips at the sound of Alfie's voice. I smile. He used his manners – Mum will love that.

I snatch my head and shoulders back from the bannister for fear of being seen from below.

'Oh, hello... yes... *Holly?*' I imagine Mum standing aside from the open door, turning and hollering up the staircase. Oh, to be a fly on the wall to witness her expression, her smiling yet puzzled face complete with her over-the-top hollering voice.

I wait before answering. I need to linger and pretend I'm not on the landing. Hannah rolls her eyes, fighting the urge to shout a candid remark.

'*Yeah?*' I aim for nonchalant but don't quite pull it off.

'You've got a... *visitor* at the door,' calls Mum. I exchange a cheeky glance with Hannah, who continues to smirk. A visitor? Well done, Mum.

'OK.' I bounce down the stairs two at a time, to be greeted by two different smiles. My mother's is wary yet pleasant. Alfie's is bright and eager, illuminated by the drive's security light. He looks like a model dressed in faded jeans and a checked shirt. 'Hi, Alfie. Mum, this is Alfie – we're off to youth club. I'll be home in a couple of hours.' I step straight out of the door to stand beside him on our block paving. I cringe as the net of optic fairy lights adorning our lounge window changes colour and flashes simultaneously.

'See ya, both,' says Mum as Hannah joins her on the doorstep.

'Bye, Mum.'

'Bye, Mrs Turner.'

I see Mum's 'nice boy detector' flicker to life.

'Bye, Alfie, nice to meet you.'

We hastily stride down the driveway escaping the security light; neither one of us speaks until we reach the road. I know that Mum and Hannah are still hugging the doorframe, refusing to close the front door.

'Thank you,' I say as we cross the street and head towards the corner.

'Pleasure. Your mum seems nice, though a bit surprised when she opened the door.'

'Mmmm, I hadn't told her,' I say, grimacing. 'I'll get pulled up for it when I arrive back, but hey.'

'Yeah, don't worry, I get it.'

'Will your mum give you the third degree also?'

'Oh, no, I mean I get the whole "not telling mums stuff" thing,' says Alfie, zipping his jacket. 'My mum isn't living with us at the minute. She left back in January to do her own thing.'

I hear a break in his voice as he says the last part.

'Sorry, that must be difficult. My grandad died just after New Year and my mum has missed having her parent – even at the age she is.'

Alfie gives a shrug.

'Come on.' Alfie grabs my hand in his and we begin to do a slow run past other homes' tastefully adorning fairy lights and front gardens boasting real Christmas trees. We nip past the school's green fencing and towards the wooden shack community centre positioned alongside the far playground. My hand fits into his; there are no gaps, no holes and no awkward sensations. It feels warm, safe and natural.

*

Angie

The apartment buzzer sounds bang on eight o'clock. Nick is on time.

I quickly survey the lounge – everything looks neat and tidy – before I depress the wall-mounted release button.

It will take him minutes to climb the three floors, so I calmly walk to the front door, and stand with my hand on the latch, and wait.

I dashed home from the office, showered, dressed and dried my hair all before quarter to seven. I tried to pace myself by reading a magazine but ended up cleaning the lounge, kitchen and bathroom as tonight will be the first time Nick has seen inside my new home.

It feels like our uni days all over again, when we circled each other for twenty minutes, leaning again various objects and walls in my single dorm. In those days, Nick would eventually seat himself on the end of my bed and I would claim the only other place available – the desk chair.

I suddenly feel sick. I can hear all six feet four of Nick pounding up the staircase, the man I know so well and yet, I still feel overcome with nerves.

'Knock, knock.'

I pause, though my hand is already on the latch, and count backwards: ten, nine, eight, seven, six... bugger, can't wait... open.

'Hi.' I aim for casual, but it sounds fake.

'Angie, these are for you.' Clean-shaven, cologne *and* a new suit. Nick lifts a bunch of cellophane-wrapped white lilies from his side like a staged magician. Lilies, my favourite. From a proper florist too, not garage or supermarket stock.

My stomach flips.

'Thank you, come in.' I step aside, breathing in the fragrance of the flowers. Nick goes to remove his shoes, as we used to do at his home.

'No need, honestly.' I hadn't planned on us stopping for longer than a hello and let's go!

I close the door.

'Come through, while I put these into water,' I say as I lead the way. I'm relieved that I cleaned the kitchen as well as the lounge; he wouldn't have been impressed earlier.

'Nice place... oh, you've already got your tree, I see.'

His surprised tone catches my ear. I need to explain, I just don't want to.

'Yes, I bought it on Sunday from the usual place...'

'A Blue spruce.'

'Yes, a Blue spruce.' I know the significance won't go unmissed. He knows how long I have waited to get my own way.

We stare at the blue-green giant in the corner.

'And yet, no decorations?' In two strides he's crossed the room, to touch the outstretched branches.

I need to explain. He might read the wrong message otherwise.

'I ran out of time on Sunday. It took all my effort to drag it up the stairs and then being at work all day yesterday and today... I've watered it each day as instructed by the care leaflet but no decorations, not yet.'

'You should have called... I wouldn't see you stuck, Angie.'

I lean against the door jamb, lilies in hand, and stare at my ex-husband gently stroking the blue-green spruce.

'I know. It didn't seem right to ask... so, I managed.'

His eyes look sad as they look back at me.

'Anyway, let me put these into water and we'll head out...' I dash to the sink unit, and rummage beneath for a vase.

'Beautiful,' I say, carrying the vase to the breakfast bar and placing it centre stage.

Nick smiles. His sadness seems to have melted.

'Your favourites... I believe,' he says.

*

Holly

As we near the youth club shack, the doors are already wide open and a huddle of teenagers stand about outside chilling in small groups despite the cold weather. Paris and her cronies are there, chewing gum and texting.

I see one girl nudge Paris as we walk by. Their heads turn, the whispers start and their evil stares bore into the front, then the side and finally, the backs of our heads as we pass. Alfie doesn't seem to care. I keep my eyes straight ahead. I'm holding Alfie Woodward's hand; there isn't much else I care about.

'Holly!' I turn on hearing Demi's voice.

'Hang on a sec,' I say to Alfie, who immediately stops and waits at the entrance. 'Demi?'

Demi cuts through the rabble and stands before us, her smirk as wide as mine, her eyes as twinkly, if not more excited, than I would allow mine to be.

'Alfie Woodward... what a surprise. Together, are we?' she asks coyly.

Alfie glances at me before answering, a wry smile dressing his features.

'Well, yeah, I'd say so...'

I don't hear the rest of his conversation with Demi. My stomach convulses, my legs go weak and all I can think about is how I am going to explain my teenage date to my mum tonight when she is staked on the doorstep awaiting my arrival home.

A yank at my hand pulls me back to reality as Alfie walks me inside. A large wooden hut, a scattering of old sofas, oversized blaring music speakers and gathering groups of teenagers equates to a youth club. He wanders towards the drinks counter, saying hello to everyone he passes along the way. Some I recognise from our year at school, others must come from a neighbouring school across town. Our hands are still joined and I delight at being attached in public to Alfie Woodward.

'What drink do you want, Hols?'

Hols? He called me Hols. It sounds so natural, so us. I like it.

I lean forward and scan the selection.

'Diet Coke, please.'

Alfie frowns.

'Don't you want a Zube tube?'

I shake my head.

'Diet Coke is fine, thanks.'

'You're not one of those, are you?'

'What?'

'A calorie warrior who insists on diet everything… because they think they are just *so* fat!'

'No, and wait till you see me in the vicinity of chocolate. Trust me, you'll laugh that you asked such a question.'

He smiles.

'Good. I don't do that whole fat-talk business.' He leans over the counter and attracts the guy's attention. 'Two cans of Diet Coke, please, and a large bag of strawberry laces, cheers.' He grabs a fiver from his pocket. I instantly pull one from mine too. At which he shakes his head. 'You can pay another time. I invited you so fair's fair.'

'OK, but only if you stand by that.'

'I will. We'll do something come the weekend, if you're free, that is?'

I nod. Words fail me as explosions of joy cluster and burst deep within. Alfie Woodward, you have no idea how fabulous you've made a boring Tuesday night by holding my hand, buying me a Diet Coke and shortening my name.

*

Angie

'Madam?'

The festive fragrance of cedarwood and cinnamon fills the air as I follow the maître d' along the train's dining carriage until he indicates our table, to the right of the wide aisle.

My eyes take in the art deco surroundings, the wood panelling, the table's crystal chandelier, pristine white linen and burgundy velvet padded seats. The ultimate in high-class dining. This wasn't my expectation when we arrived on the platform to be greeted by a fuggy smell of burning coal.

'Nick?' I gasp as I slide into my seat, before the maître d' ruins my napkin sculpture with a hand flick to release it upon my lap.

'Sir?' I watch the waiter; he repeats the napkin flick like a matador, before draping the linen across Nick's lap.

'Menu for madam.' The leather-bound menu is heavy in my palms; the pages edged with gold contain delicate script to entice my appetite. 'Sir.' With a bow and a nimble step, he is gone and we are alone, smiling inanely over the tops of our menus.

'Nick, this is fabulous... I didn't expect anything as lavish as this for our first date,' I say, trying to act sophisticated and yet feeling very underdressed compared to the other dining guests.

'A guy at work mentioned it a while back. I always planned to bring you here, but we... well... you know...'

I nod. I don't need reminding; I left.

'Well, it's exquisite. It's a vintage steam train, right?'

Nick nods.

'A three-hour wine and dine journey – we can visit the cocktail lounge later, if you wish.'

'It feels like the Orient Express.' I giggle, trying to hide my delight.

'Not quite as expensive, though.' Nick laughs. I'm no expert on boys' toys, but when the train had arrived at the platform, I had instantly recognised the old-fashioned design of the locomotive. 'I wanted something special, for us.'

The train whistle sounds, cutting into the dark night, as the carriage gently sways to a rhythmical rumble upon aged tracks.

Our very first date was a night in the union bar at uni some twenty years ago. I'd hoped for somewhere far more glamorous then, but hey, he'd been short of cash and original ideas, so we'd crashed in the corner with numerous cans of Hooch and a plate of cheesy chips. And I'd had the time of my life. I had spent the evening chatting with the most interesting man I'd ever met. We'd laughed, talked serious and smooched non-stop while the jukebox played endless tunes. Afterwards, he'd walked me back to my room and had had the decency not to push his luck but to leave straight after a goodnight kiss.

That's Nick. My Nick, the old Nick. The man I fell hopelessly head over heels in love with. The man I was so desperate to marry. The guy that I fell pregnant by as soon as the wedding ring was on my hand. And, the forty-three-year-old that I left, one cold miserable night back in January. What a fool I was.

'*Angie?*'

I jump with a start. Nick looks concerned.

'Sorry, I was just enjoying the moment.' I return to my menu. The glorious array of food is mind-boggling: Brittany lobster, salt marsh lamb, braised venison and seasonal turkey. This must be costing him an arm and a leg and he's done it all for us. Me and him. Our *second* first date. I can't even focus on the menu selection, as my brain has turned to mush, much as it did when I was pregnant with Alfie.

*

'So, how's this year been?' asks Nick, washing his fingertips having consumed his bowl of fresh mussels.

I dab at my mouth, ensuring all signs of melba toast are brushed away.

'I've learnt a lot… a lot about myself. I have very little emotional intelligence where relationships are concerned

106

and…' I pause. I have no idea if he wishes me to air such feelings on a first date, but he asked so I need to be honest. 'I have experienced modern dating – which is an eye-opener.'

'Really?'

'Oh, yeah, things have changed since we…' I add, unsure if he wants to hear more. But he's attentive, he's leaning in, he's focused and silent so maybe he wishes for me to continue. 'It's all online profiles, side swiping or ghosting nowadays.'

Nick's brow furrows.

'I know… confusing… There's a whole host of dating lingo and…' Should I be honest, or keep a little back? I go for it. 'Lies. It's a minefield, in fact, but I did have a couple of nice dates and met some interesting people.'

'Men?'

I nod. I watch as the information registers. Yes, men, Nick. I've been dating men. Men of all ages. Some older, some slightly younger, with different backgrounds, situations and interests.

The silence grows.

I see his expression reboot and revive.

'That's good, Angie… and that's helped you to realise…?'

I nod.

Phew! Being honest isn't easy, is it?

'It has. Don't think there's been hundreds of dates but there's been a few… and yes, they've helped me to realise what I actually want in life and that, maybe, I've been at fault for previous mistakes.'

Nick nods. I think I've said enough for a first date. I could do with a conversation changer.

'Did any lead to a romantic attachment?'

Oh, my God, he's going there. Honesty is the best… could be the best policy. Eeeek!

I take a deep breath.

'You could say I've experienced a romantic revival… that I wasn't aware was lacking.'

Nick's mouth is straight and mute, awaiting my answer.

'*Sorry*, was that hurtful to hear?' My voice fades as my cheeks burn. 'I was simply being honest. And you?' I throw him a line.

'I've pretty much stayed the same as I was when we were… but no, I've not been romantically linked with any one.'

'Since January?' I ask in a curious tone, as the waiter removes our spent plates.

'Since January.'

'No dates?'

'Nope.'

'Nick?'

'Angie?'

'Seriously, no one?' I sit back and stare. He's aged well, he presents himself well and yet, he'd stayed at home each night. I honestly thought he'd venture towards pastures new once the divorce was finalised, and yet, he hadn't.

Nick coughs interrupting my internal monologue.

'Sorry, if that sounded hurtful. That was slightly more honest than I should have been, but you asked, Nick. I've definitely become more honest and open about my feelings and… needs.'

Nick nods. I know he's unsure of what to say, because he's Nick and I'm Angie. That's how our old marriage worked for eighteen years.

Nick readjusts his seating and leans forward; his hand stretches for mine.

'That's good. Honesty is important in a marriage.'

Back then, I wasn't honest or open. Back then, he wasn't sure what to do, what to say, or how to behave. The end result was a meltdown and a walkout. Both conducted by me, of course.

＊

'Thank you for such a wonderful evening, Nick.' I'm smitten, all over again. He's been attentive, curious and engaging. I've been honest, open and welcoming. I finish my sentence hoping that he'll lean in a little.

Then he leans close, placing a reassuring hand on my forearm, and gently kisses my forehead. I catch my breath hoping he does nothing more. *That* is perfect. The briefest of touches, yet the meaning is there.

I smile. He moves backwards, and smiles at my smile.

'Goodnight,' he whispers.

'Goodnight.' I want to burst with excitement. Oh, Nick, you have learnt so much in the last eleven months. I want to congratulate him; instead I remain silent. Could our divorce really help our relationship?

I unlock the lobby door and give a contented smile as Nick stands back from the doorstep, and I gently close the door behind me.

Five

Angie

Wednesday, 12 December

'Boy, from whose bed did you spring this morning?' asks Jilly, looking up from her tinsel-adorned screen as I charge at a super-speedy pace from one task to another about our tiny office.

'Nobody's!' I sing at her, swiping a pile of payroll queries from the incoming tray and eagerly begin to separate them.

'Christ... surely not the query tray... Are you delusional?' She removes her reading glasses, allowing them to swing from her gold chain, and peers at me, bemused.

'Nope. Just in a good mood, that's all.' I busy my hands as my mind begins to replay last night's fabulous dinner date. Nick has been a true gent. The guy I always wanted him to mature into. There were no awkward silences, no arguing or point scoring... no mention of

Alfie. Just the two of us enjoying a fabulous meal, in wonderful surroundings… a date to remember for all the right reasons.

'What's his name, then?' asks Jilly, pushing her keyboard aside for an impromptu break from entering overtime data.

I give her my best smile.

'Seriously, you're not going to share?' Her greying bob tilts sideways as if pleading to hear my news.

I smile even more.

'Bloody hell, he must be good. In the last eleven months, I've heard about the Italian stallion, the Mr Thong guy and that ultra-sexy stud from the builder's yard but you're now staying silent. *Angie*, what are you up to, woman?'

'Arrr, wouldn't you like to know?'

'Yes, please! My life consists of the weekly excitement that is *Bake Off* and *Strictly*. My Chris has given up the ghost regards romance so, yeah… spill those beans.'

'Nope!' I say in a comedic fashion. I have no intention of sharing anything about this one. She is right: I shared regarding Fabio, the Thong-guy and screamed it from the roof-top about young Matt the builder, but this… is private. Special. Sensitive. Jilly can guess all she wants; I'm not breathing a word.

'I'm thinking first-night sex, right?' she whispers from behind the tacky Douglas fir ornament decorating her tiny desk.

I shake my head as I begin slotting the queries into date order.

'No! All-night sex?'

I frown, without even looking up.

'Was there sex at all?' asks Jilly, getting up from her seat and drifting over from her chair.

'Mmm… let me think,' I ponder in my best acting style and finally laugh. 'No!'

'So, what the hell are you so damned happy about this morning?'

'Life!'

'Phuh, don't give me that crap, Angie. Since the beginning of this year your life has been one long shag-fest.'

'Date-fest actually!'

'Same thing.'

'Definitely not! Actually, I'll have you know I've learnt a lot about myself this year – probably more than any other year of my life – and in recent days, I have actually realised that…' I stop. This is going to sound utterly American-talk-show-host-ish, but still. 'I think I've found myself.'

Jilly perches her M&S skirt on the edge of my desk, nudging my cheap fibre-optic Christmas tree aside, before belly laughing.

I watch her, head back, mouth wide open, snorting at my epiphany moment. I wait for her to open her eyes and acknowledge that I'm watching her.

She finally opens her eyes. Ceases to laugh, splutters and stares at me.

'Are you serious?'

'Yep. I, Angie Woodward, aged forty, can honestly say... I think, I know who I am and what I desire in life.'

'Pull the other one – it's got bells on it!'

'Nah! It hasn't.'

Jilly stares at me. She's waiting for my outburst, my emotional revelation. She's going to be disappointed. I continue with my work.

'Bloody hell.' She slides her ass off my desk corner. 'Have you seen a doctor about this?'

'Nope. *And,* I don't intend to.'

Jilly sidles back to her own desk. Her intrigue register is on high alert, in case I suddenly divulge and she needs to quickly return to my desk. She settles back at her keyboard and resumes entering numbers into the monthly spreadsheet, her gaze eagerly trained upon me.

'If you don't share, you'll pay the consequences,' she warns, pretending to pinch the lower branch of her cheap festive ornament.

'I'm not sharing, Jilly.'

'So be it!' Jilly pinches the ornament's branch. Instantly the Douglas fir bursts into life, its eyes bulging and mouth flapping, singing and swaying to 'Jingle Bell Rock'.

I smile contentedly, I can tune out the tinny music. I haven't a care in the world. This is how it must feel to be happy. I'd quite forgotten.

*

Holly

'And?' asks Demi as we walk to school. 'Did he?'

I never ask her for details, and yet she wants to hear everything.

'Firstly, I'm grounded,' I say as I hitch my school bag onto my shoulder. 'My mum wasn't happy when I got home.'

'No way!'

'Yes, way.'

Demi shakes her head.

'We got into an argument about Alfie – she called me sneaky and I said that I was allowed some privacy, which my dad agreed with, but my mum wasn't having it. She thinks she needs to know everything that I do, say, think and I raised my voice in answering her back, and now I'm grounded till the weekend.'

'Phew! If I was grounded every time I raised my voice in our house I'd be in solitary confinement till I was twenty-six!' Demi laughs. 'And Alfie?'

'She doesn't seem too bothered by him, more the fact that I didn't confide in her.'

'She's going for the "let's be all pally-pally with mother-daughter secrets", but it's false, isn't it?'

'Yep, totally false. I think she liked him, to be fair.'

'But she's not gonna tell you that, not yet anyway.' Demi pauses. 'So…?'

'Oh, my God, Demi Walker... yes, he kissed me. OK now?'

'And...' Demi stops walking and turns, her face looming into mine, much as Alfie's did last night.

I giggle.

'You did tongues, didn't you?'

'Stop it!' I know my face is scarlet.

'Holly and Alfie sitting in a tree K-I-S-S-I-N-G,' sings Demi as we link arms and continue on our way.

I tell her how we bumped noses, how I was embarrassed by my train-track braces and how his breath tasted of strawberry laces.

'Did he say anything about school?'

'He said I could hang with their group... but I don't think I want to.'

'Good. For one minute, I thought I was getting dumped as your bestie.'

'Demi, no way.'

'Just saying. Anyway, if you're grounded you won't be able to come out tonight. We're thinking of nipping up to the tree farm for a few cheeky ciders. Spud walked me home last night after sharing three cans.'

I shake my head. Cheeky ciders amongst a group of trespassing teenagers is not my kind of thrill but, even so, my mum will enforce her grounding from the moment I arrive home anyway.

We arrive at the school entrance and pass through the double green gates. As we enter the driveway, Paris and her gang are standing beneath the nearest tree. They simultaneously turn and stare as we walk by.

I stare straight ahead; Demi turns to acknowledge their interest in us.

'Don't antagonise them,' I mutter.

'Bloody hell, what's the attraction?' Demi laughs, turning to the front. 'Unless she has designs on Alfie.'

As we enter the playground we hear a hastily-garbled remark shouted by the mean-girl group.

'I've got food tech with Paris later – I'll spike her cake mixture with salt, if you like.'

'Nah! A waste of energy.'

'*And* good salt,' adds Demi.

*

Nina

Rap a tap tap. I hear Zach's knuckles upon the frosted glass announcing their arrival for day two.

I can't do it, but I can't ignore them.

'Morning,' I mutter, unlatching the cottage door.

'Nice to see you've kept the place looking lovely,' remarks Bram, poking his head around the lounge door, 'even if it was simply overnight.'

'If you can't face a second day of cleaning, take yourself out for a while – we'll crack on,' offers Zach, unpinning the kitchen door from its hinges. 'Seriously, we don't mind.'

Two concerned faces stare at me, both with clear grey eyes, muted smiles and a warmth that no one else can deliver.

I shrug. I'm dumbstruck. I don't deserve such friendship.

'We'll put aside anything that might be precious or needs your opinion,' adds Bram, pocketing the hinge pins as Zach passes them over. Bram manoeuvres the wooden door, leaning it against the hallway wall. 'We won't throw anything out.'

'What are you doing?'

'Have you seen how tiny the kitchen is? We'll have more room without the door in place,' explains Zach.

In unison, we stare around the small kitchen. I see it with fresh eyes. Every ceramic tile, cooker ring and cupboard handle now reveals itself in a furry, fuzzy light. In fact, as I stare at the ceiling lights I see the extent of the dirt – even the spotlights have a covering of yellow grime.

'How have you not been ill?' asks Bram, leaning against the door jamb, wary of entering. 'Do you actually cook in here?'

'*Sometimes*, but lately it's been fridge food, warmed through,' I mutter.

'What about when your dad was here?' he continues.

'Bram!'

'What?'

'Give it a bloody rest,' says Zach.

Bram stares at me, before answering.

'She's fine, man... I'm not upsetting her. So, stop being so bloody tetchy on her behalf.'

I pray Bram doesn't mention the Friday night date – wheedling out of that one today might send me over the edge.

'I'm fine, Zach, honestly. I still have my moments every day but for the majority of the time I'm OK talking about Dad.'

Zach nods, almost as convinced as I am by my words

*

120

'I suggest two clean in here and one hits the upstairs,' offers Zach, pulling his gloves on.

'Bagsy upstairs... if anyone belongs in her bedroom, it's me!' announces Bram, with a cheeky wink. Zach and I exchange a glance before we both stare at Bram.

'I don't think so!' I retort. 'Zach, you upstairs. I'll stay here with Casanova.'

'OK, but I'll start the bathroom first, Bram... or did you forget that is also located upstairs?' says Zach.

'Seriously, Nina, I was only joking... just trying to bring a bit of sparkle and joy into your day, that's all. Don't get the hump.'

'I haven't.'

We can hear Zach thumping up each stair above our heads.

I open the back door and pin it wide with a hard-backed chair, allowing a whoosh of cold December air to enter the kitchen.

'Everything out, clean and then return, is it?' asks Bram.

'Yep, even the lino... let's rip it up and I'll replace it at a later date.'

I am amazed how quickly tears spring to my eyes when Bram opens the top cupboard and I spy the piles of white cardboard boxes with my dad's prescription labels attached. Two shelves filled with neatly-stacked boxes. Boxes that I was never allowed to touch. When I was a child that cupboard had housed our biscuit barrel filled with lemon puffs and pink wafers, but those treats were relegated to the pantry cupboard for safekeeping and replaced with a multitude of his medication.

I wasn't supposed to notice or ask any difficult questions. So, I didn't ask questions for nearly five years, until it was blindingly obvious that I should have asked them sooner.

It takes an hour and a half just to empty the cupboards of forgotten saucepans, trifle dishes and soup tins.

How can anyone stash so many tins of tomato soup and not ever eat?

I ooze cream cleaner onto my cloth and smear the newly-discovered red floor tiles in opaque white.

*

'Shall I drag the junk out from the cubbyhole under the stairs?' asks Bram, opening the tiny wooden door.

'No!' I dash into the hallway, hurting my hand as I slam the tiny door closed, dislodging his grip. 'There's no junk in there!'

I don't want anyone touching under the stairs. It is precious and doesn't need disturbing. My fixed gaze blurs with tears as Bram's bemused face stares at me. For the second time in two days I lean and bury my head into a male's solid frame whilst his arms wrap around my shoulders.

I appreciate the twins' help with the house cleaning, but it's all too much, all too soon.

*

Justifying my decisions whilst others strongly suggest solutions to my current circumstances finally gets the better of me. It isn't entirely Bram's fault; his Christmas tree suggestion is simply the final straw after a difficult two days. I snap.

'I'm never having a Christmas tree again!' I shout at Bram's frozen expression. 'There'll be no sparkly lights, or colourful tinsel, not even a holly wreath on the door. Never!'

'OK, I hear you, no need to shout,' mutters Bram, backing away from me. 'Just saying it would be nice, that's all.'

It wasn't the craziest suggestion, given that his father traditionally gifts each of his workers a spruce come Christmas Eve. Boss Fielding wouldn't be surprised or offended – he and Jackie understand my reluctance to join in with the season's festivities. Wasn't that what Sunday's little chat was about?

My mood doesn't improve once they've gone home, taking all the bin liners to the rubbish tip on a short detour. As I watch TV, I feel lonely, ungrateful and thoroughly miserable. I look across to Dad's seat and, for the first time since he's gone, I can't imagine him sitting there any more. The seat is empty. I berate myself for letting the twins rearrange the lounge furniture. The room feels alien, uncomfortable in every way, from every angle. Not how my dad would remember it. I know he's never coming back, he's dead, but in the world of make-believe my mind throws up strange comforts. It feels as if I've lost him all over again.

At eight o'clock, I go to bed and cry.

*

Angie

'Alfie, it's Mum.' I wait for his reaction to know how to proceed.

'Hi.'

'I was wondering when you're free... so we can hook up for a chat.' I can hear the TV blaring in the background despite it only being four thirty. Shouldn't he be doing homework?

'Dad's working late... suppose we could get some pizza later.'

Hallelujah, an answer. I snatch a glance across the office. My desk and in-tray are clear, Jilly's computer screen is blank, so she's winding down for the day too. I could pack up and leave bang on five.

'OK, how about I pick you up in forty minutes?'

'Could you make it an hour or so? I'm kind of busy right now.'

Great! Don't rock the boat and wreck it.

'OK, that sounds perfect... We'll head into town for pizza, if that's your choice.'

'Excellent. Cheers!'

'Alfie... I...' The phone went dead. Well, blow me, does no one say goodbye any more when talking on a mobile? It is beginning to be like the American soaps where everyone simply puts the phone down and cuts you dead. 'Bye, Mum, bye, lad... see you in an hour,' I say sarcastically aloud to myself.

*

Holly

'That was my mum...' says Alfie, shoving his mobile into his blazer's top pocket. 'What time have you got to be back home by?'

We'd gone round to Alfie's house straight from school. Alfie had let me in with his own key. My mum wouldn't trust me with a goldfish, let alone a door key. I'd met their dog, Rolo, who is now sitting begging for titbits. I had tried to focus on the dog while Alfie was talking to his mum.

'Five o'clock otherwise I'll be in trouble with my mum about being grounded,' I say dolefully. I don't really want to go home. It's peaceful here. I'd much prefer to stay here in Alfie's kitchen drinking hot Ribena and scoffing waffles.

'I'm heading out for pizza with my mum... awkward or what?'

'Is that not your usual routine for Wednesdays?'

'Nah! I haven't seen her for months. She's trying to build bridges before Christmas arrives. She'll probably be all hyper pretending she saw me only last week.' He doesn't look at me as he explains, but fiddles with his mug handle.

We sit at their breakfast bar; a fruit bowl filled with plastic bits, keys and string sits between us. My feet swing on such a high chrome stool, my pleated school skirt bounces at my knee.

'I stayed with Dad... which annoyed the hell out of my mum but, hey, she was the one that was unhappy with us, not the other way around.'

I nod as he speaks. Complain as I do about my mum, I can't imagine our home without her.

'I'm sorry, it sounds dreadful,' I say, not knowing how else to be supportive.

Alfie shrugs in a nonchalant manner.

'It was *her* decision. Me and Dad have got along without her... She doesn't understand how tough it's been, but she's not witnessed it, has she?'

'But she's your mum.'

'Exactly. A mum that left me for...' He hesitates before continuing, 'Dad reckons she was having an affair... someone at work.'

I see the sadness flicker about his eyes. Funny how you don't suspect a classmate of having a bad time when you see them laughing and joking with their peers in lesson. There must have been times he didn't want to be in school, let alone be the popular boy with the funny banter.

His eyes flicker to meet mine.

'I'll never know, will I? Unless I confront her. Did my mum choose some good-looking boss over me?'

'Alfie... I'm sure...' I fall silent. I'm not sure of anything in this world regarding adults. I only know what happens in our house and desperately hope my parents stay the course without having affairs with their bosses. An image of both their bosses springs to mind. I want to giggle at the ludicrous idea, given that my dad's boss at the garage is Mr Evans, with bushy grey eyebrows that overhang his face. My mum's is a baby-faced bloke at the local café where she works part-time.

'Can you imagine doing that?'

'Me?'

'It's not a nice lesson to learn about people you think you know... I suppose I expect everyone to leave.' He stares at me.

My brow furrows. He's obviously hurt by her actions, but still.

'Sorry, that was a bit heavy. It's just how I feel now. I might be a teenager, but she's changed how I think about people.'

'I get that... but please don't think all girls... women act like that. My mum has never been away from my dad and they've been married for sixteen years.'

'Mine did eighteen years – it didn't stop her leaving.' He stares at me; silence lingers. I can see he's calculating the maths.

'Yeah, she was eight months gone with me by the time they got married.'

'I just got that.' He laughs. 'Parents... they aren't *that* clever, are they, despite what they say?'

'Exactly.' I laugh. 'My parents are forever lecturing me on the rights and wrongs of life and yet they couldn't use a condom properly.'

Alfie smiles; his hand reaches forward and gently strokes my cheek.

'I'm glad they messed up,' he whispers, a slight blush appearing on his clear complexion.

'Me too.'

*

Angie

He's grown so much since I last saw him and he holds himself differently. One thing that hasn't changed is his appetite. Alfie wolfs down his pizza like a starving dog. He doesn't stop to draw breath but inhales each piece – Frankie and Benny's pizza was always a family favourite.

His jawline looks different; the downy fluff has gone. Has he started shaving? Surely not, he's still at school.

'What?' he says, midway through a bite.

'Nothing.'

'But you're staring, Mum.'

I shake my head, admit nothing, the ultimate defence to being caught watching. He continues eating his pizza while I toy with my bowl of carbonara pasta. I can't even taste the creamy sauce, but I ordered it because this was always *our* order. Our order when we were a happy family unit, before I trashed the family portrait.

'So, how's school?' Usually a safe question.

He rolls his bottom lip. That's not my Alfie. That question usually fills a fifteen-minute silence as he rattles on about History, Physics and sometimes Maths. More if you nudge him as regards sport.

'*Really?* That good.' I rack my brain for the next conversation lead. 'How's young Neil doing?' I ask. The pair have been inseparable since playgroup.

'He's got a job as a glass collector at weekends but he's started smoking stuff... so, I don't see—'

'My God! At sixteen? Does his mother know?'

'Sure, Mum, he told her first off... Of course she doesn't know.'

'I've a good mind...'

Alfie stares at me.

'What?'

'I haven't seen you in months but you've a good mind to dash around their house to inform Jenny of his weed habit. Cheers!' He puts down his pizza slice. 'Maybe I should have joined him with a joint or two.'

'Hey, cut it out. It was your decision not to see me. I wanted visitation weekends.'

'When, Mum? When in the last six months have you offered to see me, talk to me or do this?' He waves his hand in the gap between us.

I'm taken aback. Since when did he argue like his father? All logical and factual.

'Alfie—'

'Leave it. I don't want to hear it.' He resumes eating his pizza slice.

I push my unfinished bowl away, grateful for an excuse.

'Alfie, I have every right to be happy... I wasn't happy.'

'True. But I have every right to have a mother I can rely upon... but, hey, you chose to ignore me while you had your fling.'

'Has your father told you that? Is that what he's saying?'

'It's what I've heard him say on the phone.'

The phone? Who the hell would Nick say that to?

'To Gran?' I ask.

Alfie pulls a face.

'Like she wishes to discuss *you*!'

I balk at his remark. Julia and I had always got on; surely she understood where I was coming from?

I breathe deeply. This isn't how I envisaged our meal. I expected the usual laughter, happy chatter and jokes with my son. That child seems to have grown and developed an opinion of his own, or one spoon-fed to him by others.

'Do you want me to explain?'

'Nope.' He wipes his mouth with the green serviette, and swigs his Coke.

I watch his Adam's apple dance as he does so. When did that appear so prominently?

I try another tack.

'Has your father spoken to you since the weekend?'

'Not much. He's worked late tonight...' His eyes flicker about my face before he continues. 'He had a date last night, so I didn't see him before bed.'

That was with me. Why didn't Nick say?

I give a nod, unsure how to proceed.

Alfie takes the lead instead.

'This morning over breakfast he said she was nice.'

'Did he?' I eye him. Alfie's watching my every move. Is he toying with me or testing me for information?

'Have you met her?'

He shakes his head profusely.

'First date, I think.'

'Has Dad had many dates?'

Alfie smiles.

'That would be telling.'

I stare. I can't believe my own son is toying with me as regards his father's actions. I know, he's told me he hasn't seen anyone in the entire time, and yet...

'I'm glad. It's about time your dad started to see other people... move on with his life.'

Alfie nods, a little too eagerly. Thanks, I now know which camp he supports.

'Exactly what I said. He's spent too long moping around the house, trying to figure out how to move on, but he seemed happy at breakfast. He was whistling again.'

My ears prick up.

'Was he?'

'Oh, yeah, I took it as a good sign – he'd had a decent night. Though he hadn't brought her back to ours for a coffee or anything.'

'He might have... she might have slipped out before you woke.'

'Nah. I was wide awake listening for him to come in. He was alone when he came back.'

Isn't it supposed to be the other way around?

'Would you have minded?'

'If he'd brought her back?'

I nod. Now who is testing who?

'Not really... I suppose it's what I expect him to do when he finds someone. You must have taken people back after a night out?'

My mouth works at an answer but fails miserably.

'See. Why should Dad be any different?'

'Dessert?' I literally bail from the conversation. I can't talk in this manner with my son. He's not even left school and yet seems to know the ins and outs of adult relationships without ever bloody being in one.

He shakes his head.

'I'll have a coffee though... if you're having one.'

Since when did my son say no to a dessert but wants coffee? I try again.

'You love that chocolate brownie dessert...'

Alfie shakes his head.

'Too sweet.'

'Too sweet?' I laugh. I'm stunned. 'You used to wolf it down. Boy, how you've changed!'

I cease; he's watching me.

'Lots of things have changed...' His voice fades. 'More than you realise.'

'Alfie, come now.' I reach for his hand. His eyes follow my touch and he stares as I try to take his dead hand in mine. Under his gaze, I retract my hand and sit back.

He's very different from the boy I waved off from the doorstep each day. Adolescence is difficult in lots of ways; I suppose he's confused entering another phase of life. No longer the child but certainly not an adult.

I call for the bill. We sit in silence waiting, but it feels like an eternity.

'Are you interested in any young ladies?' I ask, trying to end on a good note.

He eyes me before speaking.

'Nah!' His eyes flicker, as if he's lying.

'Really? At your age most of the lads are cute on someone.'

'If this is heading towards a chat about the birds and the bees – I'd quit now, I've discussed it with Dad.'

He sees the interest in my features.

'I don't think you've ever been a guy, so there's really no point you trying to explain… stuff.'

I nod an acknowledgement. Useless and redundant in that department too, am I?

The young waitress nips the bill wallet to our table. I flip the cover to view.

'Are we going Dutch?' asks Alfie.

'No!' I'm horrified. When did my son start using that phrase?

I pass the waitress my debit card.

'Look, Alfie, whatever has happened, I remain your mother. You are the child and I am the…' I don't finish my sentence.

'Well, there's the problem. You should have continued to act as my mother when life got tough, but you didn't, you… you bailed.'

The waitress doesn't know where to look, and neither do I.

*

'Thanks, Mum.'

I kiss him on the cheek, the ultra-smooth slightly fragrant cheek, which has been scraped bare by a man's razor, before he escapes from the passenger seat of my car.

The house looks empty, albeit for a dim light around the edge of the lounge curtain. Is Nick home or not? Is Alfie now a latch-door kid? Am I a bad mother for having feelings of my own? Or is Alfie still naïve regarding emotions and desires?

I half lean across the passenger seat, expecting him to turn and wave at the gate. Maybe the doorstep? Before the door closes? Nothing. He is gone, door shut.

I pull away from their kerb, drive into the next street, pull over and park beside a stranger's kerb… and sob. An uncontrollable, gut-wrenching sob.

I've lost my baby.

A dog walker passes by. He bends slightly to view the mess in the driver's seat, clutching her steering wheel and wailing. From outside I must look like a tragic mime artist, mascara seeping down my cheeks, but without the gloves. He hastily walks by, tugging impatiently at his dog to hurry up.

I sit back, dry my eyes and stare at the road ahead. A pristine street, similar to ours... *theirs*, with neat front gardens, privet hedges and reverse-parked cars awaiting the routine of tomorrow morning. I stare aimlessly at each set of drawn, fully-lined curtains, all hiding the stage show of a family. Those happy, sad, desperate families protected from public humiliation by the face they project to the neighbours. The cheery good mornings shouted across the manicured lawns, the polite nods to the nameless few. We, the Woodwards, were once one of these decent families, until I blew our shit wide open to the neighbours by packing two large suitcases and plonking them on the block paving. Boy, that must have given Mae over the road a new topic to discuss at coffee morning with her WI ladies.

Six

Nina

Thursday, 13 December

'How did it go?' asks Kitty as we ready ourselves in the snug by dressing in layers for yet another cold morning on the farm.

'Emotional… but cathartic,' I say. 'I'm surprised how good it felt this morning coming down to a clean home.' One with fewer reminders plastered on every surface.

'A job well done, then?'

'Absolutely. Twenty-seven black bin liners of… removed from the house.' I can't bring myself to say rubbish, but still.

'And?' Kitty continues, her face spreading into a beaming smile. 'How were the fellas?'

I attempt blasé, but she continues to watch me as I add another jumper.

'I'm waiting.' Kitty gives a giggle, her blonde fringe dancing.

'They were amazing, and really caring...' I fade to silence.

'And yet?' Kitty stands, hands on hips, bulging in a puffa jacket, extra padded trousers and large boots. She looks quite comical.

'Bram was his usual cheeky self, asking for a date, but Zach was amazing, comforting me whenever I got upset.'

'So?' she urges.

'Shouldn't I feel something more?'

'Duh! Yeah!'

'That's the problem... I don't.'

'Nina!' cries Kitty. 'I thought... you were getting the whole...'

'Heart-racing and stomach-flipping sickness?'

'Yeah!'

'Nah!' I grimace.

Kitty's eyebrows are lost into her fringe as she shakes her head.

'That's not good, girl.'

'I didn't think it was. I always hoped I'd feel the whole shebang when I met the right guy but...'

'I know that feeling,' Kitty says, unable to keep back her glowing smile. 'Ahh, my legs turned to jelly ten times over. I knew the minute I saw Connor that...' She ceases to speak. She doesn't need to finish her sentence; her expression says it all. Kitty is in love, head over heels, totally smitten. Her face comes alive the moment she

140

thinks about Connor, like an internal light bulb that beams. Each night he collects her from work. She can't wait to be with him, so jogs over to his car, hastily shouting bye to us. They've been together for a couple of years and still the magic is alive. That's what I want. Someone who ignites my world, and I theirs.

The snug door bursts open. It's Shazza, gasping for breath.

'The boss is spitting feathers out here. You're both late and he wants all hands on deck – the herd of reindeer have arrived early,' she calls.

'In a minute,' says Kitty, eager to finish the conversation.

'No, now!' says Shazza. 'He's in a devil of a mood. They weren't due until tomorrow and he's just discovered that the kids have cut through the fencing *again* and had some kind of winter barbecue amongst the spruce. There's cider cans and aerosol canisters everywhere.'

'Is this happening every night?' I ask, pulling on my embroidered jacket.

'Virtually,' says Kitty. 'Shazza, tell him we're on our way.'

Shazza disappears, with an unconvinced look on her face.

Kitty rubs my forearm and gives me a puppy-dog look.

'So now what do I do?' I mutter.

*

Holly

I stare at my mobile: ten text messages all from Alfie about his pizza night with his mum. Doesn't sound like it was a fun night, and I can completely understand that.

It's 7 a.m. Do I reply? He must have fallen asleep only three hours ago – how is he going to get through double physics today?

I ready myself for school, pack my book bag and dive downstairs for breakfast. It's the usual scene: a cramped huddle about the breakfast table all shouting for Frosties and sharing the decreasing milk, eyeing the remaining amount left. I'd love to live in a house that has plenty of milk. We *never* have enough milk. I squeeze in at the breakfast table between Hope and Hettie, though I fear for my school uniform given the way they dribble and throw their cereal around. Dad is scooping milk from a bowl, while trying to pour orange juice; Mum is frantically trying to spread sandwiches on a Formica sideboard that is covered in an array of plastic lunch boxes. When I'm older, much, much older, I won't be having *this* many children. I look around the table. Having six sisters is probably the best contraception I could ever wish for. Living amongst this amount of pink is probably more influential than those safe sex film shown at school. Two babies, even one, might be enough.

'Morning, Holly!' says Dad finally, looking up from his spent bowl. 'Are you wearing make-up?' He peers at my face then turns to view Mum's anxious features, her butter knife suspended mid-action.

'A bit… just mascara.'

'Hump!' snorts my mother, returning to duty.

'Mum says he's got nice manners…' jibes Dad, adding his bowl to the mountain of dirty crocks on the drainer.

I raise my eyebrows. This feels so foreign. I expected him to lecture, to ban me from having a boyfriend, but to compliment, wow!

'He comes from the Rowland's Way Estate,' I say, as if that explains everything Dad needs to know.

My parents exchange a glance and pull a face.

'La-di-da, is he?' asks Dad, circling the table and giving out kisses before he dashes to work at the garage.

'No! Pretty down to earth, actually.' He annoys me with that comment. What's la-di-da got to do with having nice manners? He makes Alfie sound like a posh-weirdo.

Dad comes closer to plant a kiss on my forehead before speaking.

'Maybe you want to invite him over for tea one night. I'm sure his mum won't mind,' he says.

'It's just him and his dad. His mum left.'

My mother whips around from her butty duty, her eyebrows high.

'Single parent family?' she mutters, and shakes her head.

'It's not his fault, love,' adds Dad, smoothing his newspaper to take with him.

'Exactly. I'll ask him, Dad.'

'Any attempt to get a boy in the house.' Hannah laughs, and Dad pretends to swipe her with the folded newspaper.

'Ha, ha, young lady. We may ask to trade him for *you*. Maybe his dad would like a daughter for a while before sending you back!' Hannah pulls a face, as Dad gives Mum her final peck on the cheek. I like the fact that they openly kiss in front of us. I think it's how it should be when you're married. I wonder if Alfie's parents had stopped kissing in front of him. Maybe that's stage one towards the divorce courts.

Within ten minutes of Dad leaving, I'm back upstairs faffing about trying to get Heidi dressed. She won't wear her woollen tights, she won't have her hair brushed and at this rate I'm going to be late calling for Demi.

'Stop wriggling about and get dressed properly,' I snap. I see her eyes widen. As little as she is, she knows that's not me. 'Sorry.' Heidi gets dressed without fuss; she knows when she's crossed a line with us older ones.

My mobile bleeps, which distracts me from my guilty conscience.

It's Alfie.

Walk to school?

I answer, not wanting to push my best friend aside.

What about Demi?

His reply takes ages to arrive. I stare at my screen, willing him to answer, as Heidi pulls her woollen tights over her scabby knees.

Her too.

Right answer, Alfie. I'm thrilled. I've never like it when friends get blown out just because two people start dating. Demi's unaware of the fact, but she's done that to me a couple of times and it feels like the pits. Then the minute they get dumped they call you up to go down town as if nothing happened. I've always gone with her when she's asked but I've had the hump inside for days. I quickly reply.

OK ☺

'Come on, slow coach, race you downstairs!' Heidi belts from her bedroom and dashes downstairs. I follow, leaving her in Hannah's capable hands, grab my coat, kiss Mum and shout goodbye from the open doorway.

*

Alfie waits on the corner of Raveloe Drive, his rucksack lolling from his shoulders and his new fringe swept to the side, chomping a bacon roll from the corner shop.

146

'Is that your breakfast?' I ask, on approaching.

'It only costs a quid,' he says. I hesitate. Are we at the 'kiss you on greeting' stage or just when in private? 'How are you?'

'Good, though my sister refused to get dressed this morning... so I feel tetchy as hell! Come on, otherwise Demi will think I've stood her up.'

We fall into step side by side, him nearest the road side of the pavement and me on the inside. His free hand links into mine. My fingers wrap around his like a glove.

'My dad said you can visit for tea one night if your dad's OK with that,' I say, unsure of how he'll feel. A household filled with screaming girls and Barbie dolls in comparison to being calm, peaceful and surrounded by computer games.

'Cool, I'll mention it when I get back. Next week would be better for my dad – I know he's home early for the rest of this week.'

My mobile bleeps; it's Demi.

Where the hell are you?

I instantly feel guilty. *Dawdling*, that's where.

'Come on, we're late.'

We do a stupid jog-speed walk action as we cross the road and head towards Demi's.

*

147

'I see. Like that, is it?' calls Demi as she slams the porch door behind her.

'Morning, Demi,' calls Alfie, in a jolly voice.

Demi gives him a sly stare.

'What?'

'Has Spud said anything to you?' she says, joining us on the pavement.

I didn't think she was that keen on Spud.

'Boys talk,' warns Alfie.

'Demi?'

'Hasn't she told you?' jibes Alfie, releasing my hand. 'Well, Spud's saying that on...'

I stare at Demi, who has gone decidedly pink beneath her tinted moisturiser.

'Shut up, Alfie Woodward. You know nothing. He's lying.'

Alfie raises his eyebrows at me.

'Boys talk, do they?' I ask, cheekily.

'Not me. I don't,' he quickly adds, taking my hand as we trundle back along the street towards the school gate.

*

Nina

'I daren't ask whose bloody stupid idea this is,' grumbles Old Bill, the farm's eldest and long-suffering handyman-come-gofer, as he loads the final wooden pallets onto the truck's trailer.

'Mine,' I offer, keeping my head low, knowing that my suggestion has caused additional work for others.

'Cheers, Nina... as if I haven't enough to do around here,' says Old Bill, quickly fastening the strap ties across the pile of pallets. He heads for the truck's cab, hitching up his baggy corduroy trousers as he walks. I could complain, I could grumble too, but I'm not going to. I follow suit, jumping into the passenger seat.

Instead of a day in the sales yard, I am helping Old Bill create a new festive attraction.

'Every other year the traditional grotto that's been stashed in the end barn has always been good enough, but oh, no, not this year!' mumbles Old Bill. He draws breath and starts again. 'I don't stop fetching, carrying and building sodding projects on this damned farm, you know?'

He drives across the sales yard and through the gate towards the spruce growing in the north fields.

'The boss wants something attractive for his customers. They don't want the same old thing every year, do they?' I offer.

'Boss wants something new then leaves it until two days before opening to assign me the time to build it. And as for those bloody reindeer – have you seen the size of them?' His white overgrown hair shakes constantly as he talks; everyone knows when Old Bill is not best pleased.

'Bill, you know what it's like around here come Christmas time – it's always manic.'

'Seriously, you girls with your bright ideas. It'll not secure you one of the twins, you know?'

'Oi!' I snap, as he touches a nerve. 'You've no idea what you're talking about. Plus, we're all busy. I'd much prefer to be on the sales yard amongst the customers and spruce than *this*.'

'Phuh! Wait till you have to muck out the reindeer – then you'll be moaning about being busy.'

'We are! Jackie's got a Christmas Eve wedding to organise, Shazza's trying to plan the perfect carol service and, despite it being my great idea, I've been lumbered with helping you build the new grotto.'

'Who has a bloody wedding this close to Christmas, I ask you?' he scoffs, navigating the muddy pathway.

'I think a winter wedding is romantic,' I answer, staring from the passenger window at the rows of growing Norway spruce.

'Like there's shed loads of snow about to fulfil her winter wonderland dreams,' grumbles Old Bill.

'True, if the bride's wanting snow it looks like she's picked the wrong year,' I say, noting the abundance of muddy brown earth and emerald moss carpeting the ground amongst the passing spruce.

'The forecasters are always bloody wrong. Mark my words, there'll be no snow this year despite what the boss says.'

'Jackie's the queen of weddings – she'll deliver whatever the couple have asked for. Anyway, you don't even work the weddings so what are you chomping about?'

The cab of the truck wobbles us back and forth as the chunky tyres grip the uneven terrain. It's not the same spruce-lined meandering pathway that the customers will walk whilst visiting the grotto, but it's the widest path for a vehicle to deliver the pile of raw materials necessary for building.

'Bloody good job. I've been here thirty-seven years and never have I known such nonsense as this. And that sodding carol service… whose bright idea is that to move it from the usual seated arrangement and make it a lantern procession?'

'I think it's nice.'

'Phuh! It's all a bloody gimmick, if you ask me. The customers don't know half the carols anyway… they'd be silent without the song sheet stuck under their noses.'

'Bill, December is the busiest month. We might not like events but that's what we have to do to get through the year.'

'Phuh!'

'Without the extra money, some of us would be out of a job!'

'Mmmm, and I suppose you think that about the bloody rental shacks down by the lake?'

'I think you'll find they're log cabins, Bill... and yes, I do quite like them, *actually*.'

'Utter bloody nonsense, if you ask me, folk paying good money to stay in a glorified shed – what's so wrong with staying in their own homes? That's what I say.'

I remain silent.

'We called it camping in my day and we did it under canvas but not now – your generation think they're so daring and adventurous sleeping in a heated shed.'

I'm sure he's about to start complaining about our designated task again, and I don't want to spend the day justifying why I think it's a cracking idea. Plus, I can't afford to add fuel to his fire, as I'll never live it down if *this* project goes wrong.

So I am thankful when we drive in silence amongst the spruce until we arrive at our designated spot.

*

Angie

Nick indicates left and pulls the car into the sweeping driveway, drawing up behind a long queue of cars. Why is the zoo so busy on a weekday in December?

I've taken the day off work by calling in sick. Nick has taken the day off. I feel guilty; Nick doesn't.

'The zoo?'

He nods eagerly.

'In eighteen years, we've never visited Twycross zoo and yet live fifteen minutes away,' he explains.

'We just never got around to it, that's why. There was always something more important to do. Life on your doorstep is never important during the holiday seasons... so, why now?'

Nick draws the car forward, chasing the bumper of the car in front.

'Why not?'

'Because we didn't even bring Alfie here – the school brought him on an away-day trip in primary school.'

'Well, that was wrong, Angie. Parents should take their son to the zoo, not the bloody school. It's not their job to raise our lad.'

I watch his side profile; he's staring ahead, having disappeared back into yesteryear. My yesteryears revolved around SATS, chicken pox and endless play dates. Is this the new Nick or a hidden remnant of the old?

'What?'

'Nothing, just thinking. What else have we missed over the years, Nick?'

'Loads… we got lost along the way, I think.'

I reposition the seat belt across my breastbone and stare from the passenger window. Did we?

Nick steers towards the beckoning hand protruding from a fluorescent coat standing on the grassy car park area. He drives in as directed and pulls the handbrake on before killing the engine.

We walk the short distance to the payment kiosks, Nick rummages in his pocket for his debit card.

'Morning, two adults, please?' Nick offers his card to the young lady.

'Any children?'

I watch as she glances over the kiosk ledge at the empty space between us, expecting to see little ones.

'No.' Nick laughs.

We're about twelve years too late on that parenting duty. Nick enters his pin code into the hand-held machine as I wonder what we did instead with our toddler. Probably sat at home, snuggled on the sofa watching animated crap on TV. A wave of guilt snags in my throat. Would Alfie be more forgiving if we'd taken more family day trips? Were we always destined to fall apart as a family?

'Cheers.' Nick takes the offered receipt from the attendant, and unfurls the offered map as we walk through to the entrance.

'Were we happy when Alfie was a toddler?'

'Bloody hell, Angie – you know we were.' His voice is soft, caring and sure.

I nod. I honestly can't remember.

'I just remember how rushed we were. Like ships in the night, dashing here, there and everywhere and yet we *never* did the things that mattered to him… or us. And now…' My voice fades.

'Angie… you can't beat yourself up about stuff from sixteen years ago.'

'Can't I?'

'No, love, you can't.' He glances at my puzzled face. 'Seriously, just focus on the here and now.'

I look up to view his intense gaze.

I nod; he's right.

Here and now. That's all we ever really have, isn't it?

*

Nina

It takes four hours to build the new festive grotto. Whenever I watch DIY programmes on the TV, nothing takes longer than ten seconds to build. Several times during the morning, I'm tempted to ask Old Bill if he can rattle a nail gun as fast as Tommy Walsh, but I suspect he'll answer with: 'Who?'. So, I help where I can and fetch tools from the truck or hold wooden panels at right angles, where necessary. I watch intently as his weathered hands bring the jigsaw together. Eventually, a large shed made of used pallet wood, painted white and topped with the cutest apex roof, is free-standing amongst the Blue spruce. Old Bill starts to erect a tiny rope-and-post fence to organise the queuing customers and I add suitable decoration inside our two-roomed creation to imitate an icy igloo. I nail-gun swathes of white wadding to every interior wall and ceiling in the hope that it looks like compacted snow. Strings of sparkly fairy lights and a collection of wrapped fake presents are stacked high as a fitting backdrop for Santa's chair. I've even added a set of shimmery, sparkly door ribbons leading from the foyer area into Santa's throne room, purely for effect, and I like the way the colours twinkle in the fairy lights.

'There, that looks grand,' I mutter as we stand back to admire our handiwork.

'Are you happy now?' grunts Old Bill, collecting his tools from the surrounding earth patch. 'Suitably decorated for single occupancy to meet and greet his visitors – when I get time, I'll deliver his throne and organise a larger generator.'

'I am and I'm sure the boss will be too,' I say, chivvying him along. 'You've got until Saturday, so don't worry.'

'Good, because that's taken far longer to build than necessary and I don't need to remind you that we have a second, identical one to build on the south side of the farm.'

'Hmmm.'

'Yes, surprise, surprise, we're having two grottos.'

It was my clever suggestion said in jest, when our panel couldn't choose between two identical roly-poly Santas. Surely two Santas would halve the queuing time, which would be a bonus for any family with excited children, resulting in a more memorable visit rather than the rush-and-push visits witnessed in most Santa's grottos. The only downside would now be the number of elves descending on the farm. I hope this plan pays off, otherwise I can wave goodbye to my Christmas bonus.

*

Angie

'Nick, Alfie hates me,' I moan as we stare at the empty gorilla enclosure. There's no sign of a majestic silverback and his mate, just tree trunks and plastic bottle crates. Obviously, the pair have more sense to be cosy inside their indoor enclosure, unlike us.

'Angie... he doesn't hate you. He's trying to come to terms with what has happened. What did you expect him to do? Fling his arms around you like a three-year-old?'

'Err, yeah – he used to.'

'He used to wet the bed too but, hey, that ceased years ago.'

'You didn't even tell him it was me you went to dinner with the other night. Do you know how embarrassing it was to listen to my own son telling me the details of your mysterious date, knowing it was me?'

'Angie?'

'Nick... seriously, he was playing games with me, suggesting he was OK with you bringing back some bit of stuff for the night.' My voice has risen three octaves so I am glad that we're the only folk viewing the empty enclosure 'And then—'

'Stop, Angie.' His voice is edgy and cold. 'Alfie's got his own opinions. He's finding his own way in the world and sussing out the boundaries. What do you expect me to do?'

'Talk to him, Nick, make him understand about us, me and you…' Instantly I feel stupid defining 'us'. 'That we're trying again. He needs to stop with these ideas of you and another woman… Nick?'

'Don't you think that would be pushing it a bit fast given we're only on our second date?'

'Nick?'

'I think it's best for everyone concerned if we leave things as they are for now… See how we fare first before telling him that we've decided—'

'Nick!' I can't believe he's saying this. I thought this was what he wanted. What he's hoped for, for months and months, and now I'm some sordid secret kept from my own son.

'What?' He sounds tired again.

'I think I've paid the price for my decision back in January. I'd like Alfie to know.'

'I'm not saying you haven't but… you weren't here, Angie. You haven't seen what the lad's been through and I don't want to raise his hopes in case we… don't make it for a second time. I'm putting Alfie first. That's what we need to do.'

I am fuming. I wish I hadn't called in sick to spend the day with him.

'We need to focus on us, Angie. If we take our time, make sure we're sure… then telling Alfie will be the best thing ever. He'll understand. He's not a kid any more.'

Obviously not, given his relaxed attitude as regards his father's potential sleepovers.

*

Holly

'Are you OK with your dad dating?' I ask as Alfie grabs bags of crisps from their kitchen cupboard. Their dog, Rolo, watches him intensely as if he's anticipating a treat.

'Oh, yeah. He hasn't left the house for months, yet today he was singing in the shower.'

'Ah, that's sweet.'

'It is from a middle-aged guy. Seriously, I haven't got an issue with it but I think my mum will go spare.'

I frown.

'Surely, she has no say.'

'You think?' He laughs, leading the way to their lounge, which is as neat and tidy as their kitchen. 'Take a pew.'

I look around at the large leather couches in warm creams with contrasting mocha cushions, surrounding a glass coffee table complete with an array of remote controls.

Rolo follows us and flops onto the floor before the fire hearth, his big brown eyes noting our every move.

How lovely to have a choice of seat from which you don't have to pick up and move a pile of plastic: baby dolls, jelly shoes or bricks. I choose the sofa opposite their large plasma TV and sink into the plush cushions –

it takes me by surprise. Alfie flops down beside me and offers me a choice of crisp flavours.

'Cheese and onion or salt and vinegar?' He holds the two out.

I like both but want to be generous.

'What's your favourite?'

'Cheese... but you can have them.'

'Nah. I'll take the salt and vinegar ones, please.'

'You sure?'

I snatch the bag and open it before he can play the gallant gent. He laughs, a sound that I'm beginning to enjoy hearing. We sit crunching crisps, which gives me chance to eye their lounge and him time to play with the remote controls, flicking from channel to channel. They haven't any decorations or a tree yet and it's halfway through December.

We don't talk, just munch crisps. Even with my sisters this would feel weird, as if one of us had to speak or joke to fill the silence, but this feels right. It feels nice to be beside Alfie, saying absolutely nothing.

I spot a wedding invite card on their mantelpiece exactly the same as we have at home.

'Are you invited to a wedding on Christmas Eve?' I ask.

'Yep, the bride's father was my dad's uni lecturer – it sounds weird but dad was such a good student that they kept in touch and remained friends.'

'Us too! Isabella and Luca?'

Alfie nods, but scowls.

'I'm bridesmaid, if that makes you feel any better about attending.' I laugh.

'It's not that... We're supposed to be going as a family, Mum included.'

Oh, I see.

Silence lingers.

'Would your mum return, given the chance?' I finally ask, unsure if that conversation has truly finished.

'Nah! It was her decision to leave... She wanted out. Dad was gutted when she left. He'd have taken her back but reckons she'd met a guy at work and then shacked up with him until...' His voice fades. I can't imagine how it must feel when parents go their separate ways. 'He probably dumped her after having some fun.'

'Oh. You don't know for certain, then?'

'Not exactly. I think she'd met someone else but when he ditched her she had to figure out how to save face so stayed as she was.'

'And is she happy?'

'Nope. The other night she stared at me when I said that Dad had finally plucked up the courage to take someone out. It's not as if he's not tried to win her back, he has, but she's turned him down each time. Then I've been the one lying in bed at night knowing he's downstairs drowning his sorrows with whisky.'

I listen in silence. The words flow from him without thinking or effort.

'It got quite bad when she'd been gone for a month or so, then he picked up, but then when the divorce papers came through the post he was back to square one. She hasn't a clue what she's done to him, she really hasn't.'

'Maybe she was hurting too?'

'Doubt it. She hasn't called me in ages, months, and then out of the blue she wants to go on a mother-son date... She expected me to drop everything. I said no way, but still she phoned again for pizza, so I agreed to go.'

'Maybe she's realised how bad it looked?'

'Maybe.' He falls silent, and stares at me. 'You've got a crisp.' He picks at the corner of my mouth.

He flicks the crumb onto the carpet, and leans forward. My breath stalls. His face nears mine; his eyes have tiny flecks of yellow amongst the blue. Such white eyes, such huge pupils... His lips are on mine. I can taste the cheese and onion crisps. I wonder if he can taste salt and vinegar. His right arm lifts up, over and around my shoulder as our lips work, pulling me slightly closer towards him. I can't believe this. I'm sitting in Alfie Woodward's lounge, kissing him in the middle of the afternoon, when I'm supposed to be grounded.

*

Angie

'Sorry.' It seems the only feasible thing to say as Nick quickly indicates and pulls into the busy traffic just after four o'clock.

'No worries. We've had a good day. We didn't get to see many animals in their outdoor enclosures, given the turn in the weather, but it makes a change from The Rose.'

'What do you expect in December? The poor bloody animals had more sense than us.' We visited every outdoor enclosure and the majority were empty; only the Amur leopards, the two female elephants and the playful baby Orang Utan were obliging to brave the elements, like us.

'Things are freaking me out... How can we go behind our son's back and date without there being a shadow over the beginnings of this new relationship?'

Nick nods.

'I thought we were going for honesty here, Nick. I really did.'

'We are. We both need to learn from our past mistakes but if I were dating someone else, which I'm not, I wouldn't have introduced her to Alfie after the first or second date, would I? Or is that the norm nowadays – meet, date and immediate contact?'

Is he actually asking me? Or was that hypothetical?

'Angie?'

Oh, he is.

'No, but I'm his mother!'

'I know. That's why we are trying again after a separation, a costly divorce and several months.'

Is he never going to let that drop?

I smile.

'Angie… don't give me that look. I get that it's difficult, but think about Alfie. If we say we're back together he'll assume you're moving back into the house… and that's not how we're playing this.'

I shake my head. I can't speak for fear of an outburst of tears.

'It's best this way until we are one hundred per cent sure that we both want the same things, the same life, the same goals and the same—'

'Did we ever have that much in common?' I ask, without thinking.

Nick shrugs.

'So, why's it necessary the second time around?'

'Because the first time around we both wanted to start a family, finish our degrees and find a lasting relationship. Second time around I think some things have possibly changed, Angie.'

I stare at his profile before asking.

'What is it you want, Nick?'

'I want happiness, security with someone that loves me, and I want to embark on the latter part of my life with a strong foundation. I know I don't want the upset I've had this year reappear in my later years.'

Good answer.

'And you?'

I take a deep breath.

'I would like... no, I *want* my independence, the space to follow my goals in life and...' I hesitate; my nerve has gone.

'Yes?'

'A better sex life than the one I had when we were previously married.'

'You weren't satisfied?'

'Satisfied with what I knew about but... but...' Why do I keep doing this? I know exactly what I want to say in my head and yet the minute my mouth is brought into gear the words fade.

'But?' encourages Nick.

'I tried to say this the other night, but... I've realised how little I knew about life or relationships.' There, it's out in the open and Nick can make of it what he likes.

He nods and remains silent. Clever tactic. You can't make a false move whilst silent, or put your foot in it and ruin stuff.

I watch as his expression deepens and the cogs turn.

'Nobody we know, was it?' he finally asks.

'Good God, no!' I retort. 'Nick... what do you think I am?'

'Just asking… I always thought Phil held a candle to you over the years.'

'Phil and Carol, Phil?'

Nick nods.

'*Really?* Oh, no.'

A smile cracks upon his taut features.

'You honestly thought that Phil Clarke, with his huge hands and bandy legs swathed in Bermuda shorts, is the kind of fella I'd go for?'

Nick smiles.

'Nah!' A small gallery of men flickers through my recent memory – I won't be divulging the full details but Phil Clarke isn't amongst them.

Seven

Nina

Friday, 14 December

'I haven't told him yet,' I whisper to Kitty as we dress in our layers.

Kitty winces, which makes me feel worse. I should have spoken to Bram before now. And thanked him for being so amazing at the cottage. We could have talked any time during the week but I'm not completely sure about how I feel so the best bet is avoiding such discussions altogether.

'I feel awful,' I mutter, pulling on my sweater. 'I don't want to go and yet... he's picking me up at eight.'

'Nina, you need to stop worrying about Bram's feelings and think about your own.'

'But, Kitty...'

'But Kitty nothing... you've put this off for long enough.'

The cabin door closes behind her. I'm alone. As there is no 'get out of jail' card coming via my friend, I need to buck myself up. Tonight, it looks as if I'm going on a date.

*

Angie

As I settle at my desk, Jilly swivels her office chair around to stare.

'*And?*'

'It's getting complicated... with each date we have.'

I don't bother feigning recovery after yesterday's absence; Jilly knows I pulled a sickie. She'll take a duvet day when it suits her family.

Jilly pedals her feet, bringing her office chair and her morning coffee to my desk.

'Tell me more.'

With our heads together, obscured from the rest of the office behind my tiny fibre-optic Christmas tree, I quickly fill her in on the 'me and Nick' situation.

'So, you're in a relationship... not content with the dating stage?'

'We are... but just further along on dates than we were on our original set of dates.' I pause; I hear my ludicrous remark. Thankfully Jilly keeps a straight face, so I continue. 'Basically, we're dating as if we were strangers, but it's damned hard trying to forget the details of a man that I've known all my adult life.'

'Confusing, then?'

'For starters, we keep bickering about Alfie – who wasn't a consideration the first time around.'

'But still, Angie... he's going to fly the nest in the next few years – are you sure your future lies with Nick?'

I nod. I am certain. If we can just rebuild the good bits, resurrect the foundations of what could have been – I know we'll be happy.

'I could never have returned to my Mike, not after the divorce,' says Jilly, pursing her lips. 'I knew once it was dead, it was dead.'

'And you never regretted it?'

'Never. Even when our Nina refused to come with me, I knew I'd never go back.'

'That must have hurt though, Jilly?'

'It did, when the family court asked who she wanted to be with and she came straight out with it, 'my dad...' I was cut to the quick but, still, it was her choice.'

'How long afterwards did you meet Chris?'

'Four, maybe five years... but in that time, I never wanted to go back home.' Jilly watches me as her words linger.

'I didn't... until recently,' I say.

'Maybe it's the time of year. Christmas time can do funny things to folk... brings up a lot of sadness and regret in some,' she adds.

I watch as Jilly's eyes glisten and flicker before recovering in an instant.

'Are you not going to contact her?' I ask, unsure if I should bring up the daughter she rarely mentions.

Jilly shakes her head; the age lines cut deep around her mouth.

'I don't know anything about her, do I? I suspect she's still at the cottage. She's big enough to make her own choices now. She knows where to find me.'

'Maybe she felt torn when her dad was alive – loyalty and all that.' It's rarely mentioned but I know Jilly's ex-husband has now passed away.

'Possibly, I should have fought harder, insisted that she visited at weekends, but the constant friction gets you down, ruins everything and puts a stop to visitations.'

'That's been my mistake, I've lapsed as regards my time spent with Alfie. I'm picking him up tonight, but I've let him down recently.'

'And now, you're paying the price. You need to push for it, Ange – seriously, lovey, otherwise it'll end up like me and Nina.'

*

Holly

'Holly?'

'Yes, sir,' I answer the register as I unpack my history book.

'Yes, sir,' a female voice mimics behind me, from the back row. I turn to look but a row of identical blank expressions, smudged kohl liner and orange foundation stares back at me. Paris is one of them, of course.

I face forward, conscious of every word I hear from the back row.

Mr Bennett begins to explain today's outcomes, drawing one of his crazy and colourful mind-maps upon the whiteboard. I'm looking but I'm not listening, which is unlike me.

Ping!

Something small hits my right shoulder. I turn around but can't see anything on my blazer. I face the front.

Ping!

It hits my left shoulder. A small piece of white rubber falls to the floor beside my chair leg. I stare at the chewed piece. Obviously, someone has invented a new game.

Within five minutes, there are numerous pieces of chewed rubber scattered around my chair. I didn't feel them all land, just the majority.

I put my hand in the air.

'Yes, Holly.'

'Can I move seats, please, sir?'

Mr Bennett looks confused. 'Why?'

'No reason... I just want to move seats.'

The teacher looks around the classroom, as if he can replay the class interaction that occurs each time he turns his back to write on the whiteboard. He can't and I'm not about to squeal.

I wait patiently as he assesses the class. He knows me too well to know that I haven't suddenly developed a penchant for moving seats. I can see his cogs twirling. He's figuring out if it's the boys beside me who are the pain or elsewhere in the class.

'Sir... can I just move?'

He nods, cautiously eyeing the class, as the back row hold their breath.

I stand, remove my belongings and move right to the front. Mr Bennett is confused but accommodating. At the front their target practice won't reach me, ruler or no ruler.

*

'Holly?' Alfie's voice sounds gruff as he calls me from the playground wall. 'What's this I hear about your history class? Bits of rubber being chucked at you, who by?'

'Forget it.' Someone has snitched in record time; the break bell has only just sounded.

'No, that's out of order—'

'Alfie, it's just silly girl stuff.'

Alfie puts his hand in mine as we walk along the top wall and down the steps to the bottom playground.

'You sure?'

'Sure. Anyway, who told you?'

'Jordan.'

Jordan Haywood is hardly a fan of mine; he often refuses to sit next to me in class since the time the health advisor in primary school sent me home with a letter informing parents that I had little visitors. Jordan has never forgotten that and I am sure Alfie will know the nit story before long.

'What plans have you got for the weekend?' asks Alfie.

'I'm working at the chemist tomorrow morning and baby-sitting tomorrow night so my parents can attend a friend's party. What are you doing?'

'I've got a work trial at Christmas Tree Farm – hopefully they'll take me on for Saturday work. It'll give me some extra cash.'

'They were run off their feet last weekend when we collected our tree.'

'You've already got a Christmas tree up?'

'Oh, yeah. My baby sister has pulled it over ten times already. My mum's not happy about it.'

The end of break bell sounds, interrupting our conversation. Alfie walks me to my English class and gives me a peck on the cheek, before attending his own class. The rest of the class, lining up outside the room, stare at me as Alfie leaves. I know what they are all thinking: how?

I join the rear of the line and contentedly smile.

*

Nina

'It didn't take long to clear the rubbish left by the trespassing teenagers,' explains Bram, sprawled upon a couch as lunch break begins. 'Though Dad is getting his hair off about it, but, as Jackie keeps telling him, "kids will be kids".'

'The police advised him to get a couple of guard dogs but he won't,' adds Zach, settling in an armchair beside the wood burner.

'He reckons Shazza knows who it is,' says Bram, removing his scarf.

I give him a quizzical look.

'Seriously, she made a comment earlier – something about her kid brother and his mates or such like.'

'She's never mentioned them to me,' I answer, unsure if such accusations should be made behind Shazza's back.

'Phuh, she wouldn't, would she?' Bram says, adding, 'She needs to warn him, because if Dad gets hold of the little swines, he'll be done for GBH.'

'Get away with you. Your dad's not the violent type.'

'He is where his livelihood is concerned. These trees are worth a sodding fortune... and to think a bunch of little scrotes are roaming around during the night,' says Zach.

'Bram, can we talk?' I ask, clutching my coffee mug.

'About what?' he says, peering at me as his hands busily twist his scarf around itself.

'Nothing.' I back out. I will find another time to let him down, or Kitty will scold me again.

Bram screws his face up.

'You're a weird one, you know that, Nina?'

I shrug. He isn't the first guy to make such a remark. Which explains why I've never had a relationship last longer than a few weeks at twenty-five years of age.

Zach glances between the two of us, before his packed lunch and Thermos flask dominate his interest.

One by one the team slowly come in for their lunch. It's the only time that all the staff break together. I sit in the cosy corner of the sofa watching the groups. It's fascinating to see the working dynamics of the cutting crew with the sales team and the general dogsbody team.

I steer clear of sitting with Kitty, in case she wishes to continue this morning's little chat. I ignore Shazza in case she wants to confess to having insider knowledge about the trespassing.

*

Time flies when you're busy avoiding everyone. I move piles of netted spruce around the yard, gathering, stacking and labelling in relation to their species and height, piling them one on top of the other so customers can select with ease. It's quiet for a Friday afternoon but there's no doubt that tomorrow will be the start of a busy weekend.

I have my eye on the clock, ready to race from the farm at the first opportunity.

My plan is to buy some new candles on the way home, cheap and cheerful ones from the local shop, to accompany a long, lazy bubble bath. Then dress for my night out, which has become my new term as regards tonight.

That's when I see him.

He is gazing at me from across the sales yard. A pair of dark hazel eyes staring from deep olive skin, topped with a tumble of brown curls and neat sideburns. He's leaning against the driver's door of a blue Range Rover, dressed in faded jeans and a thick winter coat, open to reveal cream knitwear. The scene looks too perfect, like a winter catalogue picture pose.

My stomach flips. A deep rolling sensation sloshes my heart up against my throat.

How long has he been standing there?

I instantly blush and look away as I drag a six-foot Blue spruce along to join its buddies. I sense he's still watching, as he hasn't moved an inch. I can't help myself; I want to look over again to confirm he's still staring. I look *again*. Our eyes meet. Confirmed: he's still staring.

My knees turn to jelly.

He can't be watching me. Can he?

I give a quick glance over my shoulder, because that would be extremely embarrassing if Shazza is standing behind me, and the guy is actually acknowledging her. Shazza isn't anywhere to be seen. Nor Kitty. For once in our busy sales yard, nobody is anywhere near me. Suddenly the yard feels very eerie and empty but for me dragging a Christmas tree.

Why does this happen, for the first time in my life, when I'm wearing a million layers of shabby clothing, a red tabard and a bobble hat borrowed from the snug as I've left my cute, fluffy girlie hat at home? Seriously, even I would describe me as looking particularly rough at this precise moment.

And yet, he's still looking.

I dare myself to take a third look. One, two, three... look. And there it is – a smile twitches at the corner of his mouth.

Again, my stomach somersaults the length of my insides. I feel as if my lunch is about to come back up and be delivered at my feet.

OMG! This is insane. My heart is pounding.

I return to the original pile and select a new spruce to move.

Do I know him? Is he a friend of the twins who I've met at a party? Not that I've been to many parties with the guys, not recently anyway.

I sneak another glance towards him.

Is he here to purchase a tree? In which case, someone needs to go and attend to the customer. Though preferably not me, given the current weakness in my limbs.

Or is he here to collect a specific order? I bet that's it, given the Range Rover. Some commercial businesses order a specific size tree to decorate their corporate reception areas or meeting rooms. They aren't expected to attend and purchase like the general public, so special arrangements are made for collection and invoices forwarded to their accounts departments. But why hasn't he gone straight to the cashier's cabin to hand in his order number? Why haven't the delivery crew attended to collect and help him load the designated tree? My mind is racing, much like my feet as I drag the umpteenth spruce across the yard.

A sudden thought makes my heart sink – he's obviously waiting for someone.

Bang on cue, Jackie exits the cashier's cabin alongside an attractive woman, dressed in a fur-lined gilet, faded jeans and knee-high black boots. The blonde woman bounces down the wooden steps quickly followed by two young boys dressed in identical coats and gloves. I watch their warm goodbyes plus accompanying air-kissing before Jackie hastily returns inside the cabin.

My heart sinks to my boots. I instinctively know in which direction the woman will walk. *His*.

Taken. Bugger!

I busy myself at the spruce pile and watch under cover of my lowered brow. They exchange a smile as she walks directly to him, placing an outstretched hand upon his jacket sleeve. Her hand lingers as they talk. The two boys dart to his side; play fighting by pulling each other's hoods. He's quick to step in and stop their rough play.

My heart sinks a little further. I want to cry.

I turn my back and busy my focus upon the current spruce, which won't lie flat amongst the others but rocks horizontally, making the pile unstable for the next layer.

I hear their car doors slam, the engine revs and the tyres crunch on the gravel as the Range Rover swings in a huge arc to reverse alongside me whilst I rock an unstable spruce into position.

Don't look up. Don't turn around. Just carry on doing your job.

I do both, at the precise moment that I am aligned to his driver's window.

His hazel eyes meet mine and he smiles, all the way up to his eyes.

I freeze.

He changes gear and drives off.

I stand and stare at the departing registration plate: BN68... The remaining digits and figures blur with the speed of his departure. In seconds, he is gone.

As I continue to watch the empty driveway, the first sprinkles of snow begin to fall upon the sales yard. Big, white fluffy flakes gently drift from above and instantly settle like a delicate veil.

I replay the scene in my mind.

Why didn't they buy a Christmas tree? Who leaves our farm without a spruce when driving a Range Rover?

I look from the empty driveway towards the cashier's cabin, the snow beginning to fall faster and denser than before.

I have a good mind to go and ask Kitty what the blonde woman purchased.

*

'Burr, it's cold out there,' I say, entering the cashier's cabin. 'And it's just started to snow.'

The fumes from the small gas heater make your head spin before the warmth is fully appreciated.

'Has it? I told you to wrap up earlier. Have you much more to do outside for today?' asks Kitty, perched on her usual stool punching sales figures into her calculator.

'Not really, it seems dead out there today.'

'Yeah, Boss has sent most of the staff over to the grottos to ensure they're ready for tomorrow. He's paranoid that the kids' parents will come across a stash of cider cans whilst queuing.' Kitty laughs.

'Or, worse still, the Santa will find a stash of cider and quickly repeat last year's disaster,' I add, unsure of the true facts due to my absence.

'Exactly.'

I clumsily change the subject.

'Did that woman not collect her corporate order?' I ask, attempting a nonchalant tone.

'The blonde?'

I nod.

'No, she dropped off an order for wedding garlands – the size and requirements are quite specific, so she needed to speak to Jackie in person.'

'Oh.'

'Why?'

'Nothing.'

'Do you know her?'

'Just thought I recognised her, that's all,' I lie.

Kitty grabs the ordering clipboard from the wall hook and flicks through the details.

'Garlands of holly with extra-long, broad red satin ribbons, double-tied bows and a robin perched on each. It's for the Christmas Eve wedding.'

'Mmmm, very specific,' I say, leaning on the countertop trying to read Jackie's handwriting upside down. I quickly scan the surname box: Romano. Sounds a tad Italian. His olive skin and dark eyes reignite in my memory – it fits.

Bloody typical.

'Are you working it?' asks Kitty, returning the clipboard to its order hook.

I shrug. I haven't been asked to work a double shift on Christmas Eve, but given the date Jackie probably daren't ask. She is usually pretty good at organising her wedding staff ahead of time. A double shift would mean working the sales yard from early morning till lunchtime then showering, changing and returning to the farm to work till late at the wedding banquet alongside her hired catering crew. Christmas Eve is unlikely to be a favourable day as regards me working.

'Hasn't she asked you to waitress?'

I shake my head.

'I'm not bothered. I'm a Christmas tree seller not a silver service waitress, unless it suits. You?'

Kitty nods. She always helps Jackie organise the fancy events. They are usually one-offs, mainly large corporate parties or, like this, a massive wedding reception in a luxury marquee amidst our beautiful Christmas trees. Sounds magical, especially if the snow continues.

'Jackie will ask you, you know that?' soothes Kitty, covering her growing embarrassment having potentially opened a can of worms.

'I'd prefer her not to, given the date.'

'You all right?' asks Kitty. 'You seem… distant.'

'Just confused about tonight's date… about my dad… and celebrating Christmas.' I could have mentioned the weird stomach-flip moment that had just occurred outside, but I didn't.

Kitty gives a sympathetic head tilt, having been sidetracked from the wedding details.

'I didn't think life was supposed to be this complicated. As a kid, I thought you grew up, earned money and had the time of your life… when really you lurch from one bad experience to another with very little gratification in between.'

'Oh, gratification, hey… big word for you.' Kitty gives a cheeky wink; she knows how to humour me. 'Now, you'd better get out of here before the boss realises you're skiving.'

'See you,' I say, peeling myself from the counter and making for the door. At the final moment before exiting, I stop and turn.

'What did you say that bride's name was?'

Kitty grabs the clipboard again and scans.

'Luca and Isabella… Romano. Still think you recognise her?'

'Not sure I do now… my mistake.' I quickly close the door, as the name Luca spins round my head.

I return to my spruce netting, labelling and dragging duties in a very different frame of mind. Luca – it suits him. An Italian stallion who's made me go all weak at the knees. Luca Romano: very Italian-sounding, complete with a dark smouldering gaze, thickset shoulders and – I stop myself – a fiancée.

*

187

Angie

'Alfie, it's Mum. I'm outside.'

I hear his sigh and can imagine his face, much as it was when I called at eight thirty this morning as he walked to school.

'Two minutes.' The line goes dead as I wait in the car and view the street, snowflakes gently falling upon my windscreen. I'm not entirely sure what Alfie expects of the flat, but at least I've finally purchased a whole load of decorations to hang on my beautiful tree.

Come on, where is he?

I don't want to sound the horn but at this rate the neighbours will have had an eyeful of me before Alfie leaves the house. What's keeping him?

The front door opens.

Finally.

Nick appears on the step and waves.

I hold a hand up. I don't really want to chat at this moment; I simply wish to collect Alfie and be gone.

Nick comes towards me down the driveway.

What is going on?

He taps on the driver's side window. I lower it.

'Hi, Angie... Alfie's... not sure.'

'What?'

'He's nervous... you can understand that.'

'Nick?'

'I know, I know... but see it from his side?'

'Go and tell him to hurry up. This is nonsense. He agreed to a sleepover at mine, just the two of us.'

'I'm just saying in case he decides not to.' I can see this is difficult for Nick. 'I can't make him, can I?'

'Yes, *you* can, actually.'

Nick leans an arm on the roof of the car and lowers his face towards mine.

I've got it all planned: we'll drive by KFC and collect a huge bucket plus desserts. Then head to the flat, crash in front of the TV for a chill-out night at home. Just me and my son.

'Could you go and fetch him, please...? This isn't what I expected him to do.'

It hurts like hell.

Nick peels himself away from his leaning position and walks back to the house, their coach-light illuminates the driveway as he approaches the front door.

Why is everything so difficult? Everyone else just pulls up, parks and their kid comes running out, overnight bag in hand, and jumps in the car. Not mine. Mine equals drama.

I watch as the front door closes.

Alone. Again.

I busy myself staring at the neighbours' first-floor extension.

I wonder what they'll use it for.

My attention snaps back to Nick's front door. Alfie appears, his holdall hoisted upon his back; Nick is ushering him out of the door.

Oh, great, he's been *made* to come.

*

'I don't see your issue.'

We've only been in the flat for fifteen minutes and his holdall remains in the hallway.

'Seriously, Mum, I'm bored of the lectures.'

'You're a bright lad, Alfie, you've a great future ahead of you and you can't let some little girl—'

'Holly. Her name is Holly.'

'OK, then, Holly… ruin your plans.'

Alfie shakes his head, rolling his lips together as if preventing the words from spilling forth.

'Look, this isn't easy for me either, you know… so please can we just spend a pleasant evening with each other and enjoy the time we have?'

My words register as I see his eyelids flicker and avert my stare. His lips continue to roll, muting his inner thoughts.

He nods.

'And my room?'

It's as good an excuse to change tack as any.

'This way.' I swiftly lead him from the kitchen to his room along the hallway. 'Ta-dah!'

It's a simple room, decorated in shades of blue, with a single bed and a load of cushions and throws. I can't decorate it as his permanent room, given that it is a rental flat, but I've purchased all new bedding and matching curtains especially for his stay. I've tried, let's put it that way.

'Cheers!' is his only word as he throws the holdall down onto the bed.

'It's not much, but I don't really know what you're into nowadays so thought I'd keep it modern but mature.'

'It's fine – do you mind if I unpack?'

I smile. I'm crowding him; I just can't help it. This is the longest I have been alone with my son since January and my head is spinning with so many things that I want to cram into our time.

*

'And Dad, how's he?' I ask, with as much nonchalance as I can muster, while focusing on my fried chicken.

'Fine, I think.' Alfie pauses to finish his fries. 'He seems happier since he's been going out more.'

I pause, not daring to lift my gaze from my plate.

'Which is a good thing, given his experience of the past few months,' adds Alfie. His mood instantly annoys me. Should I tell him? Let it slip or would that create a bigger divide than is present?

I remain mute and let him talk.

'I don't know when he's expecting to introduce her but...'

'You're OK with that, then?'

'Yeah. It's Dad. He'll do it when he's ready. He never does anything before he's thought it through.'

Alfie smirks.

'What's that supposed to mean?' My voice has an edge, as I know he's referring to me.

'What?' His eyes lift to mine, and I know he can see the hurt.

'Don't give me, what? That is a dig at me... I'll tell you what, Alfie, you've got a lot of growing up to do and dare you ever find yourself in the same position I did...' My voice cracks, but I continue. 'Stuck in a bloody rut, not knowing what I want in life, not knowing if what I have... *had* is the be-all and end-all... then you can remember that you thought my situation was bloody funny. Just you remember that!'

Alfie shrugs.

'I won't leave my kids...'

'It wasn't just about *you* or your dad – it was about *me*!'

He stretches across the table for another piece of chicken.

'Being a grown-up isn't all it's cracked up to be, you know.'

'You try being a kid in this era, then – you'll soon see you're not the only one that matters.'

I sit back and stare. Alfie eats his chicken as if nothing is wrong.

I want to scream. I want all my fears, sorrows, regrets to come pouring out so he can witness what he thinks is so damned funny. But I can't, he's just a child. And if I don't truly understand where our marriage went wrong, why am I expecting him to?

'What?' he says, staring at me.

'Nothing.'

'You looked like you were about to say something, that's all.'

I sigh.

'I know you're fairly young, but has your stomach ever flipped, Alfie?'

'Yeah.' His answer surprises me.

'Did you ignore it or act upon it?'

'The latter... why?'

'Me too. I also acted upon it. That one moment has determined everything I have ever done, achieved and desired for my entire adult life... from that moment onwards. Then last year, for the first time, I questioned what my life would have been had that moment never happened. So much so, I couldn't bear it any longer, so January... I decided to find out.'

He puts his chicken piece down.

'And?'

'And it frightened me to think that I may have wasted my years by building my entire life on a chance meeting which made my stomach flip.'

Alfie nods.

'And now?'

I stand up, cross the floor to the fridge, grab the open bottle of wine and pour myself a large glass.

He follows my every move, not daring to speak but awaiting my answer.

I lean against the countertop, take a long sip and face my son.

'And now... I realise that stomach flip was possibly the greatest moment of my life from which everything I hold dear has come from... as if a basic instinct responded before my consciousness had time to. And now, I know last January had to happen for me to appreciate what I once had.'

Alfie breaks eye contact, staring down at his plate.

'Pity we had to feel the brunt of it, then,' he mutters.

I ignore him and continue.

'Yes, I walked out, but I've learnt a lot about myself, Alfie. And I've learnt that that *one* moment doesn't come around again as I thought it might...'

He pushes his plate away, his chicken unfinished, and stands.

I watch as his lean frame seems unsteady, beneath the weight of our troubles.

'Thanks for your honesty, Mum, but for me – I wish you'd figured that out without having to destroy our family,' he says, adding, 'I'm going to go for a shower, if you don't mind.'

I nod and sip my wine.

Alfie's got a point.

Eight

Nina

Saturday, 15 December

'I can't deal with this, Kitty. Seriously, last night has proven I'm not ready to start dating.'

'So, you went?' Kitty shakes her head, whilst dressing in her additional layers.

I nod. Bram arrived in a taxi bang on eight o'clock.

I follow suit regards dressing, as the silence lingers between us. I need her advice. I want her opinion but I know she's not pleased with me.

'Kitty.'

She halts pulling her coat on and stares.

'What do you want me to say?'

I shrug.

'I couldn't say no to Bram, not after they've been so good to me.'

'And Zach?'

'I couldn't say no to him either but he never asks, you know that.'

Kitty sighs, finishes pulling on and doing up her coat zipper. Her eyes don't leave mine. I know she's concerned: for me, Bram and Zach.

'If you were my little sister, I'd say Zach's your man —'

I begin to protest; it's not that simple.

'Hey, hear me out, Nina.'

'OK.' I lean against the coat pegs.

'We all know how deep this friendship runs, OK, I get that, but you can't spend the rest of your life dodging the one decision you need to make. Ninety per cent of life's happiness or sadness probably comes from just one decision.'

'I hear you – Zach's kind, caring, reliable... but surely I shouldn't just settle for what's purely in front of me?'

'Settle? He's a good man, Nina. You probably still view him, *them*, as teenage boys but they're not. Seriously, they're both ready to settle down, buy homes of their own and commit.'

'That's not how you got with Connor.'

'I knew you were going to bring us into it.'

'Well, it's true, you say it every time... your knees went weak... your...'

'Stop!' Her hand lifts to silence me.

'So really the question is, do I settle or wait for what you and Connor have?'

197

Kitty sighs.

'I know, it's frustrating, Kitty – but I want what you guys have, honest I do. And if either of the twins had that effect upon me – I would grab the opportunity in a heartbeat...'

'But it's not there, is it?' Her hand reaches out to gently stroke my cheek.

I slowly shake my head. I want to tell her about yesterday. I want to share what happened in the sales yard when that guy stared at me, but the words stick in my throat. Her woeful blue eyes show me how much she wants it to be me and Zach.

'Tell you what, how about we head into town one night for a cocktail or two?' she asks, a smile brightening her eyes. 'We can ask Shazza along, if you fancy.'

For the first time in ages, I actually feel alive.

'Yes, that would be great!'

'Come on, best foot forward before Boss Fielding catches us skiving.' She laughs, straightening her coat and heading for the door.

'Kitty!'

'Yeah?' She turns, her hand on the door latch.

'Thank you... for being there,' I say, as my eyes glisten.

'My pleasure... but you can thank me with an Espresso Martini!'

Suddenly, I feel eager for a night of cocktails – it's just what I need.

'Fair deal.' I zipper up my embroidered coat and hastily follow Kitty's steps.

*

Angie

We drive in silence through the snow-covered lanes towards the farm where he can escape into his new job lugging spruces around a busy yard.

'Alfie, I'm sorry.'

'I know. It wasn't exactly what I'd planned either.'

'Maybe we can have another weekend together, some time over the Christmas holidays when you've broken up from school... have some fun, like the old days?'

He gives the smallest of nods; he's not convinced.

'I know I messed up. I just don't need my teenage son to keep drilling that home for me, Alfie. I need time to show you that I never stopped loving you... despite my actions.'

He looks at my profile as I drive.

'And I need time to rebuild my trust in you...'

I nod, my gaze fixed upon the snow-covered road ahead.

'I get it, I let you down. But know this, Alfie – I also let myself down along the way by not having the time I needed to mature before I became a wife and mother.'

We continue in silence. How do you flip to discussing the weather when it's chillier inside the car than it is outside?

I indicate and pull into the farm's rutted track. A thick layer of snow covers every inch of the driveway.

'You'd have thought they'd have gritted this section.'

Alfie doesn't answer but sporadically waves to some passers-by heading towards the farm. I assume they are also part-time teenage workers who he knows from school trudging towards a busy shift.

I park up in the car park. He opens the door, allowing Noddy Holder's screaming tones to invade my space. Alfie grabs his holdall from the rear seat, before addressing me.

'See you, Mum... take care.'

There's no kiss or hug forthcoming.

'See you in a few days, Alfie.' I hold it together as he slams the passenger door and bounces off towards a log cabin.

I swiftly turn the car around, taking the driveway slower than usual as my sight blurs and my emotions overflow.

*

Nina

'Nina, wait!' Zach's voice wails as I stride towards the netting machine, to which I've been assigned for the day.

I continue to trudge in the snow, knowing his long legs will catch me in no time.

'Oi, Nina!'

'Hi, Zach... you OK?'

'Are you?' he mutters, his grey eyes downcast and staring. 'Didn't you hear me?'

'Sorry... I was in a world of my own.' I begin organising the netting feed and the plastic secure ties.

Zach stands and watches. I'm pretending to be engrossed in my task.

'Are you not talking to me?'

'Dooh!'

'Nina, stop!' He grabs at my arm, pulling me around to face him. 'What's wrong?'

'Nothing. Just trying to earn a living by doing the job your father pays me for.' I attempt a breezy tone but I can hear it has edge. He's not stupid.

'*Seriously?* Since when has my old man's bottom line been your main interest?'

'Always.' I snatch my sleeve free of his gloved hand. 'I like to do a good job.'

'*Nina?*'

I dump the cable ties and pliers onto the ground. If I have a choice, which I don't usually get, I'll be at this end removing the netted spruce from the machine – the loading end is the worst part due to the constant lifting from the pallet. Cable tying and throwing down is far easier on your back.

'What?' I snap, unsure why I'm taking this out on Zach. Though, forgive me, but he is the nearest I've come to Bram all morning.

Zach eyes me suspiciously.

'You don't want to talk, do you?'

I give the smallest of head shakes.

He nods but continues to stare.

'Zach, I'm just out of sorts... it's tough at the minute and I feel...' I pause, watching the raucous cutting team drive nearer. The wagon begins to reverse and, despite the overhead speakers spewing 'Santa Baby', the air is filled with an intermittent bleeping as the wagon reverses alongside the netting station.

'Sorry,' I mouth, as Zach's eyes bore into mine.

The cab doors open on the reversed wagon and the crew jump down.

'Nina... where have you been hiding?' shouts Bram, straightening his puffa jacket having jumped from the wagon.

*

Holly

'Would you like a bag?' I ask, emptying her wire basket.

The customer smiles but doesn't answer.

'There'll be five pence charge if—'

'No.'

I press the till for the total to charge.

'Nine pounds, thirty-three pence, please.'

The ten-pound note is delivered with a quick flicking action of her wrist. Serving the general public isn't a joy first thing on a Saturday morning, but it helps to give me a little extra pocket money.

My customer swipes her goods into her own shopping bag before departing. I bid her goodbye. She ignores my farewell. I smile, awaiting my next customer, and that's when I see them. The group of mean girls standing at the end of the hair and beauty aisle staring at me. Gawping, in fact. All dressed in tight jeans clutching their large designer handbags, primped hair and black eyeliner skilfully flicked, stare as if viewing an alien. Yep, me, the alien in their classroom. The one that works for her own cash, has little chance of parental pocket money and is constantly harassed by the likes of them.

They turn on their heels and flee along the aisle. I'm glad.

I can predict their post-sixteen options: A-levels, university, potentially high-flying careers, before marriage and family. My journey will probably skip to the final two options unless I'm lucky.

Becca, the cashier supervisor, sidles towards the till as her mahogany-rich bob swings with each step.

'Can you see the CCTV monitor from where you're standing, Holly?'

I nod.

'Can you check aisle five, a bunch of teenage girls – they're acting a little strange beside the gift boxes. I don't want any funny business, not today.'

My heart stops.

I look at the grainy image on the tiny screen below the countertop. The group of girls huddle together into a tight rugby scrum; an arm stretches from their mass of bodies towards the shelving unit, grabs an item and quickly withdraws amongst the crowd.

They have a bloody nerve. Do they think they'll get away with it?

'Well?' asks Becca, ready to do her bit as store detective.

I nod.

Becca is gone in a flash. She flies around the corner of the aisle and I hear her shout for assistance. I'm staying back on this call. There is no way I can get dragged into their situation purely through knowing them. Plus, I'll never live it down in school.

I watch the store manager and his deputy run to attend the apprehension of the mean-girl group. Six sulky teenagers are frogmarched towards the manager's rear office. I stand at my till and watch the doleful faces pass by one by one. Each one stares at me in turn, as if I'm solely to blame for their predicament.

I watch as Becca plus the two managers escort the group into the rear offices. I know the routine: they'll call the police, await assistance and then call parents.

How embarrassing. My parents would kill me for pulling such a stunt. They each receive way more pocket money than I'll ever get and still they steal!

'Holly, could you come through, please?' calls Becca, standing in the doorway. It turns out the store manager has other things to do, but the group need to be watched until the police arrive.

'Becca, I know them,' I mutter, not wanting to be involved. 'They're in my class at school.'

Becca shakes her head. It makes no difference.

I have to stand in the manager's office while six of my classmates are accused of stealing two boxes of hair dye, three Dove box sets and a selection of nail varnishes.

The police are stern, taking all six back to the police station to process and inform their parents. I am deeply ashamed purely by association of gender and age. As they file out, one by one, they drop their heads except Paris, who eyeballs me in a threatening manner.

Wait till I tell Alfie; he won't believe it.

*

Nina

'Nina!' A cry from the equipment barn fills the air. I drop the Norway spruce that I am stacking, turn and run through the snow to the barn.

Zach is inside the donkey pen, his back pressed against the railings with beads of sweat decorating his forehead. I instantly understand the situation and grab a carrot from the food stash by the entrance and rush towards the far side of the pen. Gertrude isn't the issue, it's Arthur. The billy goat's stance is dominant; his chest thrust forward, head lowered and his mighty horns primed for attack.

'Arrrrthur,' I sing, in a loud and distracting voice, whilst waving the carrot through the railings at his eye level.

'Hurry up, he's angry!' splutters Zach, the whites of his eyes growing wide.

'Arthur... what's this, old boy?' I frantically wave the carrot. 'Zach, you might need to run for it.'

'No shit, Sherlock, I hadn't thought of that. Wave the carrot a bit higher to distract him. He needs to cease this behaviour or he'll be getting his nads chopped off.'

Arthur's front hoof cuffs the straw.

'Zach, get out of there!'

The same hoof repeats the action.

Arthur aggressively launches forward, his weapons drawn, charging at full pelt, as Zach bounces over the metal railings just in time to miss Arthur impaling his left thigh. Zach lands on my side of the pen, straightens his jacket and sweeps his hair back.

'That was close.'

'Too close,' I add, throwing Arthur the carrot.

'Don't reward him for behaving in that way. No wonder he keeps doing it if you give him the sodding carrot.'

I ignore the remark. Arthur doubles back from his charge and parades his glorious horns before locating the thrown carrot.

'He needs an afternoon with the vet for a castration job – he's becoming a sodding menace.'

'He needs a mate, more like.'

'Don't we all?'

I ignore him for the second time in as many minutes.

'Why won't your dad just call the vet in?' I ask. 'He's getting worse.'

'Male pride, I think.' Zach laughs, straightening the legs of his work trousers before standing tall. 'You've been avoiding me.'

'I'm just not ready for social situations, Zach. It feels like I'm entering another phase.'

'Another stage of the grieving process?'

I've done the anger, feeling isolated, being in denial, being the victim and the aggressor, and now I'm consumed by the melancholy phase with a touch of restlessness thrown in.

'When will the happy phase start?'

Zach raises his eyebrows in a comical fashion.

'I'm serious, Zach.'

'I'm serious too,' he says, adding, 'You're in control of your own happiness, no one else.'

'Thanks for that gem of wisdom.'

His grey eyes portray such compassion in one gaze.

Why can't life be simple? If I could have a Christmas wish it would be for a peaceful existence, the way life used to be: me, Dad and the cottage. Dad's mood swings overshadowed our memories, his physical deterioration didn't help matters but life had a regular pattern. I feigned my role as an unofficial carer pretending not to have a care and Dad understood his – together we simply plodded along.

'Fancy a pint tomorrow night in The Rose?' I ask.

His eyebrows lift in a questioning manner.

'I thought you couldn't handle social situations.'

'A quiet drink with you is different.'

'And last night's date with Bram was...?'

'Difficult, awkward... hasn't he said?'

'He doesn't tell me everything, you know.'

'Ah, but I do, is that it?'

'OK. The Rose... at eight.'

'Deal?'

'Deal,' he repeats, before heading from the barn into the snowfall.

*

Angie

It felt like a good idea but in sixty minutes, I've learnt that Fabio is still using his dating profile. He's also lost a tonne of weight unless that's an old photo and he has ventured on a recent holiday with a woman who happens to resemble his wife.

So, he's still playing Casanova amongst the single women in the area.

Great.

I close the laptop. I wish I hadn't looked now. My initial task was to find an interesting date on which I could invite Nick. Somehow, I was distracted.

It shouldn't be this easy to find and follow people online. It shouldn't be allowed for married people to actively seek affairs via dating websites.

My wounds reopen. The edges slowly tear apart and gape, wide and unattractively raw. I never imagined this could happen but it has.

I need a task that will successfully distract me from the likes of Fabio. Fabio and his ladies. Fabio and his wife. Fabio and his glorious carnal knowledge.

I count the shopping days remaining until Christmas – not enough – but still I don't feel like competing with the crowds purely to please my gobby young pup. Is it too late to use online for everything and get it delivered in time?

I can decorate my Blue spruce. Yep, that's what I'll do – decorate my tree, which has stood naked for a week.

The tree that is supposed to be a treat for me to enjoy and I've neglected it.

I quickly collect my box of new decorations, which I'd hoped Alfie and I would have emptied last night in a mother and son bonanza night of family bonding. But sadly, we didn't.

I open and unpack every box of silver baubles, tinsel garlands and white fairy lights, laying the decorations on the lounge floor before slowly and purposefully hanging each item upon the blue boughs. I stand back to admire the silver against blue combination – it looks impressive, but I can't muster my original spirit for doing this alone. In my head, I envisaged happy times, decorating the tree with my Alfie… *This* feels wrong and pathetic. How has my glorious spruce become a symbolic gesture of pathetic loneliness and spinsterhood? How?

An image of Fabio's tight torso fills my mind. His sturdy, powerful thighs and that cute manner of curling his lip.

Why do I do this to myself? I've consciously decided to focus on Nick. Rebuild my relationship with Nick. Me and Nick. Nick and me. *And* Alfie. So why do I bother looking for past lovers? Nothing good ever comes of searching for an ex online. Nothing.

My train of thought follows a downward spiral: dates that equalled nights out. Nights out that led to nights in, which led to the memories of passionate nights tumbling between sheets.

Stop it! Angie, just stop! I'm annoying myself.

I need to be stronger. I need to focus on my future with Nick, not look backwards... A happy family Christmas filled with tradition and fun – that's what I need.

I run through the list of top-ten dates I found on the web: sport event, yoga retreat, camping, adventure theme park, horse racing, NEC exhibition event, music concert... I will choose one and plan the perfect night out for us. Me and Nick. The zoo visit, though pleasant, wasn't the day he'd have hoped for but his dinner date on the steam train was amazing.

Amazing nights with Nick, that's what I need to focus upon... no more thoughts of Fabio.

<u>Nine</u>

Nina

Sunday, 16 December

When I arrive at work, I stare in horror at the staff notice board. I thought today would be a busy Sunday, not only for spruce sales but as day two of our Santas' grottos, so why am I relieved of my usual duties on the sales yard? Instead, I am honoured with the task of helping Shazza decorate the nativity scene. Not my idea of fun. I'd complain less at being dressed as a grotto elf for the day.

Worse still, I'm to help groom Gertrude, the donkey, who will be rehomed during opening hours within the festive nativity scene. I instantly feel sorry for Arthur; he'll miss her dearly, and no doubt he'll protest with more aggressive head-butting and charging. Unable to think up an excuse from my allocated task – I'm not allergic to donkeys, can scrub and clean despite recent suggestions and fully appreciate the festive traditions

214

here at Christmas Tree Farm – I collect the keys and head to the tiny barn in the corner of the yard to transform a hovel into a believable scene with Shazza's help.

*

'I hate this job,' moans Shazza, sweeping the empty barn clean of spiders' webs and last year's dust. Her discarded debris blackens the surrounding snow at the entrance to the tiny barn. Thankfully the continual snow has ceased for the time being, one plus point of the morning.

'It isn't my favourite either,' I mutter, crouching with a dustpan and brush in hand. 'I'd much prefer to be selling.'

Within twenty minutes we are surrounded by buckets of hot soapy water, standing amongst a crowd of life-size plaster cast figurines.

'What the hell?' I mutter, staring from the faces of three wise men into that of the Virgin Mary and the infant Jesus. A thick layer of grime covers each one, denying their finely decorated glaze chance to shine.

'So, grab a wet sponge, squirt on some cleaner and away we go!' instructs Shazza, demonstrating as she talks. I watch as the cream cleaner oozes onto the giant yellow sponge. Shazza swiftly applies it to a Balthazar's face and begins a circular motion. 'See?'

'That smells like lemons.' I laugh, feeling ridiculous at my suggestion.

'It is – lemon bathroom cleaner.'

'No way!'

'Yes way – I used it last year and it worked a treat... look.'

She's right. Balthazar has a clear complexion and a gleam to his cheek and temple.

'Shazza, you're not expecting me to smear the Virgin Mary with bathroom cleaner, are you?'

'Mhuh.'

'I can't.'

'You can... they're only statues,' moans Shazza, topping and tailing the baby Jesus.

'Forgive me,' I mutter, acknowledging my guilt for what I'm about to do to an angelic face. I wet my sponge and squirt the cream cleaner as demoed by Shazza. I feel all the painted eyes staring at me.

I step back in horror.

'No. I can't.'

'Nina, don't be so daft.'

'Shazza, I'm not devoutly religious but even so... cream cleaner!'

'All right, use washing up liquid, then, if it makes you feel better.'

'No – I'm out of this!' I look around the busy sales yard in panic, not sure where an answer would lie. This isn't right. Surely, the boss will object; Jackie definitely will.

A throng of excited families swarm around the yard happily inspecting, measuring and, some, arguing about their perfect Christmas tree. The staff are running back and forth across the snowy yard answering questions, filling in sales dockets and distributing mulled wine and warm mince pies.

I'm in a trance, watching the activity in the busy yard. That's usually my domain, running between customers helping where I can. Why couldn't I have been selected to wear green tights and a pointy felt hat, with attached ears, directing excited children towards Santa? More fun than this job!

'If you're that uncomfortable, you can start decorating the inside of the stable. I'll finish the figurines.'

I come to, relieved by her suggestion.

'Are you sure? My dad raised me to show respect to...' I point at the figurines. 'So, I literally can't do *that*.' I switch my index finger to the cream cleaner.

'I'm sure,' she mutters as I make a hasty exit to collect bales of hay and a wooden crate for the manger.

Our barn to nativity scene transformation takes three hours, and once it's complete we position the statues in a pleasing arrangement around the wooden manger. It looks good, despite the whiff of lemons.

'I just need to groom Gertrude and then walk her across,' I say.

'Make sure you tether her away from the statues, otherwise she'll demolish the lot.'

Shazza drapes her arm over my shoulder and we stand back to admire our handiwork.

'Beautiful,' whispers Shazza, staring at the twinkling fairy lights, the thick bed of straw and a super-large star pinned to the apex.

'Even so, we're still going to hell for using bathroom cleaner on the holy family.'

Shazza laughs.

'You might be but not me. I've done a few good turns that guarantee me a place up top.'

'Shazza, I doubt it, love,' I say, before calling Boss Fielding over to view our efforts.

*

After lunch, having spent an hour brushing her dusty coat and clipping her mane, I attempt to lead Gertrude across the snow-covered yard to introduce her to the new festive stable. We weave in between the busy crowds, some purchasing spruces whilst enjoying their complimentary mince pie and mulled wine. Other families are buzzing with excitement at the prospect of seeing Father Christmas, as two queues stream through separate gates, each leading to a winterland grotto.

Gertrude happily leaves her pen as I lead her across the snowy sales yard. But then she grinds to a halt. Her hooves are planted to the ground and I'm tugging at her reins as if my life depends upon her moving, but nothing. She isn't impressed by the snow, evidently.

How embarrassing! Customers turn and watch my struggle as I wave a carrot before her muzzle.

'I'll fetch you a larger carrot. I'll rub your belly. I'll even tickle your ears, if you wish,' I promise the donkey, with no effect.

I push at her rear end, pull her reins from the front. Nothing. Gertrude is stuck fast, refusing to budge.

A Range Rover pulls into the yard, scattering a layer of snow in its wake, amidst my dilemma.

I do a double take on recognition. Luca, the guy from the other day. I avert my eyes as he reverses, parks and exits the vehicle. Alone.

My innards melt at the sight of him.

'Come on, Gertrude, this is not the time to show me up,' I hiss.

From between Gertrude's twitching ears, I see him glance around the yard and its bustling crowds before proceeding. He doesn't head to the cashier's cabin like the blonde lady had, but directly towards my immoveable object and me. The only difference in his appearance is the coloured jumper; otherwise he's groomed like a model in an advert.

'Hi.' His voice is as deep as they come.

'Hi.' I give a weak smile, adding, 'The donkey won't move.'

His dark eyebrows lift as he views the animal.

'I was wondering if someone could give me some information about the types of trees you have for sale.' I watch his bottom lip, rounded and edible, form each word.

My stomach leaps into my chest.

Great, my area of expertise and yet I'm busy fighting with Gertrude. It grieves me to call Shazza, but needs must as she finished the nativity scene, minus a donkey, a while ago.

I watch as Shazza bounds over, all expectant smiles for our guy; he in turn gives me a sideways glance and hesitates before accepting Shazza's warm invitation to, 'Follow me.'

'Thanks,' is his parting word to me. 'Thanks' for not helping? 'Thanks' for brushing me off onto your colleague? 'Thanks' for acting the prat by pushing a donkey across a sales yard? Or simply, 'Thanks'?

I watch Shazza be all bubbly and vivacious with him, flicking her hair back and giggling as she directs him to the pallets of cut spruce. I want to shout after her, 'He's taken,' or even 'He's the groom for the Christmas Eve wedding,' but I don't. Instead I silently cringe as my brain taunts me by replaying my classy 'the donkey won't move' line.

As I watch him, Gertrude gently nuzzles my hand and slowly begins to plod forward.

'Thanks, Gertrude, why couldn't you have done that five minutes ago, freeing me up to serve him, Mr Stomach-flip?'

Amidst the bustling crowds, I lead the donkey to her new home and tether her, ignoring Shazza's advice, where she immediately begins nibbling at the hay in the manger – despite the swaddled infant already nestled in there.

'Please don't eat it all, Gertrude,' I say, tying her leash to the nearest anchor point. I quickly scan the yard, with the fanciful idea that I'm now available to take over the information pitch from Shazza, if I dare. I watch as Shazza eagerly explains and points at various spruces, explaining the differences, Luca nods, listening intently, his hands dug deep into his jacket pockets.

Lots of families pass in between my position and his stance; I crane my neck to keep him in view between the bodies. I pray that no one asks for my assistance as regards the difference between a spruce and a fir.

In no time, he's thanking Shazza and is striding towards me faster than I can decide what I am supposed to be doing. Minus the stubborn donkey, I'm adrift in the middle of the yard, lingering amongst the crowd with Luca heading in my direction. I just wish I had something, anything, to busy myself with so that I can casually pretend that I just happen to be present as he walks by towards his vehicle.

I glance up at intervals, when he's twenty paces away, ten paces, five and two.

'See you, Nina,' he says as he passes in a fleeting stride.

He knows my name! How does he know my name?

'Bye.' My hand lifts to give a stupid half-wave. What the hell was that wave for? I blush. Did he ask Shazza? Did Shazza mention me? I need to know.

And he's gone. *Gone*.

*

'Shazza, did that guy not want a spruce after you'd explained each species?' I ask in the snug as we change at home time. I waited all day to ask but don't dare arouse her suspicions – when have I ever asked about a specific customer's conversation?

'Who?' she asks, peeling her layers off and dropping them into her plastic storage box.

Who? What the hell? As if he didn't stand out a mile from the numerous customers she served today.

'The guy with the dark curls... I called you over when he asked for an explanation but Gertrude was refusing to walk, so I couldn't assist...'

'Oh, *him*,' she says, adding, 'He said he needed to go back and relay the information, before he could purchase a tree.'

Great, that must be to his wife-to-be.

Shazza hangs her coat on its hook – her name is embroidered on the back above the Christmas tree logo. My heart sinks a little – *that's* how he knew my name.

'Did you run through the aftercare routine?' I ask, trying to cover my inquisitive nature. I know Shazza rarely includes it in her explanations. She'll happily talk through each species, but customers need to know how to care for the Christmas tree once purchased and at home.

'Yeah, but I can't see him returning. Who visits the farm, asks for details and then doesn't buy on the day but promises to come back another time?' She shakes her head profusely. 'A waste of time.'

I disagree. Why wasn't he with his wife-to-be? Why am I even thinking about a guy that has simply said, 'Bye, Nina' and is out of my league, and very soon to be attached forever?

Shazza is staring at me.

'What?'

'Nothing...' She looks away quickly, a wry smile dressing her lips.

'Seriously *what*?'

'I could be wrong... but I swear, I just saw something...' She smiles again, before giving me a doe-eyed expression.

I turn away, just in case she spots it again.

*

223

Holly

'They'll get a caution and a record of the incident at the police station – so, that really wasn't worth it, was it? Fancy having a reputation as a thief for the rest of year eleven,' says Alfie, as we walk hand in hand along the snow-covered Long Street.

I thought the same thing, so I'm pleased that Alfie is on the same wavelength as me. We only have school until next Friday – surely I can avoid getting into sticky situations with the mean girls in that time.

'Let's forget about them.'

We head towards the memorial car park so that Alfie can practise his skateboarding tricks alongside his mates. I brush the snow from the nearest bollard and perch, huddled, watching, in awe that my boyfriend can actually perform such complicated stunts.

*

'Holly?' Mum's voice sounds angry through my mobile speaker.

'Yes.'

'You need to come home at once.'

'Why?'

'Can you just do as we ask, please?'

'Mum, can't it wait? I'm out with Alfie.'

'As I suspected. No, it can't wait. I expect you home in the next ten minutes.'

My phone went dead.

'Alfie, I need to go home. My mum wants me back straight away, so I'll phone you later. OK?' With a swift kiss I leave, concerned that my mum sounded pretty annoyed.

The police car is parked before the house, partly on and off the pavement. I walk up our driveway, which my dad has carefully cleared and gritted, wondering what has happened.

As soon as my key enters the Yale lock my mum opens the latch from within.

'Into the lounge, young lady,' she says; her tone has an edge. The house is unusually quiet – where are my sisters?

In the lounge sits a female officer, and a young male officer stands by the window. My dad is sitting in his favourite armchair bouncing Hope on his knee.

'Holly, this lady would like to talk to you. Sit down,' says my dad, nodding towards the female officer.

'Hello, Holly, how are you today?'

'I'm fine, thanks.' I sit myself on the sofa, facing my dad.

'Good, good, we just wanted to ask you a few questions to clear up a matter of interest. Is that OK?'

I nod. My mum stands beside my father's armchair. Her knuckles are white, and her eyes are on the brink of tears.

'Do you work at the chemist on Long Street?'

'Yeah, on Saturdays.'

'And you like it?'

I nod.

'Yesterday there was an incident, wasn't there? Tell me what you saw of it.'

I explain that I saw the girls together, then Becca mentioned a possible theft, the CCTV image, and then I had to stand in the office until the police arrived.

The adults glance at each other as I speak.

'Holly... the girls claim that you were part of the theft.'

I stare at her. I don't understand.

'Is there anything you'd like to tell us?'

'Such as what?'

'Are they correct? Were you part of their group?'

'How can I be part of their group? They don't even like me.'

'Holly, did you do it because you're frightened of them? Did they pressurise you into joining in?' asks Mum.

'Mum!'

'You only have to say, darling. Teenagers do stupid things simply to fit in with the cool kids.'

My face prickles with heat. I can't believe my own mother is asking such a question, or suggesting I want to hang with the mean girls.

'Seriously, I know nothing about their plans. They stood staring at me a little time beforehand, but nothing else – they didn't even speak to me... Haven't you watched the CCTV?'

'We have.'

'So, you'll know I was serving on the tills.'

'Given the camera angle, it shows you nodding towards them, as if acknowledging and maybe indicating...' Her words fade with meaning.

'I never.' I repeat the phrase numerous times, until tears flood my cheeks. 'I don't even like those girls at school. They are mean to everyone including each other.'

My dad is out of the armchair in seconds.

'Enough, you've asked your questions and she's given an answer,' he says, patting my back.

'Steve!' cries my mother. 'If she's involved, then I want her to have the same consequences. I blame that boy!'

'Are you serious? Alfie had nothing to do with this. The girls are lying just to get me into trouble alongside them. They don't like me because I'm seeing Alfie... but I haven't done anything wrong, so I don't see why I should be punished for things I'm not involved in.'

I keep repeating my story for another fifteen minutes. I can tell only Dad believes me.

Eventually, both police officers thank my parents; neither one says anything else to me. Rude, having accused me and then not even saying goodbye.

Angie

Nick grimaces when I mention ice skating. 'Anything but,' are his actual words.

'But, Angie, what's the point when I can't even stand up? I'll spend the entire evening on my ass.'

'Try, Nick. All it takes is a little effort.'

'I have never had good balance and to put me on blades – you're asking for trouble.'

I stood and watched animals – or no animals in some cases – moping around at the zoo.

He has little to argue about, given that we are already at the ice rink, part-way through the turnstile.

We queue for skates, hand over our own shoes and then the fun begins.

I feel like a kid returning to the ice after a very long time but Nick is a different case, entirely.

The cold atmosphere hits us as we near the ice rink. The surface of the ice glistens under the bright lights. We hold hands and gingerly make our way towards the rink. We sit on a bench, tying our laces around our ankles.

The crowds whiz around in one direction, limbs flying, feet out of control, and in between them swerve the graceful skaters whizzing back and forth with their expert moves.

We stand at the gate edge waiting for a traffic gap to appear big enough for both of us to cut in and survive on our feet. We make several attempts but at the last minute we snatch back to the rail without risking our lives.

Finally, we take our lives in our hands and go for it.

My hand clutches Nick's. Our arms are stretched and lengthened in all directions but secured by a knot of ten digits.

*

Within fifteen minutes, the seat of my jeans is wet through, my teeth are chattering but we're laughing – my ribs hurt and cheeks ache. The kind of laughter that brings two people together in the quickest space of time ever.

'I've missed this,' mutters Nick as we cling together at the barrier edge.

'Ice skating?' I grimace, unsure if I've ever seen him in skates since we met.

'No. *Us.*' His face is inches from mine, staring into my eyes. His breath warms my face.

My stomach flips. It's weird that this one man, in the history of all men, has the ability to do this to me with a word, a phrase or simply a look.

'And me.' I drop my head forward, to cover my blush. Nick leans closer. I feel his breath increase on my skin. If I stay as I am, head down, I might ruin this moment. Look up. Look at him.

Instantly, I look up.

Nick kisses me. Kisses me hard. Gone is the polite exchange, the gentle meeting of skin; instead I can feel the depth of feeling, the passion, the reason why this man, and only this man, makes my stomach somersault. His right hand lifts and slides around my neck, earlobe and into my hairline, gently pulling my face towards his. His kiss is hungry. An underlying passion surges to suggest a need and want. It's not Nick's usual offering: soft and gentle. Vanilla is how I used to describe it, but this... My lips respond to his. I want him to know for sure that this isn't a faddy attempt to reignite us. It isn't a rebound situation. I want my marriage back, no, correction, I want me and Nick back. The Nick Woodward and Angie Howard of yesterday, before the wedding, before the house and baby. That's what I want.

Nick's mouth slowly eases from mine, a gentle nip to my bottom lip as he withdraws into his own space.

I smile as his face returns to focus.

He smiles, looks about the vicinity at the crowds of laughing faces, all ages.

'It's easy to be happy surrounded by other happy people, isn't it?'

I nod.

'I haven't had a moment of happiness since—'

I raise a finger to his lips, as if muting his words can alter his feelings.

'I know. I'm sorry.'

He nods.

'If it makes you feel any better, there were times in recent years when I wasn't happy either, you know,' he says.

This is news to me.

'Oh, yeah, plenty. I've had moments when I would wonder if it was worth the sacrifice... but I never wanted to be without you, so never got past the acknowledgement that we weren't happy.'

I can't speak. My eyes are fixed on his expression. There is a deep sadness that is surfacing for the first time and I'm not about to trample on his moment. I want to know. I need to know that he understands and experienced doubts similar to mine.

He pauses, gives a weak smile and inhales. It isn't easy for Nick to be this open; he is the ultimate closed book.

'You never said,' I whisper, hoping he continues.

'Was that my job to say, to complain about my lot, or simply get on with the life I had?'

'Even so, you should have told me.'

Nick lowers his gaze and stares at his skating boot kicking the wooden barrier.

'Nick.'

He returns his gaze to mine. It isn't the best place to have a heart-to-heart but, given the expanse of ice covered in one night, it feels right.

'Tell me, *please*.'

232

*

Nina

We sit at the corner table in the busy lounge of The Rose pub, with a glass of mulled wine and his Stella, amidst open packets of peanuts. Overhead the speakers play Christmas tracks, much like the farm's music loop.

'Was it that bad?' asks Zach, after his first sip of Stella.

'Worse. I lacked conversation, interest and knocked my red wine over the white tablecloth.'

'*Classy*. And Bram?'

'*Really?* You want me to discuss this with you?'

'Sure – you'd say if it was another guy you'd dated.'

I take a deep breath.

'We had a decent meal, he chatted about the fishing trip he's planning for next spring, and we laughed about antics on the farm...'

'But?'

'It just didn't feel right. Then as we walked across town there was a homeless guy...'

'On the benches by the library?'

'The exact place. Anyway, as we neared the guy looked up and muttered something. Bram rummaged in his pocket and brought out a handful of change. He picked out a two-pence piece and flipped it in his direction and said to me, "It makes you feel like a king, doesn't it?"'

234

'It makes you feel like a king?' whispers Zach. His face distorts with disgust. 'Bram said that whilst donating to a homeless person?'

'I thought he was joking at first, but he carried on walking.'

'What did the guy do?'

'That was the worst part. Sitting alone in the dark, he actually thanked him for flinging a two-pence coin at his feet. I've never been so embarrassed in my life... and after he'd just spent a shedload of cash on our meal.'

'What did you do?'

'I couldn't walk past him. I opened my purse and quickly gave him a note. I just kept apologising. Bram kept walking but then said I was being stupid because it wouldn't be spent on food but probably on drugs.'

'I'd have done the same as you... and the guy?'

'He blessed me for being charitable. From that point on, he was all I could think about. He hadn't a home, a decent sleeping bag or warm food in his belly. This is the season of goodwill and yet people can't be charitable towards others. I've never seen that side of Bram before. I know he can be brash with his comments, egotistical sometimes, but that was simply mean.'

'That's not like Bram. Do you think he was trying to impress you with a joke and got it wrong?'

'A couple of quid would have impressed me. It ruined the evening, Zach.'

'Did he walk you—?'

'Hi, Zach, where's Bram tonight?' interrupts the newcomer to our table.

We look up to view Selena Hall, her red glossy pout and extended eyelashes fluttering provocatively.

'At home, I think,' says Zach as I return her polite smile and a head-to-toe glance over. Every item of her clothing, from her tiny leather jacket, tight bejewelled top and killer heels, screams expense, unlike mine.

I glance around the lounge and spot a table of females agog beside the inglenook fireplace. Their group looks full of festive cheer, which complements the garland decorations adorning every aged beam.

'Any plans for him to join you?' she purrs, running her finger along the back of the spare chair.

'None. He was out last night on a date so I doubt—'

'A date?' she gasps. Her painted mouth drops wide. I want the floor to swallow me whole. 'Are you joking me?'

Zach shakes his head, collects his pint and sips.

Selena stares from us to her table of friends and back again.

'I can't believe that... Do you know who with?' she asks, feigning a nonchalant tone.

Zach replaces his glass to the table and shrugs.

'Selena, I'm not my brother's keeper, am I?'

'Do you know?'

She catches me unaware. Selena Hall never speaks to me, ever.

'Me?'

She waves a dismissive hand in my direction.

'Never mind. I'll catch up with him later.'

I simply nod.

'Anyway, tell him I said hi,' she adds before strutting back to her friends.

I glare at Zach.

'What? She was all over him like a rash last Saturday night. If he's interested he'll make his own plans, won't he?'

'But still.'

'Phuh! Bram's only got eyes for you at the minute... question is whether he's messed up what could have been a very merry Christmas?'

'I'm not *doing* Christmas. How many times do I have to say?'

'Even you can't cancel Christmas, Nina.'

'I can and I will!'

'Don't you fancy reconnecting with your mum this Christmas?' asks Zach.

'Why?'

'Because...'

'*Because* she fled as soon as she couldn't cope with MS?' I say, grabbing a load of peanuts.

'Because she's your mum.'

'Phuh! She's not. How were we supposed to cope with MS as a two when she couldn't cope as a three?'

'*Nina.*'

'No, don't Nina me... me and Dad did MS together for seventeen years. Jilly made her decision a long time ago. She's made a new life – she can live with it.'

'But...'

'But nothing. End of.'

We sit in silence, sipping our drinks and crunching peanuts.

'Is this any better than last night's date?' asks Zach, after a ten-minute truce.

I stare from beneath my fringe.

'No, but at least I feel more like myself with you. Last night didn't feel comfortable... which is why it can't happen again.' I look across to Selena, laughing with her girlfriends by the open fire. 'He's probably more suited to the likes of her than me.'

'Maybe, but he thinks differently.'

'And you?'

Zach shakes his head.

'See, you never answer a straight question, do you?'

He sighs heavily.

'Nina, it's not what I think that counts, is it?'

Ten

Nina

Monday, 17 December

Everyone in the village knew that Dad was ill. They just didn't know what he was suffering with, despite their efforts to find out. For years, he refused to be drawn into their conversations. Like the stubborn git that he was. His rationale was that if they didn't know, they wouldn't interfere, but he was wrong. People had eyes in their head. I think it became a guessing game for most of the village folk, so they interfered more than he desired.

Having had a few good days after cleaning the cottage, I can't go backwards. I'm supposed to be happier.

It's three o'clock in the morning; the cottage is silent – it's the worst time of night for a trip down Memory Lane.

'Is it the "c" word?' a kid once asked me during school break-time. 'My mum reckons it is.'

My lack of reply only induced more stares, nodding and whisperings around the village. They'd talk even more during his lengthy remissions, when he'd appear 'better' than before.

Hardly surprising that I've locked myself away for the last twelve months like a cocooned lava hiding from the world, whilst deep inside change is occurring.

The seventeenth December, this time last year, we had just eight more days before he died. I'd have worked a busy shift at the farm, walked home to change and gone straight to the hospice. Did we watch TV? Talk? Or argue? We argued a lot, in a bickering manner, when we got on each other's nerves. I can't remember. I'm no psychologist, but I reckon it's a coping mechanism to numb the pain.

A year on, have I resurfaced?

The thick fug of grief hasn't lifted, so maybe not.

I won't sleep now so I get up, make tea and search for the biscuit barrel, returned to its original and rightful home in the top cupboard.

*

At seven thirty I enter the yard to the merriment of 'Last Christmas' piping through the overhead speakers. I'm the last person who should be encouraged to reminisce about last Christmas.

'Nina!' hollers Zach, his hands cupping his mouth, standing before the snug. 'Quick!'

'The boss is calling a staff meeting,' beckons Kitty, standing beside him. I can see other staff wandering in the same direction, so hastily follow suit cutting through the snow. It's not as if I'm late for my work shift – I don't see what all the fuss is about.

We cram into the snug, where it is standing room only. I search amongst the faces, so many contract workers that I don't know or rather don't know their names. Where do they all go after December?

'Where's Shazza?' I ask Kitty.

'Bram said she's called in sick,' comes her reply.

We're all exchanging quizzical glances; we never have staff meetings. Boss Fielding stands at the far end of the cabin, and begins to call for order with Jackie by his side. This is unusual for them; they don't usually address the staff en masse.

'Sorry to bring you together so unexpectedly, but I wish to make you aware of the current situation that...'

We're losing our jobs. We're all being sacked. Christmas has been cancelled! Yay! Fanciful ideas flit through my head.

'As you know, we have a group of local teenagers who are trespassing during the evenings, which is causing us concern. Last night, they cut through the fence *again* and we've found a selection of cider bottles and spent fireworks scattered up at the south clearing. We need

241

you to keep your ears open for names of the culprits – this needs to stop. Someone is going to be hurt and the onus will be on us should that happen. Later today, we'll be meeting with a security team to discuss our options to monitor the premises after closing each night, so if you hear anything in the local community please come and report it. If we can provide the names the police have agreed to visit the teenagers for a chat and warn them of the dangers.'

A round of head nodding occurs before we are dismissed to get ready for the day.

'Seems serious,' I whisper to Kitty, as the boss sidesteps through the crowd to leave.

'In today's blame and claim culture he'll be in the firing line if someone gets seriously hurt.'

'Makes you wonder why Shazza's off today,' I add. 'It feels underhand mentioning it, but the twins are convinced she knows what's what.'

Kitty pulls a quizzical face.

'All eyes and ears open, is what I suggest,' says Kitty, departing towards the cashier's cabin.

'Nina!' calls Boss Fielding, from the door of the snug. 'Can I see you in five minutes, please?'

*

'Morning,' I say, as cheerfully as possible to cover my melancholy, as I approach Boss Fielding brushing fresh snow from the wooden steps outside his office.

'There's a change to the notice board tasks... as you know, Shazza's just called in sick so...' I watch as he turns back inside his office door, grabs a plastic storage box and hands it to me. The box is filled with a jumble of green Lycra fabric. I glance from fabric to Boss and back to the fabric before he speaks. 'Could you do a couple of hours of elf duty at the grotto? It'll be a quiet day given it's a school day, but we've got two minibuses arriving from the local nursery as part of a Christmas outing.'

I simply stare at my boss.

'Elf duty?'

My muddled brain suddenly screams, 'Elf!'

The boss turns, attempting to go inside his office.

A sudden panic fills my body.

'Oh, no, no, I couldn't. Seriously, Boss... please, no, not today,' I protest, offering the plastic box back to him.

He turns around swiftly; his brow lowers.

'Now, Nina, only yesterday you said you'd prefer—'

I know what I said; I don't need reminding.

I stare up at him with woeful eyes.

'Switch between the two grottos, please, and make sure it's a good day for the kiddies. Quick now, chop chop.' His hands gently push the box back into mine.

How am I going to muster up the spirit to entertain nursery children when it's difficult enough climbing

243

from my bed, dressing and attending work each day?

*

Holly

'I'm not happy about this, Holly,' says Mum over breakfast. 'A day away from school won't hurt your grades and those girls will get their just desserts.'

My mouth falls open. My mum never allows us to have time away from school. She hates the idea of enforced snow days.

'No way. If I don't go in today everyone in the year group will jump to the conclusion that I was involved. If I'm present, at least I can correct any false facts. Otherwise, they'll play judge and jury, condemning my reputation forever. No, Mum, I'm going,' I declare, across the cornflakes.

'Phew! Like you'll hear the gossips today… It'll all be snide remarks behind your back and whispering in the toilets,' adds Hannah, giving a knowing smile.

Hannah's not wrong. This issue isn't about to blow over, but still, I need to save face, stand up to my accusers and attend school.

*

Demi's face tells me she doesn't need bringing up to speed.

'The word on the street is that you've been nabbed colluding with Paris and her girls—'

'And since when did we believe the word on the street?' I ask, my eyebrows lifting.

Demi shrugs before asking, 'Are you grounded?'

'Kind of. My mum thinks it involves Alfie. I've told her countless time it doesn't but, hey, you know my mum.'

'Knows everything, your mum,' mutters Demi, kicking up the snow as we walk.

'She thinks she does!'

We both fall into a fit of giggles. Demi gets it.

*

Angie

'"Tell me, please?" – that's what you asked him? You shouldn't have said that, Angie, surely that's one can of worms you don't need to hear about?' mutters Jilly as I relay the ice skating story. Instantly, I regret sharing.

When will I ever learn? Why can't I be a strong, silent, independent type that keeps her inner goddess in charge of all her precious secrets? But no, I have to blurt and share... then, once criticised, I feel wounded. Stupid for sharing.

'*And?*' asks Jilly, eager to hear the details.

I hesitate. Is there still time to put my inner goddess in charge? Or have I missed the boat?

'Angie?'

'Jilly, maybe I shouldn't... you know, some things are private... I really shouldn't have said.'

Jilly stares and giggles.

'Says the woman who once told me many moons ago about Nick's insatiable liking for—'

The office door bursts open and in walks Troy, the latest intern, his neatly trimmed beard hiding the face of a teenager.

I breathe a sigh of relief. What the hell was Jilly about to say? Silk? Massages? Ice cubes? Or... I gulp, then blush. Yes, I do remember sharing some fairly intimate moments during a lingerie party at someone's house after a few too many white wines. So what, if handcuffs and chocolate sauce had been our thing in the early days, surely it's everyone's thing at some point?

I watch as Jilly peers at the paperwork Troy offers her. She must have the memory of an elephant to have squirrelled away that piece of information for so long.

Even I'd forgotten that little detail.

Jilly flirts with the youngster before he dashes from the office to escape the older woman.

'What?' she says, looking bashful.

'Toy boy?'

Jilly frowns.

'I'm old enough to be his bloody mother and then some.' She gives a cheeky wink, before continuing. 'Anyway, where were we? Ah, yes, *your* Nick.'

'No more… I have work to do.' I busy myself as my mind replays last night's scene in my head. It may keep my mouth from blurting details across the office to Jilly.

But really, I need to get my head around what happened last night. What I told Jilly wasn't the whole story. In fact, Nick took me by surprise.

'Do you remember when Alfie was about six and we were having a rough time coping with all the changes of routine and each weekend was bicker, bicker, bicker?'

I nodded. How could I forget? I was literally the stressed-out new mum at the school gate, with my hair scraped into a ponytail and no make-up, being the morning's entertainment for the others.

'I thought about leaving the marriage back then.' His tone was sombre, hesitant and yet loving.

I nodded, taking in this new revelation.

'You thought it was all about you when the reality was...' he inhaled deeply '...I'd met someone at work...'

Was I hearing this correctly?

'She started working in the draft office downstairs and we got chatting... and a polite good morning turned into regular coffee-break chats and before I knew it, I felt I was... falling for her.' He looked up and held my gaze. 'Do you get me?'

I nodded, speechless. My mind drifted back to that awful time. With a young child, full of energy who I was convinced had some hyperactive condition, an aversion to sleep, a death wish and a fondness for attending A & E. I was a total wipe-out as regards anything outside Alfie's routine, be it my own health, socialising or even my husband. I was closed, insular to everything other than my Alfie.

'Nothing happened, I want to make that quite clear, but... it *could* have, very easily. I felt...'

Don't you *dare* say it, I thought.

'...lonely and misunderstood.'

He bloody well said it! My blood boiled. How sodding misunderstood could a man be who left the house every morning at eight and returned at six o'clock to clean shirts, a cooked meal and a freshly vacuumed lounge? If anyone was misunderstood and lonely at that time it was me, stuck at home all day waiting for a child to come home, so my exhausted body could entertain, educate and nurture some more. There were months when I never left the house apart from the school run or grocery shopping.

'Anyway, I suggested that we stopped meeting for coffee before we hurt other people and... well... she left the company soon afterwards.'

Be mature, talk it through, don't lose it now, not when he's got to this stage of the game. Listen. Respond calmly.

'And you've never met up with her since?'

'No. Never.'

'And thought about her?'

'Sometimes, but never in the way you probably think.'

Bloody hell, how honest is he? I couldn't have admitted half that and I've done so much more. Is it me or is my blood boiling more this morning as regards Nick's confession than it was last night?

'Angie... are you wanting coffee or not?' asks Jilly, waving at me across the desks.

'Oh, yes, please.' I watch as Jilly leaves our section. I make a mental note to not discuss my private life at work. I'm having a hard enough time keeping up with the revelations as it is.

*

Nina

I'm dressed from top to toe in green Lycra, complete with a pointy hat adorned with a pair of pixie ears, freezing my ass off, in the company of twenty-four children aged four and below. I want to die. The screaming, whining and wailing is on a par with the soothing decibels created by a pneumatic drill. Six nursery assistants are busy nattering in a huddle, oblivious to the hullaballoo that is occurring around their knees. I am aware of every single voice. Though I am more aware that, given the nature of stretched Lycra, my underwear is clearly on show every time I turn about. I know, despite the averted eyes of the grotto team: all svelte beauties who are wearing suitable underwear because they've been 'elfing' since Saturday, that my red M&S briefs with lace detailing *are* the topic of conversation. Who knew that even little children could understand that 'the lady's underwear' shouldn't really be on display, but can't refrain from pointing and whispering? I've done my best to stay positive and smile throughout. But I can't keep this up for much longer.

I've ushered along a group of children, creating happy and lasting memories, much to the delight of my boss. The second group appears to be noisier and more excited, if that's possible.

'Hello and welcome to Santa's grotto,' I yell, dredging up every ounce of enthusiasm I can muster. 'Who's ready to meet Santa?'

A deafening cheer fills the sales yard. How can such tiny bodies make so much noise?

In crocodile style, I lead them along the grotto path, their wide eyes looking warily around at the giant spruces looming overhead, the diminishing light and unexpected flight of disturbed birds. They all jump out of their skins when the chainsaws of the cutting crew make a surprise start in the distance.

I slow the pace as we approach the snow-covered grotto.

'Now, boys and girls, I need to see your best fairy steps as we near Santa's grotto,' I whisper with dramatic effect. 'Santa's happy when he hears tippy-toes in the snow.' The children react with chuckles and smiles, eager to please the elf in the red pants. I am trying my hardest, knowing that the expectation of any event is sometimes the greatest and lengthiest part of a childhood memory.

Their tiny eyes grow wide, catching sight of twinkling fairy lights amidst brightly coloured fake presents stacked high either side of the entrance. Old Bill and I created an amazing winter scene befitting any Santa, and Mother Nature has been kind enough to put the icing on the grotto by topping it with a generous helping of fresh snow each night.

Everything seems to be going so well.

Standing at the entrance, I am systematically feeding two children at a time into the inner section, where a relay of elves asks for their first names before secretly squirrelling the information to Santa in preparation for the initial meet and greet where he magically knows their names without asking. Squeals of delight can be heard as two little bodies, supervised by their nursery assistants, are led around the corner to the great throne to meet Santa. Other elves take it in turns to capture the images on digital cameras to be saved and emailed to the nursery later on.

But now, I wish I were anywhere else but here.

For here, striding towards me, his tumble of brown curls bouncing, his winter coat flapping wide, is Luca, the Range Rover guy. Worse still, each hand is clasping a young boy's hand, last seen play fighting each other.

I rarely pray, but it seems the natural thing to do.

Please, dear God, let the earth open wide and swallow me whole. Now. Now, please. Now!

It doesn't.

My cheeks burn as he steps nearer. He automatically smiles at me before doing a double take and staring. His eyes travel down the length of my body to my toe-curling elf boots and slowly back up. I watch in horror as his mouth twitches uncontrollably and he tries his damnedest to fight it.

Seriously, someone kill me now!

'Hi and welcome to Santa's grotto,' I say, in my cheeriest elf voice. 'If you'd like to step inside, my elf friends will organise your party in preparation for meeting Santa.' I speak directly to his left ear. His dark eyes are somewhere to my right, staring straight at me. I break my focus and busy myself eagerly smiling at both children; boys aged about five and seven. The older one sticks his tongue out at me, but his father fails to see or correct as he is still staring at me, and probably my red underwear.

Now is the moment when I need a busy queue. So I can happily hurry along to the next family and repeat my practised lines. But there is no one else, given that it's only five past three on a school day. How has Luca arrived so early?

I linger, looking beyond the party of three. Who should be following my instructions to enter the foyer but haven't. I look around the trio but still no one else for me to welcome. Pity.

'I see you're a jack of all trades,' he remarks as he continues to stare.

'I help out where I can,' I say, averting my eyes to avoid his gaze, *again.*

'And Santa's most grateful, I'm sure.' He tilts his head to fall into my line of vision.

'Mmmm.' I can feel my cheeks getting hotter by the minute. Why can't I ever be as cool as the svelte beauties inside the grotto? I bet they never get flustered when a

254

good-looking guy speaks to them but me, I turn myself inside out with sheer embarrassment.

Again, I sweep my right hand aside, indicating they can go through to the grotto. Luca ignores it; the two boys are fidgeting on the end of each hand, causing his body to sway and jolt.

'Donkey whisperer one day, Christmas tree sales expert the next and now this... Wow, if I return tomorrow what will it be?' I know he's trying to be sociable. I get it, but for some unknown reason this guy seems to be the catalyst for my unexpected innate reactions; I am simply out of my depth. He's out of bounds, totally off limits and taken by the beautiful blonde so why, oh, why am I feeling this level of magnetism towards him when I know nothing about him?

'Hopefully, I'll be enjoying a day trip to London away from this grotto,' I reply, but on hearing myself I cringe a little more as it sounds a tad arsey.

'Well, Nina the elf, enjoy your day off – you've certainly earned it. Come on, lads, in we go.' He gives a warm smile before tugging the boys' hands in the right direction.

I give a sigh of relief as he passes by. A shiver runs the length of my spine as the smell of citrus cologne fills my nostrils. *Davidoff's Cool Water*, if I'm not mistaken.

How ridiculous am I? A total bloody stranger and I'm quaking at the knee like some teenager over the latest boy band. What's worse is that he can somehow sense it and keeps going out of his way to speak to me. Maybe these are his final tricks before the big day occurs? His last chance to witness the effect he once had upon females before he settles into married life.

I want out of here.

I check my watch: quarter past three.

I poke my head inside the grotto entrance. Luca is just disappearing through the silvery shimmery door ribbons to receive a warm welcome from Santa, and I grab the attention of the svelte-like elf adorning the prep area, shared with two scoffing reindeer.

'I'm just nipping to the loo,' I mouth.

She nods. Little does she suspect I have no intention of returning.

I dart from my grotto post and run as fast as I can, through the snow, back along the northern pathway heading for the sales yard. I sprint to the gate and hastily open and close, giving it a good bang to close the latch.

'Oi, Nina! I like the pants,' shouts Bram, stalling his work at the netting machine and nudging his co-worker. 'Very fetching.'

I pull a face at his confirmation. I've spent hours trying to kid myself that only I can see my underwear. Bram confirms the obvious... everyone has seen my underwear today. That's a staggering forty-eight nursery pupils, six helpers, five svelte elves, two Santas, two small boys, a yard full of work colleagues... oh, and Luca. *Great!*

I rush towards the snug, stomp up the steps and burst in on Kitty and Zach decorating the room in tinsel and holly garlands.

'Hi, Nina... we're attempting to jolly up the place... D-do you know that you can see...?' stammers Kitty, looking instantly uncomfortable on my behalf.

'*Really?* I hadn't realised. Thanks for noticing,' I yell as I head for the staff toilets.

'Bloody hell, Nina, you could hardly miss 'em.' Zach laughs, shaking his head as he fails to move a heavy sofa single-handed.

I slam the toilet door shut, slide the bolt and stand against the door. Is this really what my life has become? A daily battle to dress myself, breathe in and out while entertaining the masses and hiding my grief?

I stare round the cubicle. There's a load of graffiti on the side wall, it's dismal and furnished with a white porcelain toilet, yet for the first time today I can actually breathe.

Bang! Bang!

'Nina! Can we talk about the other night?' calls Bram.

*

257

Holly

'*Holly!*' my dad hollers up the staircase just after five o'clock.

'Yeah!'

'Phone!'

I descend the staircase two at a time. Who'd not call my mobile?

'Hello?'

'Hello, Holly, Mr Fairbright here from the chemist...'

After a ten-second conversation, in which I say very little except for 'yes' numerous times, he ends the call.

I walk into the hullabaloo that is our kitchen.

'Holly, you OK?' asks Dad, looking up from the table where Mum's about to dish up the evening meal.

I settle into a chair, before I speak.

'I've just been sacked!'

'What?'

'You're joking?' asks Mum, pan in hand, straining carrots.

'Seriously, that was Mr Fairbright. He said that, having given full consideration to the incident that happened at the weekend, they have very little choice but to let me go,' I repeat his words as accurately as I can.

'Oh, lovey,' swoons Mum, returning her pan to the stove before stroking my hair. 'I'm sorry, he's obviously jumped to the wrong conclusion, as I did.'

'Bloody ridiculous! Did he accuse you of stealing?'

'No, he said that the police had mentioned the accusation made by the girls but that he did believe me, but even so—'

'Even so… you're sacked.'

I stare around the table.

'I've done nothing wrong.'

'We know, babe, but these things happen and—'

'I've got a good mind to go around there to speak to him,' says Dad, bristling in his chair.

'Steve, please.'

'Seriously, he's siding with those little bitches – surely he knows Holly well enough to know she would never stoop so low as to steal?'

My mum's doing her comforting nod.

'What am I going to do for extra money?'

'Shhhh now, it's not your fault… Let's have dinner and we'll think of somewhere you can apply to afterwards.'

*

Angie

I curl up on the sofa and listen to Nick's phone message for the tenth time today.

'Hi, Angie, wondering what you are doing tonight? Maybe... if you're free we can meet up for last orders at The Rose... Let me know. It's Nick, by the way.'

As if I don't know.

I can't bring myself to delete and ignore, that's childish, and yet I could do with a night off. I glance at the clock: eight. I have two hours to make up my mind. Two hours to listen to the message a few more times before... declining? Accepting? How immature am I being?

I listen to the message again. He sounds nervous, hesitant. Does he suspect that his confession has upset me?

My mobile rings whilst in my hand. I stare at the screen: Nick.

Shit. I fight the urge to depress the accept call button. Instead, I wait.

The tiny screen illuminates, indicating another message has been left.

I quickly listen to his tired voice.

'Angie, Nick... call me.'

Short and sweet. I re-listen.

How judgemental am I being? I can accept his errors, can't I?

I press the recall button.

*

'Tell me, what made you stay?' I ask as he places my second vodka and cranberry juice before me. Finally, I've plucked up the courage to ask.

'I thought so... has it bothered you that I was so honest, last night?'

I shake my head and lie.

Nick settles beside me in the alcove facing the pub crowd.

'I had responsibilities, didn't I? There comes a day when you must grow up.'

'I thought that was the day we had Alfie?'

'It's supposed to be but, sadly, it wasn't. It was the day I walked away from an invitation that would have led to nothing but heartache for my young wife and child... Seriously, it was the first adult decision I ever made.'

I sip my drink to silence my tongue. A pain stabs at my chest. That confession actually hurt. He felt something for someone else other than me. And I didn't even know.

'Thank you.'

'For what?' he says, looking up from his pint.

'Staying with us… It was more than I did.'

Nick nods.

'I think you were simply bored, Angie… nothing more.'

'But I didn't walk away from temptation, did I?' I leapt straight in and left my husband and son behind. And now, my son's making me pay a dear price. 'How is Alfie?'

'Loved up to the eyeballs.'

I sit up. That wasn't the answer I was expecting.

'Hasn't he said?'

'Nothing about it being serious.'

'Still with this Holly girl, from the estate… getting serious, if you ask me.'

'At sixteen?'

'Yes, at sixteen, Angie… You know what puppy love is like, all or nothing.'

I think back, as far as I can remember, and it isn't particularly clear just how my puppy love was. Awkward – yes. Confusing – yes. True love and serious – no, *obviously*.

'He spends half his time in his room texting her, or in the bathroom doing his hair to go and visit her. Literally the day revolves around Holly.'

'Then you need to straighten him out. That's not healthy.'

'It's what I did at his age.'

'Doesn't mean to say it is healthy. He has schoolwork to focus upon, university places to gain – he can't go messing it up fawning over a girl.'

'Fawning over a girl... Angie?'

'Seriously, Nick... before we know it she'll be getting ideas.'

'Like what?'

'Girls these days, Nick...'

'Don't kid yourself, Angie!'

'You might want to remind him that he needs to protect himself if they... should they...' The words hang in the air like a dirty secret. 'You know.'

Nick shakes his head.

'Seriously, Nick... he needs to focus on his studies, not some girl.'

'Holly, her name is Holly, and she sounds very sensible, actually.'

'I don't care... if it's the real thing she'll wait for him.'

Nick sips his pint of Guinness and ignores my reaction.

'Anyway, how are you fixed for dinner tomorrow night? Alfie's staying around a friend's house for the night so I can cook for you, if you'd like?'

That would be nice. If there was one complaint I'd had, it was that Nick never helped about the house. I understood that he was busy, I understood that he was raised to think that certain jobs were women's work, but still... cooking could have been shared.

'I'd like that. Anything special?'

'Nothing fancy, just simple home-cooked food,' he says, which sounds wonderful to me. 'I could have a chat with Alfie... about us, beforehand.'

Eleven

Nina

Tuesday, 18 December

'Morning, Nina,' calls Boss Fielding over his shoulder in a cheerful voice, as I climb half asleep into the farm's aged minibus, parked before the snug.

'Morning,' I mutter, unsure if five o'clock in the morning aligns itself to morning or middle of the night. My definition is the latter. 'It's nice to know the exact time to avoid the Christmas music.'

I tug at the seat belt before acknowledging the presence of Bram and Zach. It takes even longer for me to register that a series of seats has been removed and replaced by an array of ladders and tool boxes. I haven't missed the twenty-foot giant Nordman fir, wrapped in plastic netting and lying supine secured with haulage strapping upon the lengthy trailer.

'Early enough for you, is it?' asks Bram, cocky and wide awake.

'Not really. Am I allowed to sleep or would that be bad manners?'

A combination of, 'Bad manners,' and, 'Sure, do as you wish,' are shouted at me by the three men. I'm grateful. I'm still processing Bram's explanation from yesterday that, 'It was a joke, Nina,' and, 'Seriously, surely you know I've got more compassion than *that* for the needy.' He wore a sheepish look throughout the explanation to which I listened. Surely, actions speak louder than words?

'To be honest, I don't remember volunteering for this task or trip,' I say, folding my coat into a pillow roll.

'You didn't. We nominated you to come to London with us. It's not every day you get to visit the prime minister's pad by private invitation,' explains Zach, touching my hand. 'Much like you've been nominated to show the new girl the ropes come the weekend.'

'What new girl?'

'Yep, Dad thought it would ignite your festive passion,' says Bram, pointing to his father. 'Yesterday, young Alfie asked if his girlfriend could have some hours over Christmas.'

'Great! He's obviously made a lasting impression on you but I'm really not in the mood to train teenagers for part-time work, Boss,' I chunter, as I settle against the window to sleep.

Boss Fielding shrugs as he steadily drives through the village lanes heading for the motorway.

'It might lighten the load on the sales yard to have another teenage gofer around the sales yard,' adds Zach.

'It won't help, but I appreciate the sentiment,' I say, yawning. 'Wake me up when we arrive in London.'

For the first time in ages, a cosy warmth envelops me and I drift off to sleep amidst the sounds of the Fielding guys bantering between themselves.

*

Never before have I undergone such a security check.

As our minibus pulls up at the black gates of Downing Street, the burly guards armed with huge machine guns swarm around the windows asking for ID.

'We are expected,' Boss explains, showing his business details and documents. 'We're delivering this year's Christmas tree.' Back in October our farm won the British Christmas Tree Growers' Association 'Grower of the Year - Champion Tree' award, and the new wooden sign made for the entrance gate was given pride of place. The accolade entitles the winning farm to donate and deliver the Christmas tree to the prime minister's front door.

We wait while clearance checks are made and eventually the black gates are opened for us to drive through, into the snow-cleared street. It is like entering a film set, surreal knowing that behind each polished door important state decisions are made and rubber-stamped with top-class authority. The railings are pristine, the door knockers sparkling and the carriage lamp at the entrance to Number 10's door shines like a beacon.

'*We*... are in Downing Street,' declares Bram, from the passenger seat.

'You see it so often on Sky News and yet look how tiny it is,' I add, peering at the wall of photographers, three bodies deep, banked upon the one side.

'There is nothing tiny about those protection officers.' Zach laughs. 'Good luck taking those guys on any time soon.'

We are beckoned towards the end of the street and instructed to park.

'All out!' shouts Boss, heaving his frame from the driver's seat.

After a brief introduction from a suited and booted Downing Street official, we are allowed to unload the Christmas tree, or rather the three men do. I stand back pretending I'm busy supervising and wait for them to stand the Nordman fir upright, soak its roots and place it carefully in a suitable display stand. A wall of camera flashes occurs the minute Larry, the official Downing Street cat, strolls over to inspect the mighty spruce with a feline sniff.

'She's all yours, Nina,' cries Boss, opening a series of decoration boxes provided by Downing Street staff.

'Me?'

'Bloody hell, woman, you've got some uses with your creative flare... now, jump to it. We need to hurry up if we're to miss the traffic on the M40,' he continues.

Oh, great! I turn to view the throng of pavement reporters and news crews all watching the proceedings. It is one thing being creative on the sales yard but before an audience is another issue.

'Chop chop,' he mouths, nodding frantically. 'We're all having our picture taken once you've dressed her in some finery.'

Zach holds my ladder firm and steady, while Bram fetches and carries from the selection of boxes – symbolic given our friendship: Zach always offering support while Bram repeatedly offers me the glitz and glamour.

'It's comforting to know that even the prime minster and co. have some crappy ornaments that linger in the decoration box that will never see the light of day again,' says Bram, holding up a feeble excuse for a tinsel garland.

'Hurry up, lad... stop wasting time,' moans his father, supervising the decoration.

*

Angie

I park my car two streets away from Nick's house in a small cul-de-sac and walk the familiar route back to theirs, that was once ours. The snow has a dirty walked-upon look, as it lingers between snow and yellow slush.

Parking elsewhere feels strange but necessary. I don't want to give Nick's neighbours anything to call me about should they recognise my car. They have no reason to involve themselves, but you know what neighbours can be like – they think everything is their business over a morning coffee and a shared packet of Bourbons.

I approach the house as nerves jingle in my stomach. I've shaved and moisturised my legs; there's no pretending, tonight could be a special night. I've even bought condoms in case Nick hasn't.

I note that the winter heather under their lounge window has thrived since planting. Good choice, but who'd have imagined as I planted it last autumn that it would look so impressive the first year after I left.

He opens the front door looking flustered and browbeaten. Our old brown Labrador, Rolo, fusses around Nick's knees.

'What's wrong?' I ask, my senses heightened with the anticipation of tonight's dinner date. 'Hi there, boy.' I reach down to pat the dog but Nick bundles me inside unceremoniously.

'Alfie... he's running late. He and his girlfriend haven't gone out yet!' explains Nick, nervously looking over his shoulder and up the staircase as he speaks.

Great! I take it the father and son honesty chat went well, then.

'I thought you said he was stopping at his friend's house.'

'He *was* but their plans fell through and... he called his girlfriend around instead. He said they are going out in a minute to the pictures.' Nick ushers me straight through into the lounge before hastily pushing me towards the kitchen door, from where an aroma of gorgeous cooking is wafting. I trail clumps of snow through the house, having not had time to wipe my feet properly on entering. Rolo lolls closely behind us. Nick firmly closes the kitchen door behind us, before he exhales.

Double great!

'Nick. Stop!'

I look around the kitchen that took me six weeks to choose from a showroom, two years for us to repay the loan for; my gaze falls on the breakfast bar on which I'd left my 'Dear Nick' letter.

'You did speak to Alfie? You told him?' I edge away from the door, but Nick stands guard, his hand snared to the door handle should Alfie attempt to enter.

271

Nick balks.

The dog looks between us and begins to pant.

Sodding hell.

'Not exactly... I was going to, honest I was, but we started the conversation and...'

'You bailed out. Friggin' hell, Nick – this isn't the way for him to find out about us.' I snap, trying to keep my voice low but wanting Nick to know just how annoyed I am.

'Sorry, it just went wrong.'

'How?'

Nick leans his shoulder against the wooden door to add weight.

I see the embarrassment rise in his face.

'I began by saying that I started to see someone and that I was liking the closeness we had and...'

'He mentioned me, didn't he?'

Nick slowly nods.

'You might as well tell me.'

'Before I could say any more he jumped in with, "That'll put Mum's back up."'

'Are you serious?' I don't know whether to laugh or cry. And from my own son, too.

'How could I carry on with my planned speech? He'd thrown me off track and I couldn't stop the conversation trail.'

'Tell me more.'

'He just kept saying that you'd never believe that I was fortunate enough to meet and fall in love with someone else other than you and...'

'Our son said that?' I've a good mind to snatch the door wide open and march up to Alfie's bedroom to prove exactly what I think about his father falling in love. Bloody teenagers – he's had a girlfriend for all of ten minutes, now he thinks he knows it all. Boy, an unexpected visit from me would wipe the smile off his face.

A banging occurs on the kitchen door.

'*Dad!*'

We both freeze. Nick leans his shoulder against the door.

'Yes, Alfie,' he calls with a nonchalant tone, holding a palm up to me.

Bloody cheek.

'Dad, we're off now. I won't be late back. The film finishes at quarter to ten so I'll walk Holly home but... well, enjoy your dinner... with your *friend*.' I hear Alfie's tone change on the word 'friend'. I can imagine two teenagers giggling on the other side of the door. They won't be giggling in twenty years' time if they have the same journey as us. Oh, no, they'll be bloody grateful for a second chance, despite what their kids think.

'Bye, Alfie. Holly. Stay safe!' calls Nick, a smile finally dawning, as we hear their bodies move away from the

273

other side of the door.

'Friend?' I'm incensed. 'A sodding friend.'

Nick shrugs.

'It's not a bad title.'

'It bloody is. Jilly at work is my friend. Phil and Carol are friends... *we* are not friends.'

'He chose the wrong word. He doesn't know what to call his dad's girlfriend, does he?'

'Err *Mum*!' I snap, feeling belittled by Alfie's shallow terminology and Nick's willingness to accept it.

'Were we not best friends when we were married?'

'No,' I retort. 'Husband and wife, lovers, partners... *never* friends, Nick – despite what other people say. Who wants their spouse as their best friend *and* lover?'

We hear the front door slam. Gone.

'Wine?'

He makes the switch that easily. I answer yes, but I know I'll be fuming for the next two hours about how our evening has begun. I expected to enter as a guest, instead I'm standing in the kitchen hiding behind a wooden door from my own son. And I still have my coat on!

Nick pours the wine as I remove my coat.

I'm about to ask where I can hang it but, given our previous history, I take myself back through the hallway. A friend or a dinner date might not know where they hang the coats in this house, but I do.

I return to find two large glasses of wine and bowls of nibbles laid out on the breakfast bar. Nick is donning oven gloves and is bending inside the oven, spooning something in a casserole dish.

'Coq au vin,' he says, returning the lid, closing the oven door and removing the gloves.

'Really?' I stifle a laugh on two counts.

'Yes, really. *Here.*' He hands me a wine glass. I note just how full it is. Definitely a larger than large glass of wine. Not expecting me to drive home, then, Nick?

'To us,' he says, chinking the side of my glass.

'To us,' I mutter, before taking a large sip and settling on a high stool.

'You can go through to the lounge if you wish. I don't have to watch over this.'

I shake my head. I'm happy here. Sitting in my old kitchen, watching my ex-husband fuss around cooking dinner is a thing I longed to see, would have given my right arm for, in fact, when we were married. I suppose, I gave my marriage up in order to see this view. A wave of sadness lifts from my stomach. My marriage, our marriage. It ended so swiftly thanks to the courts. I had plenty of time to think, rethink and change my mind, but deep down inside, did I always know this would happen?

'You look sad,' says Nick, leaning over the counter towards me, glass in hand.

'Have I messed it all up for all of us?'

Nick shakes his head.

'It's salvageable, with time.'

'But how will you ever trust me again?'

Nick shrugs, sips his wine and stares into my eyes. His silence tells me the inner struggle he's having.

I nod.

'And Alfie?'

Nick inclines his head, rolls his lips and pulls a face.

'The boy's different, Angie. You showed him the reality of relationships... before he'd had chance to experience the nice side and teenage kicks for himself. He's under no illusion.'

'Holly, is it?'

'Yeah, Holly. She seems a decent kid. She makes him laugh anyway.'

I feel a pang of jealousy. How can someone else make my son laugh?

'Live nearby?'

'Over the other side of town... the eldest of seven girls, I believe.'

'Don't they own a TV?' I laugh, shaking my head at the horror.

'She's nice. Decent family, down-to-earth types based on what Alfie says... I haven't met them yet.'

'Duh! Of course not.'

'Her parents asked to meet me a few days ago – offered us an invite to Sunday lunch. I said I thought it was too early for such tricks but Alfie seems keen.'

'Course he's bloody keen – he's copping his first feel of flesh. Christ, Nick.' My anger flares from nowhere. 'All boys are keen at *that* age...'

'Angie... he's a tad more respectful towards her than that.'

'Don't tell me what teenage boys get up to, Nick.'

We fall silent as I remember the teenage kicks I had behind the back of the shops on summer evenings with a plastic bottle of cider and a ten pack of Embassy.

'Anyway, less about Alfie,' mutters Nick, stroking my cheek. 'And more about us.'

I stare into his wide blue eyes. I can see the pain I've caused him. Would I trust me in Nick's position? I don't like my own answer but vow that, if he allows me to, I'll make it up to him and Alfie. Though Alfie may prove a tougher challenge.

The timer on the oven sounds, making us both jump.

'Take yourself through to the dining room, light the candles and I'll be in in two minutes.'

I'm grateful for a task; it can busy my hands in preference to downing my wine.

*

We lie on the sofa, lights dimmed, limbs entwined, watching a rerun of *Die Hard*. The wine bottle is empty, the two spent glasses lay toppled over beside the sofa and Nick gently strokes my neck as he stares at the TV screen and I watch his face from the corner of my eye.

'What time is it?'

'Nine.'

'Oh.'

We stare at the screen some more.

'Have you got work tomorrow?'

'Yep, the eight twenty-two train into Birmingham,' mutters Nick, his eyes not leaving the screen. His index finger continues to stroke the base of my neck.

'You got condoms?'

'What?' His tone is one of shock.

'Condoms. Rubbers. Whatever you want to call them.'

'Angie... we were married for eighteen years – have I ever used...?' I watch as he struggles to say the word, let alone use one.

'Sorry, but things have changed in recent months and, well, I need to be honest with you – if we venture down that path then it'll need to be condoms.'

Nick hastily untangles his body and sits up, grabs the TV remote and mutes Bruce Willis.

'Are you saying that... you've already slept with other people since we divorced?'

I nod. I did mention it before. I'm not shying away from this. This is the new me. The honest, truthful, direct me, Angie Woodward, honest to the core.

'Seriously, Nick, we need to talk about this. The world has changed since we were kids and bonking...

well, they don't call it that any more, but anyway, couples need to talk about sex before they decide…'

Nick simply stares.

I've caught him totally unaware. What the hell did he think would occur having shared a bottle of wine, lounged on the sofa and with the entire house to ourselves? Nothing? Oh, yeah, well, that was the good old days of our eighteen-year marriage, but this, this was supposed to be our brand-new, mark-two experience and, to be fair, I was expecting a new man.

'How many?'

I shake my head. That's none of his business.

'This is it, all you need to know is that I was safe, that I protected myself and that if I apply the same rules with you… your sexual health won't be compromised.'

'Compromised. Are you for real?' He's now moved away, sitting at the far end of the sofa like a frightened virgin at a stag do.

I raise myself to sitting. Obviously, he wasn't expecting this.

'I've had some fun, to be fair, Nick.' There, I've said it.

Nick's eyes widen.

'What's that supposed to mean?'

'Well…' I click my tongue and give a cheeky wink.

Nick looks baffled. Almost lost in the conversation. I'm not certain, but under the dimmed light he appears to pale.

I swiftly remove my earrings as he hastily leads me up the staircase. They cost a fortune from town and losing one will ruin the pair. He's in a rush, as we reach the top stair and swiftly take the second door on the right to the main back bedroom. I hesitate; this isn't where I thought we were heading.

'I moved rooms,' he mutters, pushing the door wide and entering. He doesn't put the light on, which I'm grateful for.

'Nick,' I whisper as he releases my hand and faces me in the darkness.

'Angie.'

'Is this what you really want?'

I can imagine the look of surprise on his face.

'Bloody hell, woman… *yes*.'

I don't remember removing my clothes, or his. In no time, we are on the bed – our bed, I note; he obviously hasn't replaced that – our hands snatching and grabbing at naked flesh as our mouths ferociously work at each other's face and neck.

This isn't the Nick I knew.

The Nick I knew was gentler, less hurried, more refined. This Nick is ravishing me like our wedding night eighteen years ago.

Holly

'Are you OK?' I ask as we walk back from the cinema.

Alfie shrugs, his hands stuffed deep into his pockets, my right hand adjoined to his left.

'Is it your dad?'

'More my mum.'

I wait. Alfie doesn't need pushing; he'll say when he's ready.

The streets are empty and snow has been falling for hours. I wanted to catch the bus for the short journey but Alfie wanted to walk. I stare at the orange haze around each street lamp, beyond which the moon stares as we walk the pavement.

'You think you can rely on parents, don't ya?'

I nod. I can trust mine.

'When you're little, you think they mend anything that is broken... I broke my Action Man's arm off but instantly my dad fixed it. Like in seconds, bang, as good as new.'

I know what he means. There's a story of me as a child breaking a plate that I delivered to my father in twenty or so pieces so he could fix it before my mum found out. The magic didn't work that time, but I get where Alfie's coming from.

'It's make-believe, you know.'

I learnt that from the plate.

'It's as much make-believe as the Tooth Fairy, Santa Claus and the Easter Bunny. They haven't a clue what they're doing – no more than we have, yet they pretend they do.'

'I gather that's most of what being an adult is about – pretending you have the answer when really you're bricking it inside and hoping it doesn't show on your face.'

Alfie stops dead. My hand is yanked back with his jacket pocket.

'So, why give us such a hard time?' He begins to walk again.

'Alfie, that's parenting. They're not supposed to let us know how scared they are. Look at my parents – they're all smiles and, "Hi, Alfie, how are you?" when you're there, but the minute you walk out the front door I get the full lecture regarding "nice boys", "don't be led astray" and the whole "you'll always talk to us about stuff that's worrying you, won't you?" lectures. Seriously, they like you and yet—'

'You're a girl – parents are always going to be over-possessive about girls but—'

'Hey, cut the crap!' I snap. I'm not sure if boys are always trying to be top dog or whether us girls simply stay schtum too often for them to realise their arrogance.

'Sorry, but you know what I mean.'

'I do, but your dad worries about you just as much as my parents worry about me, so don't go there!'

'Mmmm, you're right, he does.'

I wait. He's on the brink of saying something; I can feel it.

'She will hit the roof when she knows Dad has a lady-friend. Seriously, she wants to have her cake and eat it. I'd hate to be a fly on the wall when she confronts him. I won't be saying a word to discourage him and the new woman, that's for certain.'

'She can't expect him to remain single for the rest of his life.'

'I think she does.'

Common sense suggests that at some point Mr Woodward was going to run into a nice woman and pluck up the courage to ask her to dinner. From what Alfie has said he waited long enough after the divorce to even venture out of the house.

Alfie retrieves his right hand from his pocket and looks at his watch.

'Nearly ten o'clock. Do you reckon they're doing it?'

'Alfie!' I exclaim, unsure of how to answer. 'I've no idea. Nor do I want to think about two old people doing the business, thanks.'

'Nor do I, even if one of them is my old man... but I bet they are.'

We fall about in giggles. It seems the most natural thing in the world to be talking to Alfie like this and yet are we edging nearer to us taking the next step?

'If I get home and they're butt naked running around the kitchen, I'm heading back to your parents' for the night to kip on their sofa. Deal?'

'*Deal.*'

'Come on, it's getting late,' says Alfie, as we begin to jog down the road towards mine.

As we near my house the upstairs is in darkness apart from the side landing window, the landing light left on in case the little ones have nightmares. The lounge window is ablaze with the flashing netting, which my mum insisted was pinned up the minute the Christmas tree entered the house. I cringe – it's utter tack but she loves it. The halogen light blinds us as we enter the driveway. I don't attempt to complain any more but simply hasten my stride to get out of the glare.

We stop at the front door. I know both my parents are up, but I won't put the key into the lock before we've kissed goodnight. It's become our routine. The first time I slid the key into the lock, then we kissed and my mum opened the front door wide thinking I was struggling, only to find Alfie's hand on my butt. She was not impressed with his manners that night.

His mouth is moist and warm. Gone are the complaints about his mum; instead his arms wrap around my shoulders and my arms wind under and around his arms. I can feel his jacket brushing against mine. He's slightly taller than me, which is nice because it feels protective when we stand like this in the dark and kiss. It seems like we kiss for ages but I know it isn't, because when I begin to pull backwards Alfie's mouth follows mine before he releases. He wants more, I know, but no. I have my own ideas of what's decent. I don't need my parents on my back telling me over and over again not to make the same mistake they did. I hate it when they use that word; it makes me feel as if they are referring to me as the mistake. They're not, I know that, but it feels that way. They mean the mistake of having to get married so early, without all the trimmings at their wedding, the teenage holidays with their mates and the chance to buy cars and expensive gadgets. Instead they saved for prams, high chairs and sterilising units. I have my own plans. Holidays, driving licences, full-time jobs and saving for a future...

'Goodnight, then,' I mutter, knowing my parents will be watching the clock.

'One more?'

'Oooh,' I tease, knowing full well that I'll deliver. We come together in an embrace and kiss our goodbye. I pull away and this time Alfie lets me. He knows the routine. He lingers as I turn the key in the lock. He waits for me to wave from the doorstep, go inside and close the door. If I quickly open the door again, as I do tonight, I see him dash to the end of the driveway and head back through the estate, cutting into his estate.

I close the door and chuckle. I really hope he doesn't find his father in an awkward embrace in the middle of their kitchen but, on the plus side, if he does he'll be heading straight back here.

*

Nina

We didn't get back to the farm until gone closing time thanks to a snarl-up on the M40, and the snow blizzard didn't help matters. I couldn't be happier to flop onto the sofa, but I can't escape my thoughts. Today was magical, and for the first time I felt festive – I thought I'd never know that feeling again. To think our farm's Christmas tree decorates Number 10 for the rest of the month, wow!

Christmas was always such a lovely time at the cottage. We'd go the whole hog: the tree, the lights and a mountain of food for just the two of us. Many years, we'd still be eating mince pies in January and frozen yule logs come February. But every year we went overboard, to hell with the expense.

Last year, I spent Christmas morning at St Giles Hospice while the staff served me copious amounts of hot sugared tea. I brought home his unopened present, which I placed beneath the stairs. 'What am I to do with an unopened Christmas present containing a new towelling bath robe?' My dad probably wouldn't have worn it – but still.

'Should I plan for Christmas Day? Or could I pretend it was a day like every other?' I say aloud.

I look across to the end of the sofa. Empty.

Nobody is listening.

Rap a tap tap.

I cautiously open the cottage door, not knowing who would drop by at ten o'clock.

'Surprise!' shouts Kitty, dressed up to the nines and barging past my pyjama-clad frame, Shazza in hot pursuit, in similar attire. 'No arguing but you're putting these on, these on and Shazza's brought her box of tricks for your hair and make-up.'

'What?' I yawp, as Kitty holds aloft a sparkly dress, a pair of heels then points towards Shazza's carry-case. 'But—'

'She's serious, Nina. She's collecting the Espresso Martini you promised her.' Shazza laughs, closing the door and herding me towards the staircase.

'Off you pop,' orders Kitty, thrusting her items into my arms. 'Connor's waiting outside to drop us at The Edge. We'll get a taxi back.'

'A nightclub on a Tuesday night – are you serious?'

'She's serious, now go!' shouts Shazza, tweaking her blonde curls in my recently cleaned hall mirror.

*

Angie

'Alfie, is that you?' Nick's voice brings me to. I'm not aware of the time as I snuggle in the crook of his arm and wriggle deeper under the duvet.

'Shhh, Nick, don't...' I utter.

He nods and repeats his call.

'Yes, Dad, just let myself in. I walked Holly back home.'

'Good lad... you OK?'

'Yeah.' His voice seems to be moving nearer to the bedroom door. 'Did you have a nice night?'

'Yes thanks, lad. You off to bed now?'

'Yeah.'

'See you in the morning, son.'

'Night, Dad,' shouts Alfie, before adding, *'Night.'*

Nick smiles. He's as pleased as Punch about his relationship with Alfie, I can see that. But why did Alfie throw another 'night' after his dad's one?

'Was that second night for me?' I whisper.

Nick shakes his head.

'So, does he usually say, "Night, Dad, night"?'

'No, but—'

'He knows you aren't alone.'

'Angie, shhh.'

'Seriously, Nick... he said goodnight to you and then shouted night as an afterthought... to me!'

'So?'

'So, your teenage son knows you've had sex... tonight with your friend.'

'Correct me if I'm wrong, but my son, our son has a pretty good idea that I've had sex before now.'

I can't deal with this situation. I shouldn't have stayed so late. We should have eaten and I should have made my excuses... even though I'd shaved my legs, just to be on the safe side.

I begin to scramble from beneath Nick's hooked arm.

'Where are you going?' asks Nick, rising from the duvet.

'Home.'

He pulls a face and grabs at my wrist.

'Why bother? You're here now, he's gone to bed... You might as well stay the night and leave first thing in the morning.' He gives me a wink.

Common sense suggests I leave now. I instantly ignore her good advice and roll beneath the warm duvet, hoping my son remains a heavy sleeper.

*

Holly

My mobile vibrates underneath my pillow. I quickly retrieve it and read his text.

Dad's date is still here. She's sharing his room :-O

In the darkness of our bedroom, I blush. Fancy being caught by your son getting up to no good with a new date.

I hope they don't keep you awake.

I press reply before realising that, given the late hour, that must be exactly what they're doing.

'What are you giggling at?' askes a groggy Hannah, turning over to view my illuminated face.

'Alfie's dad's having a sleepover,' I mutter.

'Seriously, at his age?'

'Duh!'

'Oh! Urgh! Poor Alfie.'

'*Exactly.*'

'That's just wrong.'

'It's what adults do, Hannah.'

She turns over in bed to face me; her features are ghost-like in the escaping screen light.

'Don't tell me you're thinking of doing it,' she says softly.

'Hannah?'

'Holly, seriously… wait.'

'I don't need you to tell me what to do, thanks.'

Hannah lifts herself onto her elbow and stares.

'I'm not sharing this room with another baby if you mess up, that's all I'm saying.'

'Who said anyone's going to mess up?'

Hannah snorts, turns over and mutters, 'I bet Mum and Dad said that an hour before you were conceived.'

I stare at the back of her head. There are times I hate my sisters even more than I hate the fact that I know my parents messed up. This is one such moment.

*

Nina

'Cheers!' shouts Shazza, above the din of the music, whilst holding aloft a Mudslide cocktail.

Our three cocktail glasses clink together before we stop talking and sip our drinks.

I don't recognise myself in the bar's reflection; goodbye to winceyette-PJ-clad Nina and hello glam girl holding a Manhattan – possibly a new me, though without Kitty's shoes that pinch a little when I walk.

'I thought my Tuesday night had descended towards tragic but it's surprising how gold-painted statues, billowing chalk dust and gold lamé fabric can lift your spirits,' I reply after sipping my Manhattan.

'Does wonders for my mood,' says Shazza, dancing on the spot whilst sipping her drink.

'Mine too, especially after the day we've had,' says Kitty, cradling her Espresso Martini. 'Whereas you had a jolly trip to Downing Street.'

'That bad, eh?' I ask.

'We missed you and the twins in the sales yard... let's put it like that,' adds Shazza. 'Though guess who came back?'

I shrug, not sure what she's on about.

'Curls guy, the one from the other day. Well, guess what – he didn't buy a tree *again*.'

'Oh,' is all I manage.

'You said he was a time-waster, didn't you, Shazza?' says Kitty, playing with her straw.

Instantly, I want to defend him, but can't.

'He mulled around looking at the spruces, asked Jackie a question about needles dropping and then zoomed off in his flash car – I reckon he's got a weird fetish for spruce.' Shazza laughs.

'Or our Christmas songs,' adds Kitty.

Shazza stops laughing.

'If I have to hear Kim Wilde and Mel Smith sing "Rockin' Around the Christmas Tree" one more time, I swear I'll snap!' says Shazza, breaking her tiny cocktail umbrella in two.

'For me it's Mariah Carey's "All I want for Christmas Is You" – and yours, Nina?' asks Kitty as they both stare at me. I can't join in. I'm still pondering why Luca visited yet again whilst my stomach twirls at the thought of him.

'I don't mind them,' I lie, purely to save face.

'Are you serious? You moan more than we do about the music!' says Shazza, throwing her broken umbrella on the bar top.

'Yeah, pull the other one, it plays "Jingle Bells",' adds Kitty, before erupting into laughter. I watch the pair double up in giggles, gasping for air, their hands waving at each other to 'stop it'.

This is how my life should be – more laughter and fewer tears. They've definitely cheered me up, and not just by mentioning Luca.

*

We admire a group of men strutting by – all shoulders and biceps amidst a cloud of cologne.

'Be serious now – what's the score with the twins?' asks Shazza, her left arm slung about my neck, her right hand waving her third cocktail about.

Kitty leans closer on hearing Shazza's question.

'I'm just not sure. Growing up I imagined I'd just know when 'The One' showed up and yet, I don't. It's as if I'm consciously choosing between two options, two men. One minute it feels right... the next I'm backing away.' I busy myself with my drink as they both stare.

'But from which twin?' asks Shazza, peering at me.

'That's the problem... she doesn't know,' adds Kitty, shaking her head.

'I'm certain that Bram and I aren't a natural combination, especially after the other night,' I say, adding, 'I just don't know as regards Zach.' Shazza's left arm quickly unhooks from my neck, and she instantly stands tall, as if I've burnt her. 'What? I can't help it!'

'Nothing. You just don't know how lucky you are, that's all. Two good-looking lads chasing after you – decisions, decisions.' She laughs, before glugging at her cocktail.

'Slow down, Shaz – you'll make yourself bad,' warns Kitty, removing the near-empty glass from Shazza's lips.

'What's the worst that can happen? I might be late for my shift... like that's not the norm, given that my brother Spud hogs the bathroom most mornings.'

Kitty and I exchange a glance.

'I could die with embarrassment every time our Spud arrives home late – I just know he's been prowling the farm with his gang. I've told him, they'll come unstuck... but he's not having it. I feel so guilty when the boss looks after us workers so well.'

'Spud needs to start listening because Boss Fielding isn't a happy man,' says Kitty.

'Exactly. But hang on, where was I? Oh, yeah, asking Nina about the twins. So, anyway, which one?'

'I don't know. I always thought a serious relationship would start as friends, develop a closeness and finally, an invisible bond would draw us together, but this seems so cold, so conscious, so calculated. I just know I want what Kitty and Connor have...'

'Bloody hell, we all want true love but Cupid's arrow doesn't happen for everyone,' says Shazza. 'Twittering blue birds, cherubs and stomach flips aren't guaranteed unless you're watching Disney.'

'Maybe I should wait until such a moment comes along,' I suggest, coyly.

'Good God, woman, you could be fifty by then and life will have passed you by. Nah – make a decision and go with it,' says Shazza, emptying her glass.

'That's it, I can't.'

'So, the question may be, then, do you definitely want your life spent amongst Christmas trees...? Because that's what their future holds,' says Kitty.

'Do I want to be Jackie in twenty years' time?' I ask aloud.

'I'm willing to be Jackie in twenty years' time – that wouldn't be a bad prospect in life,' slurs Shazza, more to herself than the open mouths of Kitty and me.

＊

We stagger from The Edge nightclub at half two in the morning, arm in arm, as a new flurry of snow begins to fall. I can hardly walk in Kitty's shoes but can't bring myself to go barefoot in the snow.

As we pass him, we each simultaneously stop; turn and peer back at the young guy swathed in a sleeping bag sitting on the nearest kerbstone.

Not a word is said, but Kitty and I exchange a knowing glance, reach for our purses and return to his pitch. Shazza follows suit.

It's the season of goodwill but that notion alone doesn't fill your belly with warm food, does it?

'Merry Christmas to you!' he calls, clutching three notes in his cold hands as we three traipse happily towards the taxi rank.

<u>Twelve</u>

Angie

Wednesday, 19 December

A rapping begins at the door and I wake up, startled. Where am I?

I know I heard something.

I instantly remember last night.

'Nick,' I whisper.

'Err. What?' comes his slow reply.

The rapping occurs again.

'Dad!'

Nick launches from the bed in one move, standing behind the door in all his naked glory. I drop my head face first into the pillow.

'Yes, lad.'

'I... I... brought you both a cuppa.'

I raise my head to view Nick's look of horror.

'Well, that's... very kind of you, Alfie.'

'I'll leave the tray outside your door... OK?'

What the hell is happening here? My own son has made his father and the unknown date a morning brew?

'Cheers... are you heading out to school now?'

'Not quite. I need a shower first.'

'Nick.' I beckon him from the bed. 'Don't open the door. Don't!'

I'm begging. I feel so guilty for our actions last night and this act of adolescent kindness is sending me into a spin.

'I've left sugar and milk on the tray for your friend.'

I face-plant on the pillow, again. Could this be any worse? My ex-husband naked at the door, talking through it to our son, and me wishing that the bed would swallow me whole. Could it get any worse?

'I hope you used protection!' choruses Alfie as he moves along the landing, heading for the bathroom.

'Oy!' calls Nick, his eyes wide.

I hear the bathroom door bolt close.

I'm up in search of my clothes before Nick has time to ease the door open to check that the coast is clear.

Skirt. Knickers. Bra. I snatch at the items, ticking them off my mental list as I go. Blouse?

What the hell?

My mind goes into overdrive. Grab your stuff and go! Get out of here... I stop dead. Nick is collecting the tray delivery as if we've ordered room service.

'What are you doing?' I ask sharply, unsure whether to laugh or cry.

'He's made us tea.' His expression oozes with pride. I'd love to be sharing his moment of parental achievement, I seriously would, but what the feck am I supposed to do? Return to the duvet and drink sweet tea alongside my ex-husband and enjoy our son's generous nature, or cheek, depending on how you view it?

'Angie... he's in the bathroom taking a shower... he can't see you.'

'But he knows I'm still here.'

'Yeah, but not actually you.'

In my world it is slightly more worrying that my son can willingly accept that another woman can fill his father's bed.

Nick lays the tray on the duvet and climbs underneath.

'Suit yourself, but I'm drinking it while it's hot.' I stand, my clothes balled and clutched in my arms, watching as he adds sugar and takes the white tea and leans back against the pillows.

What was I doing before Nick spoke? Oh, yeah, blouse! I fuss about looking under the bed corner, beside the velvet ottoman and wardrobe. Nowhere.

'Here.' Nick pours milk into the black tea and adds a spoonful of sugar before offering me the mug.

'Nick... where is my...?' I suddenly remember. A flashback from the previous evening in the lounge hits me like a thunderbolt. Why, oh, why did we stay downstairs for so long before racing up the staircase?

300

We both knew sex was on the cards. We should have been more careful.

'*What?*' Nick stares from his offering to my stricken face.

'It's by the sofa arm.'

'What is?' Replacing the ignored mug on the tray.

'My blouse!'

In seconds, I have dropped my bundle of clothes and am heading for the door. It feels like a special-agent moment except that my wobbling flesh is on full show and I'm peering around a bedroom door onto an empty landing.

'Angie, wait...'

Too late. I'm out of the door, covering my nakedness as best I can, which is difficult given the proportions of my curves. The bathroom door is firmly closed. I tiptoe across the landing towards the top of the staircase. I can hear the *Mission Impossible* theme tune playing in my head. I can do this. There and back in three seconds. I can do this as well as Tom Cruise. I dart down the stairs, duck as I pass the frosted-glass front door and head for the lounge. Once inside I dart to the three-seater sofa and scour the surrounding floor. Nothing. I know it should be here; I remember Nick unbuttoning it, slipping it from my shoulders and dropping it to the floor. I lower myself, reaching under the edge of the sofa in case it got pushed underneath. Nothing. I'm on all fours in seconds peering underneath the sofa. What a bloody sight I must look! Nothing. Sitting back on my haunches, my mind whirling. What the hell have I done with it?

I hear a noise upstairs. I freeze. Oh, no! This can't be happening; it just can't!

I hear the stairs creak.

I slowly rise on my haunches. I begin to pray. Please don't let my only son find me naked in the lounge – this will put him off women for life!

The lounge door begins to move slowly. I can't breathe. I can't think. I can't look.

The dog walks through, stares up at me and... my blouse is hanging from his mouth!

I feel faint.

'Rolo, come here,' I demand in hushed annoyance, grabbing at my clothing. The dog gives an undignified look before continuing on his way to the kitchen. I scurry out of the door, duck past the frosted front door and return up the staircase to safety.

I'm halfway up the stairs, just enough for the *Mission Impossible* theme tune to fade, when I hear the bathroom bolt snap open. And there he is, my son, with a blue towel wrapped around his nether regions, towel-drying his hair as he walks from the steaming bathroom.

I freeze and catch my breath, just below the bannister level. My hand clutches my discarded blouse to my front. I halt as his hand towel is rubbed back and forth with force, flopping before his face and then revealing it before repeating the rubbing action as he walks.

I daren't exhale.

The dog rushes past me from below, pushing me aside to chase after Alfie.

'Rolo-baby!' Alfie laughs as he moves along the landing towards his room. I hear his bedroom door click shut and his thrash music comes to life.

I hurry to the top stair, peer around the bannister and charge through Nick's bedroom door.

I stand behind the door, my heart pounding like an Olympic runner. Mission complete, never impossible!

'Got it?' asks Nick, sipping his morning tea.

I wave my blouse in his direction, but instantly feel cheap for succumbing to such childish behaviour.

*

Nina

Today there's to be no chit-chat. No lingering. I will not complain about the festive music looping overhead. My head is banging thanks to the cocktails and my low mood has returned, but at least I'm in work, unlike Shazza.

Instead, I keep my head down and my hands busy for the entire morning, despite the heavy snowfall and relentless snow clearing. I harness Gertrude and successfully lead her to the nativity stable for the day, feed both her and Arthur without any head-butting incidents occurring. Using the label gun, I tag a pile of netted Fraser firs and stack them neatly, ready for customers to peruse. I'm not risking the likelihood of the boss sending me to 'elf' at the grotto for a second day, I simply can't do forced joviality today. I manage to sell three Nordman firs, a Blue spruce and two Norway spruce in between yard tasks.

As I lug a six-foot tree across the yard, the crunch of tyres on the snow distracts me. The cars have a lighter sound but the Ranger Rover sounds solid.

My heart jumps into my mouth. Today of all days?

I quickly glance around the yard; other staff are available but, today, I'll serve him. I continue to refill the labelling gun as he parks and strides in my direction. As I look up he's smiling directly at me; his eyes glisten as the sides of his temples gently crease. Behind him in the parked car, there's a shadowy outline sitting in the passenger seat. Wow, he has some nerve!

'Hello… Nina,' he says, with a slight hesitation.

'Hello. Can I help?' What a ridiculous question, but a standard cliché covers my sudden attack of nerves perfectly. I can't slip up and say his name. I just can't.

He stands a little nearer than I expect; a fresh citrus smell of cologne envelops me. I literally have to raise my chin to view his face. He has a strong presence, unlike other men. Should I step backwards? Or should he?

'The other day, I dropped by and a young lady explained about the trees…' He instinctively looks towards the stacking area where four definite piles of spruce are available for customers to peruse. 'But she confused me as regards the various types…' He stops, looks towards the parked vehicle and turns around before pulling a face. '*She* wants a traditional-smelling tree.'

Great – wife-to-be mentioned already. Though full marks for his honesty and commitment. I'm pretending she doesn't exist, purely for my own gratification. I'll take the smallest of delights wherever I can and, given today's sour mood, this could be the nicest five minutes of my day.

'So, you'll be wanting the Norway spruce, then. It has what you described as the traditional needle fragrance – which most people associate with Christmas,' I explain,

305

walking him across to the huge display of Norway spruce, pointing out the details on our display boards. My heartbeat is rapid, my throat is drying but I continue as if nothing is out of the ordinary. And yet, it is. In my head the entire solar system has simply realigned itself in awe of us conversing. 'They are easy to look after, have a nice overall shape and fine needles, which will hold for weeks as long as you water it every day. A popular choice...' As I'm explaining he's listening intently, but his eyes are flitting about my face as if scanning my features. 'It's the traditional Christmas tree that was made popular by Prince Albert introducing it to the royal household.'

A coy smile interrupts his even dark features.

'Seriously, you know the history of each species?'

'Oh, yes, I've worked here long enough to give a detailed history if a customer requires it. They are all very different.' I give a laugh. 'It's *my* job.'

'Well, yes, but the other young lady...'

'Shazza.'

He nods.

'She simply showed me the four and explained that they were different but it lacked...'

'Detail?' I suggest. 'Yeah, Shazza can do that sometimes. Oh, no, all four spruce trees are different, in fact, actually, technically speaking; they aren't all spruce, that's incorrect... We actually have two spruce and two fir trees. There is a difference...' I fall silent; his eyebrows rise as if requesting I continue. 'Well, for instance, this is a Blue spruce. See how the individual needles are sharp and pointy.' I lift the nearest branch of the Blue spruce to show the needle shape, and then walk a short distance to the Fraser fir. 'Whereas this Fraser fir has individual needles that are flat and soft along each branch. I think the difference is quite apparent. It was one of the first things I noticed when I began working here. I rarely find that the general public spot such detail.'

'I never knew that.' He laughs, looking from one tree species to the other. 'So, the Norway spruce is a true spruce with sharp pointy needles?'

'Oh, yes. And it'll have the traditional fragrance of Christmas too.'

'Sold, then.'

'So, what height are you looking for?' I say, walking back towards the Norway spruce. 'As our trees are sold by the foot.'

'I see. I'd say…' he looks along the yard, comparing the displayed sizes for each tree '… something about that height.'

'Five foot. That's a nice size. It won't dominate a room but it won't be too small that it's lost within a large room, if you get what I mean?'

He smiles; his eyes crinkle and his bottom lip protrudes slightly.

'You have to take lots into consideration when buying a Christmas tree.'

'I hadn't realised.'

'Have you never purchased a real spruce before?'

He slowly shakes his head, causing the tumble of curls to softly bounce.

My insides begin to ache. Why is he so lovely? Why is he getting married to the beautiful blonde? Why didn't we meet before he had chance to make wedding arrangements, or have babies, or build a life with someone else?

'The type, the size, the room it will decorate, the position within that room, surrounding heating and lighting. Is the stand suitable for the chosen tree? Can it hold enough water or will watering several times a day be necessary? And...' I falter, on seeing a flicker of humour in his face. Has my enthusiasm gone overboard or is the detail purely an excuse to continue to serve him? Either way, it must seem comical from his point of view. 'Anyway, all are factors that you should take into consideration before buying a Christmas tree.'

'Well... I can answer some but not *all* of those questions...' he mutters, glancing across to his parked vehicle.

Wow, she's never far away from his thoughts, is she? How beautiful to have such a commitment to another person. How lovely to be the centre of someone's world.

To know that they are forsaking all others... even when buying a Christmas tree.

'Would you mind, if I went and...?' He points towards the vehicle.

'O-of course not,' I stammer, taken aback that he should feel the need to ask. It's her tree, after all.

I watch as he strides away from me; his wide shoulders ease towards a narrower waist. His leggy stride smooth and rhythmical, he walks like a panther. If only he weren't attached. If only he were truly single, Lord knows what I would have said or suggested, but maybe I'd have taken the chance to flirt. Flutter my eyelashes and gauge his interest, but it would be simply wrong to chase or outwardly suggest such an attraction to a guy who has days until his marriage.

Boy, is life unfair.

I watch him walk to the passenger door, open and speak whilst pointing towards our display trees.

If he were single, I might have even been tempted to suggest a drink myself. I stall at my own ideas, shocked that I would consider such an approach when I've always waited for men to ask me. Yet here is a man so utterly different from anyone I've previously met, even more so because he's not free he's taken. Damn!

He steps backwards, opening the passenger door far wider than is necessary, and offers a hand to her. What beautiful manners! I'm dumbstruck to watch an older lady vacate the Range Rover in an awkward fashion, given the height of the vehicle. Her blue mac, tied at the waist, is the only shape I can see until her brown ankle boots finally touch the snow-covered ground.

I instantly look away. It's not the blonde woman, his wife-to-be.

I busy myself by pulling a five-foot Norway spruce from the pile and stand it upright so that, despite the netting, the customers can see what a beautiful and healthy spruce is before them.

Having gently led her by the arm, and gingerly walked her over amidst the snow, he arrives back at our Norway spruce display.

'Nina, this is my mother. She might as well answer for herself rather than me interpret what she wants. Mum, this is Nina...' I don't hear his explanation, I simply stand in awe as he talks her through the different species much in the manner that I did with him several minutes before. Wow, he *was* listening. The mother appears delicate, aged by poor health rather than years. I watch as she hangs on his every word. How lovely. 'So, there seems to be a lot to take into consideration.'

I nod and smile warmly at the lady's inquisitive gaze. They have the same eyes, which dart about the spruce.

'It's for the lounge, isn't it?' he asks her.

'Yes, the usual corner... but standing on the floor, not on a table,' she says, looking up at him. 'I want a proper Christmas tree, not that old plastic thing that keeps leaning and toppling over.'

'Yes, I know… you can have what you want.'

'And this one has a nice smell?' she asks, suddenly switching focus from him to me.

'Oh, yes,' I say, grabbing a netted branch, my hand crushing the needles before bringing my open palm towards her to smell.

'Yes… that's a proper one.' Her face lights up with joy. 'Yes, one of those.'

'Are you sure?' he asks her.

She gives a brisk but definite nod.

'That would be thirty-five pounds,' I offer, wanting them to know every detail before deciding.

'That's fine,' he says quickly, turning to the elderly lady. 'I'll walk you back to the car, then organise the payment.'

A quick look around the yard, and I shout over to Zach.

'Zach, could you carry this spruce across, please, so that…' I hesitate; I nearly say his name but correct myself '… this gentleman can assist the lady back to their vehicle?'

Zach comes running over, hoists the netted spruce onto his shoulder and follows the pair towards the Range Rover.

I walk towards the cashier's cabin, knowing that he'll follow in a moment to settle the bill. I wait at the bottom of the steps and watch as he slams the passenger door securely once she's inside.

How lovely. How caring and attentive.

I check my reaction. How could I have been jealous of this lady? I need to get a grip.

Zach helps him to position the tree in the rear of the vehicle before the boot slams down. A round of thanks is exchanged and Zach jogs off back to his yard tasks. Luca strides towards me, digging inside his jacket for a wallet.

'All done?' I say breezily as we climb the steps.

'She's over the moon. She's wanted a real Christmas tree for a couple of years so that's made her day,' he says, smiling.

'Perfect.'

I rarely walk customers over to the cashier's cabin but make an exception on this occasion. Kitty looks up from her orders and smiles first at him, then me.

'Could you take for a five-foot Norway spruce, please, Kitty?' I say, as if he can't speak for himself.

I watch as his long fingers open the wallet and count out the crisp notes. I notice there's no little picture under the plastic window section, just a selection of plastic cards in the leather slots.

Within seconds, he has a till receipt and Kitty is thanking him.

Is it necessary for me to stand and stare?

'Well, thank you, Nina... you've been most helpful,' he says, turning from the counter.

'My pleasure.' I beam.

Kitty's eyebrows lift and her coy smile is suppressed.

I lead the way exiting the cashier's cabin, to stand upon the wooden steps.

'Just remember to gradually introduce it to the house, maybe stand it in a porch or a garage for a day or so allowing it to acclimatise to the temperature change. Stand it in water to allow the spruce to hydrate during that time and it will be beautiful until Twelfth Night.'

He nods.

I nod.

A lingering silence occurs. I shift my stance. He copies.

'So, thanks again... you were *most* helpful,' he says.

'Thank you.'

He takes his leave. I stand and casually do nothing, pretending I'm not watching his retreating figure. Instantly, my warm glow fades, and continues to wane with each of his strides. Why can't I find a guy like that?

He suddenly stops in his tracks, turns around and stares directly at me, nods, smiles and continues on his way.

Shit!

A sixth sense, telepathy or what? Either way he has no doubts I was watching. I want the earth to open wide and swallow me whole. Ah, well, that's probably the last I'll see of him before his wedding day. If nothing else he knows that I was watching his final departure, his solitary purposeful walk like that of a panther.

*

'Any ideas, Nina?' asks Jackie as we sit around the snug at lunchtime.

I'm in a world of my own but Kitty, Zach and Bram are all staring at me.

'Sorry, I wasn't following the conversation.'

'I was asking for ideas that could bring in additional sales.'

'Oh.' My mind is blank.

'We've got the grottos, introduced the reindeer, the carol service procession is happening in a few days and the florist lady arrives from tomorrow onwards to create decorative wreaths while customers wait but...' She pauses. 'We need something a little... special.'

'Aren't the Christmas trees enough?' I ask, perturbed that our beautiful crop is being undermined by her suggestion. 'The farm won the British Christmas Tree Association's prize award – surely that holds some kudos with the public?'

'It does but... nowadays customers want more than a recognised prize or good reputation, don't they?' says Jackie.

'They want novel ideas that they can get excited about. I think we're missing that here,' says Kitty. 'We're great at what we do, but it is the same old same old every year.'

I watch as Zach and Bram nod slowly. Am I hearing them correctly? Do they not see the magic of this place? The beauty of Christmas surrounds them and yet they want more!

'So, Nina, any ideas?' asks Bram.

'You've got such a creative mind, I bet you'll come up with a corker of an idea, just like the interview questions for Santa,' adds Zach. 'So, what would you like here at Christmas Tree Farm?'

'What would I like more than anything in the whole world?' I say. Firstly, I'd like to move into one of the log cabins over the Christmas break and, secondly, to post the unopened Christmas present to my dad.

'There's two things, but you'll probably say no to the first but laugh at the second.'

'We won't… tell us,' says Jackie, eagerly leaning forward on the opposite sofa.

So, I did.

*

315

Holly

'Holly?'

I look up to see the concern in his eyes.

'You OK?' he asks.

'I know it's going to happen, that's obvious, but it really is a huge step...'

'There's no rush.'

'I know that, but still.'

Alfie's arm tightens around my shoulder; he really is older than his years. We haven't discussed where or when, but taking the next step is definitely in our future.

'We agreed, no pressure. At least we won't get caught out like your mate Demi.'

'How do you know that?' I say, surprised he'd bring her into our conversation. I'm shocked; Demi only mentioned her experience a few days ago.

'Like Spud keeps stuff to himself, yeah! He was bragging in PE theory class, reckons they were so drunk she could hardly speak.'

'Alfie!' I twist around from under his arm to view his face. 'Seriously?'

'Honestly, from what he was saying she was out of her face on drink.'

I want to cry for my friend that details of her are circulating the school yard. What a mess, but what does she expect, putting it about as she does purely to be liked by the boys? I take comfort knowing I won't be discussed during a lesson; Alfie's not like that.

'Remember that lesson where we had to put the condom on the banana?' I ask, blushing with the memory.

'I had to partner Sally Brown. She refused to touch it, let alone help me unroll it onto the banana.'

It wasn't my finest hour. I cringed and balked at the prospect but at least I understood how to do it properly, unlike others who simply blew the condoms up and threw them around the classroom.

'Alfie?'

'What?'

'The same goes for you, you know? If you feel unsure…'

'I'll say. I'm just unsure of the embarrassing stuff.'

'It's sex – apparently embarrassing stuff is pretty much guaranteed,' I jibe.

Alfie laughs.

'I'm being honest,' he splutters.

'I know.' If I'm taking this next step in the next few weeks, I want to be with someone as caring as Alfie. I just wish Demi had waited till she'd met someone who cared for her.

Thirteen

Nina

Thursday, 20 December

The sales yard is empty, the tinny overhead speakers deliver 'Step into Christmas', as I trudge through the deep snow towards the snug. I know the drill for today before the orders are given or pinned upon the notice board. It'll be all hands on deck, even the cutting crew will be selling trees, as this weekend has the potential to make or break the entire season's sales. On top of selling we'll have the carol service procession to organise ready for the big event on Friday night.

'Morning, Kitty.'

'Morning... are you ready for this?'

'Nope, but what's new?' I laugh, grabbing my box of extra clothing. 'If it's anything like last year, we'll be run ragged and exhausted by home time.'

'Ah-h-h, the joys of last year, well remembered,' laughs Kitty.

Last year the prep day for the carol service was a nightmare. The Dell, a cleared area amongst the spruce, where it was traditionally held, had been flattened in preparation for a large area of jigsaw flooring to be professionally laid. But the contractors failed to arrive on the right day – they showed up the morning after the event, much to Boss Fielding's annoyance. So, we had to lay a temporary floor, construct seating platforms and wire the electricity cabling safely ourselves – thanks to Old Bill's skill and knowledge.

'You know that Shazza's returned, don't you?' whispers Kitty.

'She texted me to say she might be in today. How is she?'

Kitty shakes her head.

'Not good. She feels she's let the team down by being off and all this talk about her brother leading the nightly trespassers is doing her head in. She's quite embarrassed, I think.'

'It's understandable, but she needs to stand her ground if she doesn't know anything. It'll stop folk speculating.'

'Morning, ladies,' calls Bram as he bursts into the snug. 'How are we?'

'Dreading today based on last year's recollection,' I say, putting on additional leggings.

Bram pulls a face.

'You ought to see the plan of action Dad has drawn up for today. NASA did less planning for space missions.'

'Are you serious?' asks Kitty, pulling her blonde locks into a ponytail.

'Serious.'

'How can a walking procession have more planning than a seated event?' I interject.

'There's more health and safety regulations as regards the snowy conditions. We need to plan for preventing people tripping, falling, sliding and breaking limbs.'

'Bloody great, this is all we need.' I sigh.

'And sales as well?' asks Kitty, dragging her arm into her embroidered coat.

'Sales as well. Sorry, ladies. He's a hard taskmaster, is the old man, you should know that by now. But one day...'

'Jesus wept... I'll be long gone from here by the time you or Zach get to play boss man.' Kitty laughs.

'Hmmm, sadly, I probably won't be,' I say.

'You cheeky gits!' moans Bram. 'I'll be the best boss you pair have ever seen when it's my turn.'

'*Really?* I can't wait.' I press closed the poppers on my tabard and fish out my gloves. 'Kitty, promise we'll take off when that happens.'

*

Angie

We sit in the school hall staring at row upon row of teachers chatting to parents, while nearby bored teenagers sit, scowling or smirking with pride.

Alfie sits alongside Nick, on my far right; he's not impressed that I'm here.

'I don't get what the fuss is about,' I remarked, from the front seat of Nick's car.

Alfie snorted in the rear seat.

Nick gave a quick glance and shook his head.

'Seriously, I'm your mother – shouldn't I know how your schoolwork is going?'

'Oh, yeah, now's the time to take an interest when there's one day left till the end of term.'

This was becoming boring. The same old story every time something didn't go Alfie's way.

I stare at the rows of animated teachers: young, old, experienced and some newly qualified if my memory serves me correctly. I watch Miss Hibbins, Alfie's English teacher, eagerly explaining some new-fangled grading system. Alfie once told me it's all digits nowadays, gone are the alphabet grades – those were the days when he wanted to chat. Miss Hibbins' cheery smile stays constant throughout the explanation, while the parents look horrified. That could be us in ten minutes.

I continue along the row of desks; many I don't know. I spot Miss Read, with her red hair and bubbly mannerisms, chatting eagerly to an upset parent.

'Alfie… is Miss Read a teacher?'

'Nah, she's on the support team – she helps if stuff starts occurring.'

'Dramas and such like?'

'Sometimes. Mainly life stuff, really.' He leans around his dad to view her corner table, situated a distance from the others offering some privacy. 'That's Melody Beale – she's been posting stuff on the Internet.'

'Alfie!' hushes Nick.

'Everyone knows… except her mum.'

I watch the interaction between the two women. There is a genuine warmth as regards help and support for both pupil and parent.

'You haven't told them, have you?' I ask Nick, suddenly aware that I don't know the line of our story.

Nick raises an eyebrow.

'Have you?'

A slight shake of the head puts my mind at rest. It's a caring school but I really don't want then knowing *our* business. It's bad enough with the neighbours judging me. If Alfie were affected by the divorce then it would be a different story, but he isn't. He wasn't, despite what Nick says.

I scan the row for other faces. I spot Mr Klym, Alfie's maths teacher. He was a newly qualified teacher when I attended here, which instantly makes me reminisce on my schooldays.

'Does Mr Klym still tell the "inflatable boy attending the inflatable school being told off by the inflatable head teacher for using a drawing pin" joke?' I ask, smiling to myself whilst remembering how my maths teacher always laughed at his own joke.

'What the… "you've let me down, you've let yourself down but most of all you've let the whole school down"?' Alfie laughs, a genuine smile dressing his face.

I join Alfie in reciting the joke's punchline. He laughs; I laugh. It's nice to connect with my boy given our recent tension. Nick sits confused, having attended St Gabriel's school in the neighbouring town.

'Mr Woodward!' I look up to see Miss Hibbins beckoning in our direction. We stand as a united trio, Nick takes the lead and Alfie settles in the centre seat before his teacher.

'Hello again, how are we?' she says in a cheery tone, shuffling her pile of papers.

Neither of us answer, both expecting the other to say.

'They're fine,' says Alfie, on our behalf.

I'm suddenly nervous.

'Good, good,' she says. 'Well, I have nothing but praise for this young man.'

I hear her opening line and exhale. Good boy, Alfie.

'He's doing OK?' asks Nick, patting Alfie's knee.

'More than OK, aren't you, Alfie? In his last assessment, he secured a grade six, which at this stage of the game is promising for his exams come next May.'

'A six?' Oh, dear, I can't remember what Alfie said about specific numbers.

'It's a secure B grade in old money.' Miss Hibbins laughs. I smile appreciatively. Nick nods. Alfie smiles. 'Alfie is predicted a grade...'

I'm drifting, not listening. I watch her kind face; her sparkling eyes shine as she talks. I wonder how many times she's repeated the same phrase tonight. How difficult must it be to tell a parent that their child is failing? She's always been honest. When he was in year seven she was fair with him, especially when he started forgetting his homework deadlines.

'Angie?'

I jump, an instant smile addressing my face.

'Any questions?' asks Nick, staring at me.

'What are his chances of getting a level eight by May?'

'Cheers, Mum, a seven not good enough for you?' Alfie pouts.

Miss Hibbins gives a polite smile.

'Alfie, I'm just asking.'

'He's doing well, very well to achieve what he has... I say try to be the best you can, but we don't want him to stress about his targets. A grade seven is very desirable... and given...' She stalls, pauses and continues. 'Anyway, I think he's done very well this year.'

'Thank you, that's good to hear. Thanks for your support too.' Nick stands, shakes her hand and I follow suit. Miss Hibbins' gaze doesn't quite meet mine.

She's being very polite, but somehow she knows about our marriage.

We shuffle from the line of three chairs and head towards the waiting area for our next teacher appointment: history with Miss Patrickson.

It feels like déjà vu as we resume our wait.

'Be back in a min,' says Alfie, jumping up and leaving us before we have chance to answer.

Nick and I watch as he legs it across the large hall and embraces a slim teenage girl. His face all smiles, her smile showing a row of metal braces.

'Who's that?'

'Holly.' Nick smiles as he watches them.

'Is he not bringing her over to speak?'

'Doubt it.'

I stare at Nick's profile.

'Why ever not? It's manners, surely.'

'Seriously, would you wish for your mother and your girlfriend to meet for the first time in front of all your teachers?'

'It's hardly serious – they're kids.' I can't look away. I'm transfixed to see this young man who I don't recognise as my own blood. He's touching her arm, leaning in, laughing, smiling... What the hell? Ten minutes ago he was seated and staring, hardly saying two words to me but now... just look at him. She's pretty. Very slim... I hope she's not one of these anorexic teenagers – our Alfie can do without such experiences as a youngster. She keeps flicking her long blonde hair. He keeps inching forward as she speaks.

'Where's her family?' I ask Nick, rattled that she has Alfie's full attention.

'Do you see the couple with the group of—?' The words haven't left his mouth when I whip around to stare at him.

'No!' I glare at the crowd of children, all girls. 'Nick, are you joking me?'

'She's very nice, Angie. You're overthinking it.'

'For feck's sake, Nick, he'll be a father before he's got his driving licence if that's any example to go by.'

'Angie, that's unkind.'

'No. Sorry. I'm not having my son being caught by some young girl who's been brought up with the idea she's just a baby machine.'

'Angie, keep your voice down, please.'

'Go and fetch him.'

'*No*. Leave him.'

'Nick.'

'Now do you see why he didn't bring her across?'

I sit back.

Why can't Nick see the influence that that young lady might have on our boy? I watch the adults amongst their group. They don't take much notice of the young couple, a slight look in their direction but no interaction. I look at the ages of the other girls – they stand like a set of steps, one after another after another. How can one couple care for so many young children? They look clean and tidy, but appearances can be deceptive. With so many children, surely, they'll take delight when the next generation comes along. Our Alfie needs sixth form and university before he starts his life. I have no intention of my son's future being altered due to a teenage infatuation.

'Have you told him about us?' I ask, knowing full well he hasn't.

'Angie?'

'I take that as a no, then.'

'We'll have a chat before Monday's wedding arrives, OK? Why spoil the next few days when I know everything will be fine, hey?'

I didn't expect Nick to be so protective. We're Alfie's parents – of course he'll be pleased we're back together. Roll on Monday when we can be a proper family together and enjoy a beautiful day out with Nick's friends, celebrating their daughter's wedding. Then we can enjoy a quiet family Christmas together at theirs and I'll supply the expensive food hamper that I've ordered. Nick can organise the basics, I'll provide the festive pizzazz. We'll make this a Christmas none of us will forget.

'Angie, Alfie's coming back,' Nick whispers.

Alfie jogs back and seats himself next to Nick. I stare, but he avoids looking at me.

'Is she all right, having a good parents' evening?' asks Nick, jovially. How he can encourage it, I don't know.

'Pretty much, though her mum's not happy with her history result. Apparently, she's gone down a grade since October so she's got to attend intervention after school.'

Nick nods, as if it's any of his concern. Personally, I reckon she'll do OK in life if she understands that babies aren't the be-all and end-all.

'Is that her family?' I ask.

'Mum.'

'Alfie, you didn't even bring her across to meet me. What am I supposed to think? Hardly a good impression, is it?'

Alfie and Nick exchange a glance. I get the message. Hardly surprising that they don't see it from my point of view; men rarely do and that's the problem.

My internal monologue continues as we wait.

*

'A grade seven is very desirable... and given...' Miss Hibbins' words keep repeating in my head as Nick drives us back to his house to collect my car.

'Miss Hibbins knows, doesn't she?' I ask over my shoulder to Alfie, in the rear seats.

'Knows what?' Alfie's head pops through the gap between the headrests, after he extends his seat belt.

'About me leaving?'

Alfie sits back.

'Oh, that. Yeah. I wrote about it one day in English.'

Nick continues to stare ahead.

'Thanks a bunch. I bet you painted him as the hero, me as the villain.'

We continue the journey in silence. I feel as if I've been awarded a grade one GCSE for my dedication to motherhood.

*

Nina

Having spent the whole day busy on sales, the farm's entire workforce stand in a semicircle staring at Boss Fielding at half six to begin the prep for tomorrow night's carol service. Due to her recent absence, Shazza has been demoted from chief organiser to one of us. I look around; there must be thirty adults awaiting instructions.

'Here's what I want. I want volunteers across the area. If each team focuses on one job, we'll be out of here in two hours. You with me?'

The obligatory mumble from tired staff is barely audible.

'I *said*, are you with me?' yells Boss Fielding, much like a rally cry for battle.

'Yes!' bawl several of the guys. I repeat my muted yes. I don't really care that he's paying me double time for this extra shift; I want to go home.

'Nina!' Zach grabs my arm and drags me across to the notice board where his father has listed the jobs. 'I've already claimed ours.'

We elbow our way through the crowd of bodies, me clutching the rear of his jacket.

'Look here…' He pulls a folded paper from his pocket and shows me the carolling rota. 'We're on lantern lighting along the driveway and then during the service we're inside organising the hot drinks and treats for the mid-break.'

'So, I don't get to be part of the lantern procession?'

'No.'

'*Great.* The one time the event is reorganised in a manner that appeals to me and I'm holed up with the catering crew serving mulled wine and mince pies, which I regularly do each weekend of our selling season to a bustling yard!' Every previous year the carol service was a seated event amongst the north growing fields, this year it would be a snaking procession amongst the mature spruces we have on the south side of the farm. I can't wait to see the candlelight procession amongst the towering trees, the farm's original crop planted by the original Farmer Fielding when Boss was just a child.

'Christ, I thought you'd be happy.'

'Nope. For once I actually wanted to join in, be part of a festive activity, given the bloody awful year I've had, but no, I'm a glorified waitress.'

Zach hastily folds the paper and returns it to his pocket.

'There's no pleasing you at the moment, is there? I don't know why I bother.' I watch as he traipses off towards the equipment barn. I know he'll cool off with Gertrude and Arthur. I'll apologise and explain later.

I rejoin the crowd and mingle amongst the working parties, each heading to different areas of the farm to undertake specific tasks. One crew needs to walk the route and clear any trip hazards or obstructions – not an easy task in the dark with just a head torch to illuminate the way. I eagerly join the crew who need to formulate the order of service and choose the carols. I hate to admit it, but Old Bill was correct when he moaned that the attendees could only mouth the words if the service sheet wasn't available, so we'll need plenty of spares.

Kitty and Shazza volunteer to organise the lanterns and candles, promising Jackie that only adult visitors will be entrusted to carry the pole and lantern contraption. I'm surprised that Jackie doesn't insist on staff carrying lanterns but, hey, it's her rules they're abiding by.

I stay in the warmth of Boss's office and help create, print and fold a huge pile of service orders on card so I can stay in the warm for once.

Sitting at Boss's desk, scoring the printed card into booklets, I see something dash past the window. I peer outside and see Zach running from the equipment barn, his arms raised and wailing.

Jumping up, I sidestep the other helpers and head for the cabin door.

'What's wrong with Zach?' I shout to Bram, who appears from the snug.

'Haven't got the foggiest but here he comes...' Nodding towards his twin. 'What's up?'

'Bloody Arthur, he's just bolted from his sodding pen. He's legged it into the south fields because someone's

332

left the gate open,' he moans. 'Dad's going to have a fit when I tell him.'

'Zach!' cries Bram. 'You bloody idiot!'

'Did you try to catch him?' I ask.

Zach turns, screwing his face up in annoyance.

'I didn't think of that! I stood my ground instead, so I could be impaled by his bloody horns. What do you think, Nina?'

'OK, don't get snappy with me. If we get a bucket of carrots or the treats he likes maybe he'll come back through the gate.'

'With tomorrow night's carol procession in the same area, the last thing we need is a rampant goat showing up!' shouts Bram.

Zach stomps off towards the equipment barn.

'I'll go and tell Dad, then, shall I?' shouts Bram, to the retreating figure of his brother.

'Do what you want, Bram,' calls Zach, entering the barn. 'You usually do.'

*

'Zach?' I enter the barn to find him leaning against the pen. 'What's up?'

His grey eyes stare at me, as I lean upon the fencing too.

'Are you ever going to tell him?' he asks.

I slowly shake my head.

'Zach… it's never going to happen between me and Bram.'

He turns towards me.

'Seriously?'

It wouldn't be right to say what I've experienced the last few days as regards the guy in the Range Rover.

Instead we stand in silence staring at a lonely Gertrude.

'Has your stomach ever flipped on meeting someone?' I break the lengthy silence.

'Yep.'

I nod, acknowledging his answer.

'Mine did recently and now I know that's the kind of attraction I'm after.'

He nods and gives me a sideways glance.

'Who?'

'It's not important, no one you know,' I mutter. 'And you?'

'Do you really need to ask?' he says softly.

*

Holly

'Shall I call for you?' asks Demi, phoning the minute I arrive home from parents' evening.

'Nope. I'm grounded till I catch up on my history GCSE work. Why, where are you going?'

'Up to Christmas Tree Farm.'

'Demi, no!'

'Yes! We have a right laugh up there. Spud brings some cans and a couple of his friends bring a bottle of wine – you don't know what you're missing. Paris and her posse came up the other night and even they were a laugh. We've gone up there most nights this week and it's a scream a minute. Last night we sat around telling ghost stories and then were all spooked by a strange noise we kept hearing... I nearly wet myself in fear.'

I can hear the excitement in her voice. I know she's having fun but I'm wary of the lads she's mixing with; they are leading her astray. If Spud is anything to go by, his friends will be replicas. What is it my dad says? 'Birds of a feather flock together.' And as for Paris and her posse, why would anyone choose to be amongst them?

'Holly, are you still there?'

'Yeah, but I'm still not coming out. Alfie says the boss knows what you're doing – the staff were saying how

335

he'd found all your empties, fireworks and the campfires you've been starting.'

'*So?* It's just a bit of fun.'

'He's thinking of getting guard dogs, you know.'

Demi falls silent. I hope she is listening. Though, deep down, I know she isn't.

'Guard dogs are a waste of money – Spud reckons they've trained their rampant goat to patrol the area!'

'Demi, please don't... Come around here and do some revision with me?'

'Nah! See you, wouldn't want to be ya!' sings Demi.

'Likewise,' I say, before my mobile goes dead. Alfie was kind enough to ask if I could work some hours come the weekend and, from what he says, I really wouldn't want to be Demi if the boss gets hold of them. He means business where his farm is concerned.

Fourteen

Nina

Friday, 21 December

It feels strange having everyone staring at me from behind a large studio window at the local radio station, but that's exactly what the production team are doing. I was ushered in ten minutes ago for an interview and I'm not comfortable with being centre of attention.

'Nina, you need to explain your thoughts so we can launch this project immediately,' explained Jackie as she drove me towards the studio. 'It's just a simple interview, sweetie. Nothing to be worried about. Forget that people are listening.'

It's difficult to forget when I'm wearing oversized headphones and a large microphone is right in front of my mouth. Not to mention that the wacky radio presenter Jimmy Diamond sits opposite me at 8:00 a.m. – I am more than slightly nervous.

'Good morning, this is Jimmy Diamond on Radio Raveloe coming to you on this crisp December morning. With me is a young lady from Christmas Tree Farm who's going to explain a very special project that she's wishing to launch, called Presents for Heaven. So, Nina, can you explain how the idea came about?' asks the male presenter in a bright and breezy tone.

Since Wednesday, everything happened so quickly. One minute Jackie was asking me a question, the next Zach and Bram's mouths widened in shock as my words spilt out explaining the pain, the loneliness and harsh reality of grief.

'My father never opened his final present from me as he died last year on Christmas Eve... and so, I'd quite like the opportunity to send his gift somewhere, anywhere, in fact... I simply want to send him my Christmas gift, and yet, I *can't*.'

'And you feel others who are in similar situations could gain comfort by doing the same?' continues Jimmy Diamond.

'Oh, yes. I know the final location isn't heaven but that doesn't matter – it's the act of sending it that will provide comfort to the bereaved. When I was a child, Dad encouraged me to write letters to Santa – in my best handwriting, sticking stamps across the envelope to send to Lapland. It's the same principle that I'm thinking of recreating with Presents for Heaven... except it's for those who have lost a loved one. It may bring them comfort and hope, and possibly a sense of continuing love for those they've lost.'

'That's lovely, Nina... but why the farm?'

'Christmas Tree Farm is where I work and it captures the magic of the season. We nurture our trees all year around until finally they are cut and sold so others can enjoy their beauty and create happy family memories. I believe that untold numbers of families in the local area enjoy their annual trip to our farm. Their visit is as traditional as baking the Christmas cake, hanging up stockings or leaving a carrot out on Christmas Eve for Rudolph.'

'And what will happen to the gifts once they are delivered to the farm?'

'We'd like each present to be clearly labelled detailing its contents and then after Christmas the farm's owners are going to find homes for each present within our local community. The gift can be wrapped as elaborately as people wish, just as their family member would have liked, as long as a label is attached. It'll make things easier for distribution.'

'So, folks, if you'd like to participate in this new project please feel free to visit the Christmas Tree Farm website for further details about Presents for Heaven. Take your wrapped present along to the farm this coming weekend. I'd like to say a big thank you to Nina for joining us today and may I take this opportunity to wish you a very merry Christmas.'

'Thank you.' I don't need to mention that I won't be celebrating.

Done.

I didn't stutter as much as I had imagined I would, but still, it has been less than forty-eight hours since the idea was born in the snug and now a new Christmas project is definitely happening.

I watch as the presenter starts a track playing before he turns to me.

'You did well. I hope it wasn't as scary as you'd imagined?'

'Thank you, it wasn't. I do believe I'm dashing off across town to speak to a reporter or two at the local paper... so, thanks again.'

'Thank you for joining us and I wish you well. The present project sounds amazing!'

Within minutes, I'm bundled into Jackie's car and, as predicted, driven across town to the offices of *The Tamworth Herald*, for a similar interview and photographs.

*

Holly

'Can we please get a move on?' screams Mum as we older girls pile into her car. This feels naughty, given that it's a school day and we're not heading for school.

I don't think I'll be missing much anyway, and it's only a half-day today. Instead we are driving into town to meet Isabella and hopefully us older girls are trying on our bridesmaid dresses ready for Monday's wedding. My younger sisters are staying at home with dad, as they don't need additional fittings given their basic shapes without a waist, a bust or hips. 'Seat belts?' is Mum's final cry before we frantically wave at Dad, stuck at home with the younger ones.

'Holly, look, there's Demi,' shouts Hannah, from the rear seats, her arm thrusting past my nose in the passenger seat.

She's right; Demi is walking in the snow amongst a crowd of uniformed pupils. As we pass, my head whips around to view who she's with: Paris and the mean girls! Great, that didn't take long for her to tag with their crowd as soon as I'm not available. Plus, she's earlier than our normal agreed time.

'She's been hanging about Christmas Tree Farm with them,' I say, to answer Hannah's unspoken question. 'She seems to think it's fun downing cider and making fires with that crowd, nowadays.'

'She'll come unstuck, if that's her game,' warns Mum, driving slowly to nudge into the stream of traffic.

I agree, for once. It doesn't make me eager to join them, but my insides feel heavy knowing that I can be replaced so easily after ten years of friendship. A warning signal goes off in my head: best not trust Demi with any new information about Alfie and me otherwise she's bound to share it with her new posse.

'Holly, can you find the website for Christmas Tree Farm and check out the details of the Presents for Heaven thing mentioned on the radio?' asks Mum. I'm glad of the distraction so pull out my mobile and oblige her with the specific instructions.

The woman sounded great on Radio Raveloe. I'd have been too nervous to speak. Alfie says Nina's much older than me so she'll look after me come my first shift. I knew it would tweak Mum's ear the minute Dad turned the radio on. She's had a tough year having lost her dad. She's a softy at heart despite her constant ranting at us.

'Right then, eyes peeled for a nice present that we'd have bought Grandad,' says Mum, her eyes fixed on the road but her mind elsewhere. I list the possible items: a warm jumper, a large quantity of pink and white fluffy marshmallows or a new flat cap. No wonder the farm is asking for specific details on gift labels otherwise handing an elderly lady a new flat cap might not be the highlight of her year!

'If I don't like my dress when I try it on, do I still have to wear it?' asks Hayley, from the rear seat.

'Of course, and you'll be grateful for being asked to be a bridesmaid,' spits Mum over her shoulder at my ill-mannered sister.

'What if I'm cold wearing it?' moans Hayley.

'Tough luck, they've cost a fortune and it's your cousin Isabella's day,' she scorns, adding, 'She's waited long enough for this wedding and there's been no expense spared so you'll be doing as you're told.'

'We've got white boleros, remember,' I add, knowing mum calls her a cousin but actually she is a distant cousin.

'The rest of the outfit is pure satin – and that's *so* warm,' continues Hayley, nudging Hannah alongside her on the back seat.

I don't care if I'm freezing cold; being measured, fitted and bought a brand-new dress is going to be the highlight of my year. The bonus that Alfie will be present to enjoy the entire day is a dream come true, though I'm mindful that we're distant family while his family are close friends of her parents. Though I'll need to finish my duties as bridesmaid first. As Mum said, there's been no expense spared.

*

343

Angie

'Candlelight is such a simple decoration and yet, so beautiful,' I say, as hundreds of flickering flames light our car journey along the farm's track. 'How can something as simple as a tiny flame be so inviting and alluring?'

Nick nods but doesn't comment.

Butterflies flutter within my stomach. It feels like bonfire night, strangers dressed for all weathers in woolly hats, wellingtons and gloves – it brings out the child in us all. I'm determined that tonight's date will be special; Christmas Tree Farm holds so many precious memories for us over the years. Tonight, I hope we'll create one more, just the two of us.

In no time, we've parked as indicated by staff dressed in fluorescent jackets. As we walk in the snow towards the meeting point, I take Nick's arm. My hand linking around his forearm feels right, where it belongs, like a hook and eye fastening.

'I'm surprised you opted for a carol service... given your voice.'

'Oi, cheeky, I can sing *when* I try.'

'Not necessarily in tune, though, is it?' Nick laughs. 'But I'm sure everyone else will forgive you.'

'I do it to make others feel better, OK?' I jibe. This is a good start – a jovial night filled with laughter and larks will help us to bond just a little more.

'*Really?* So, your uncontrollable sobbing during Alfie's first school nativity was to support others?'

'Yes! No mother wishes to be the first to cry in the audience, so I took the lead.'

Nick gives me a knowing look; he witnessed at first hand my public snot and tears display.

Alfie's days at primary school seem so long ago. But tonight, as much as I'd love Alfie to be present, we are a couple and I need to make the most of my time with Nick.

Staff wearing fluorescent jackets beckon us towards the entrance gate and check our tickets. A new-fangled ticket purchased and printed from the Internet – something I rarely do.

'Good evening, welcome to Christmas Tree Farm,' greets the young blonde woman. 'Would you like to carry a lantern?'

Nick agrees, so we pass through the gate armed with a sturdy pole from which swings a glass lantern complete with a large chapel candle. I grasp the service sheet offered by the same young woman; I never remember the words to carols.

A brass band strikes up the swirling tones of 'Silent Night' as the gathering crowd have their tickets checked and adults are strategically armed with lantern rods. Several reindeer bedecked in leather harnesses complete with tiny bells stand impatiently beside their handlers.

The farm's donkey is on a leash too. I assume they'll lead the procession. A gaggle of tiny children dressed in tea towels and bedsheets appear to be assembled for a nativity scene – I silently apologise to the tiny angel, hoping she doesn't cry should history repeat itself and I drown her out with my singing.

'Angie?' he whispers.

I turn on hearing my name.

'Yes...'

'This feels right.' He pulls me closer with his free arm and gently touches my forehead with his. 'Having spent so much time apart... *this* feels right.'

I want to cry. Nick couldn't have said it in a more genuine manner. He's a closed book where his emotions are concerned, unlike me.

'I agree. I'm glad we've taken the time out to attend.'

I stand in a growing crowd, linking arms with the only man I've ever truly loved, and I literally want to burst with pride. If he suggests that we go home now, I'll happily leave. In those few lines, he's given me what I need to hear. We're on the same page, heading in the same direction. What more do I need in life?

A gentle fluttering of snow begins to magically fall; the crowd look skywards and utter ohs and ahs of amazement.

'Ladies and gentles, children young and old,' booms a male voice over the speaker system, 'welcome to Christmas Tree Farm and our annual carol service.

346

Should you feel unwell or need assistance please make your needs known to a member of staff. So, without further ado, can I wish you all a merry Christmas and the happiest of new years?'

A round of applause erupts as the marching brass band bursts to life with 'The Holly and the Ivy', which leads us along the snow-cleared track amongst the snow-covered spruce, led by reindeer, a donkey and a parade of tiny children.

As I begin to sing, in my own beautiful way, Nick gives me a sideways glance and smiles. If that's all it takes to make my man smile, let it be. I'll spend the rest of my days singing loud, proud and totally out of tune.

The crowd swell around us, families young and old, their lanterns gently swing and our voices unite as the group saunter behind the brass band. A sense of calm envelops me. Does life get any better or any simpler than this? I could name a hundred occasions where I've made complicated arrangements, tried my hardest to impress and bust a gut organising the most amazing birthday treats – almost killing myself with the effort to get everything perfect – and yet, right here, right now is totally perfect. Costing me two five-pound tickets and a free evening to forget the rest of my life and focus on linking arms with Nick. *My* Nick. I correct myself quickly, are my defences coming down quicker than they ought? I shouldn't assume anything. I need to make sure he's right by my side as we retrace this journey back towards being us. The new improved us; the us that's happy, healthy and honest.

*

Holly

Their house is empty; Alfie's dad's out on a date night.

His forehead falls forward upon my shoulder, and lies heavy. I can feel his warm breath upon my collarbone. A soothing warmth, a steady presence and yet the tingle along my spine suggests more. His hands drape around my waist and connect at the base of my spine.

We stand, suspended in time, like a statue awaiting the arrival of lichen. Neither of us says a word. And yet, I know.

I can sense the shift in emotion, warmth and physical contact. I'm aware of every breath he takes and I can almost see each move, each line, each sentence, each moment laid before us like a script, a map that we will follow. Our map. Our route.

Within ten minutes, we are kissing as passionately as we ever have. There is no going back; there is no holding back. I want him as much as he wants me. Our mouths ravish the other's as though our lives depend upon it.

He gently strokes the base of my spine, trailing his index finger over my skin. The heat prickles under his touch. This can't be what it's all about? They never mentioned this at school.

I continue to kiss, but my mind focuses upon his hands, which gently drift underneath the rear of my tee shirt and caress my back.

My thoughts cease. Movement seems to be the only thing I am capable of right now.

Somehow, conjoined we move from the breakfast bar, through the lounge and up the staircase. We briefly separate to climb the stairs. We ignore Rolo on passing; his dark eyes lift and then drop. I sense a fraction of hesitation in Alfie's moves. Would I be offended if he chose not to keep going?

At the top of the staircase, he leads the way to his room, where there is a combination of football mania and golf magazines. It's not the first time I've entered his room, but it's definitely the first time I've *been* in his room. As soon as we are inside we close the door firmly and lean against it, as if barricading ourselves from absent adults. They're not welcome at present. Right now, nothing exists apart from Alfie.

We hit the mattress with a thud – a combination of conjoined limbs and lips.

He raises my tee shirt. I reach for his belt.

This. Is. It.

*

Angie

The carol service is delightful. All my favourite hymns are sung: 'Hark! The Herald Angels Sing', 'Away in a Manger' and 'O Little Town of Bethlehem'.

'Is Alfie staying in tonight?' I ask, cupping my mulled wine to warm my hands.

'No, he's off out to the cinema with Holly... some new film that all the kids are raving about.'

'Did he say anything about last Friday night's sleep over at mine?'

'Nope. Should he?'

I shrug.

'I'd never felt so uncomfortable. He made it clear that he's supporting the idea of you dating other women.'

'Ouch!'

'Exactly, what was I to say? He's content that we are over and eager for you to move on...'

'Don't worry, we'll have a chat, Angie.'

'But when?' I watch as he swigs his mulled wine. 'The wedding is only a few days away – he might need time to get his head around the fact.'

'He might be delighted.'

'I doubt it, Nick. He was hardly appreciative regards me attending parents' evening.'

Nick wraps his free arm around my shoulders.

'You worry too much, Angie. The lad needs to see us together to understand that if we're happy to try again, then so should he.'

'Mmmm.' I look away as my eyes begin to glisten. He makes it sound so easy. A simple chat with our son over the dining table and everything will be rosy. I'm not so sure.

A loud crackle like gunfire brings me back to tonight. The right side of the crowd surge forward and separate like the Red Sea as a huge goat with killer horns charges through the middle, with an eruption of bright white lights and exploding bangs streaming in ribbons from its behind, leaving the crowd coughing amidst a cloud of drifting white smoke.

'What the hell?' I say, clutching Nick's jacket.

'Firecrackers,' says Nick, his head craning to view the exploding area. 'Some bloody idiots have attached them to the poor creature.'

We watch as a swarm of fluorescent coats charge towards the area, chasing the frantic goat, as parents attempt to silent crying children and assure elderly relatives.

'Someone's going to get burnt,' I whisper, looking away for fear of witnessing an unsavoury image. 'Nick, how long do they last?'

'It depends how many are attached.'

Logical, as always.

The crowd moves towards our side and now strangers bustle and crush against strangers to avoid the flying sparks and white smoke. A sudden panic lifts to my throat. I feel threatened by the wall of coats filling my view. I feel trapped. I feel hot. I feel frightened.

'Nick, I don't like this,' I mutter as I am squashed towards his frame.

'Give it a second or two, it'll end in no time. No one is hurt,' he says, his blue eyes peering into my stricken face. 'It'll be fine, believe me.'

I take a deep breath and wait. I want to believe him, on so many levels.

*

Holly

His body touches the length of mine from ribcage to foot. He's muscular where I'm soft, defined where I'm hollow.

He gently strokes my cheek, his hot breath on my temple, as I stare at the ceiling. Mortified. The unwrapped but unused condom lies discarded on the carpet at the side of the bed.

'Alfie…' I begin but stop. I feel such a fool. How can you want someone so badly and yet, when the moment arrives, know in your heart of hearts that it really isn't the right moment?

'Shhhh, don't worry,' he whispers, brushing his lips against my cheek.

'But it's not that—'

'I know.'

I turn to look at him for the first time in ten silent minutes.

His clear gaze stares back. He's so honest, trusting and loveable, and yet, I couldn't. I wanted to, but I *just* couldn't.

'You're not ready. I get it.'

'But I wanted to.'

He nods.

'Thank you.'

He grimaces.

'Seriously, some lads would have reacted badly.'

'Well, I'm not most lads, am I?'

'No. Thank God.' I smile.

'Hols, it'll happen when it happens... It's nice to simply lie here with you and—' He stops talking, his attention instantly focused elsewhere.

'What?'

'Shit. I think that's my dad back early. What's he doing home at this time?'

We launch from the mattress as quickly as we hit the springs. I grab my underwear, as Alfie pulls on his clothes minus any underwear. Thirty seconds ago, life was chilled. Now, it's a frenzy. My heart rate is going nineteen to the dozen. We really shouldn't be found together up here in his room; Mr Woodward will know. Adults always know.

'Quick, here's your hair bobble,' says Alfie, collecting it from the floor. We smirk. Maybe it's a good thing that I asked him to stop once we were naked. Not only was I really not ready, as I thought, but Mr Woodward would have interrupted, that's for sure, which wasn't how I saw my first time with Alfie.

'Alfie!' hollers Mr Woodward up the staircase.

'Yeah!'

'I've got chips here if you and Holly fancy some supper.'

Alfie looks at me. Yeah, I fancy chips despite everything that has happened.

We straighten the bed for fear of interrogation.

'Holly, come here.' Alfie pulls me towards him just before we reach his doorway.

'I wouldn't want to do anything that you were uncomfortable with. OK?'

I nod. I can't speak. I love the way he's so mature. The way he has my interests at heart. If the truth be known I love Alfie Woodward a little more this evening than I did this morning, because he's proved himself worthy of being my boyfriend.

Fifteen

Nina

Saturday, 22 December

The queue of traffic snakes along the farm's track and onto the neighbouring roads as the snow continues to fall. Boss Fielding is in the best mood we've ever seen and the excitement at Christmas Tree Farm exceeds anything witnessed in previous years. In a corner of the sales yard, the local TV news reporter Kim Botterill, dressed in a pink mac, hastily delivers to camera her roving reporter piece as regards the new project, which will air across the region tonight. Who'd have thought local news would be interested in our latest project?

'Can you believe it?' asks Zach as we watch from the cashier's cabin steps. 'All this is because of your idea.'

'I know, daft, isn't it? The boss joked I'd gain a pay rise if Presents for Heaven hits the national news.'

'No, Nina, it's far from daft. It shows that families are making an additional trip on behalf of a loved one. You should be proud.'

'I wonder how many drivers are complaining because they're having to wait to reach the car park?' I joke.

'Phuh! They need to get a bit of Christmas spirit in that case.'

We watch as most cars pull past the car park area, sweeping into the temporary drop-off point hastily created yesterday, and a farm colleague takes delivery of their offered gifts. The large banner announcing 'Presents for Heaven' flaps in the wind making a snapping noise. Boss Fielding says he'll get a plastic banner printed professionally for next year but we've done our best for this year. Families, young and old, are delivering brightly wrapped presents topped with bows and curled ribbons. I expected to see many tears but very few seem upset; like me, they seem relieved at having fulfilled a need to include and remember their deceased relative in such a simple manner at Christmas time.

I watch the relay of farm workers ferry the gifts to an old wooden cart that hasn't seen the light of day from the equipment barn for years. With a garland of holly decorating the side and thick plastic sheeting lying on the bottom, it makes for an aesthetically pleasing collection point. Two teenage helpers stand upon it piling the presents sky-high; my offering was their first delivery.

Zach's arm snakes about my shoulder.

'Are you OK?'

I nod, enjoying the comfort of his embrace.

'Jackie tells me you're moving into a cabin later tonight.'

'Yep, your dad agreed I could have it free of charge over the Christmas period as only two cabins are booked for rental. It's what I want to do.'

'If you need company, you only have to come up to the house... You can join in with our festive goings-on.'

'I know. But I'll be fine.' I am determined to be fine. I've packed a huge suitcase with a host of food and a selection of reading books to occupy my quiet time. I can't cancel Christmas but I can choose to spend it how I wish.

'I saw your suitcase in the snug. Did you trundle it along in the snow this morning?'

'Yep. I felt such a fool walking through the village at such an unearthly hour.' The only witness was my robin, who flew from bough to bough a few metres ahead of me, watching me in his inquisitive manner. Despite the plastic wheels, the suitcase is heavier than it looks given that I've carefully wrapped and packaged the precious contents from beneath the stairs. I feel disrespectful, but I wasn't ready until now – now I am ready to do what needs to be done.

*

Holly

'And then?' I ask, as Alfie settles beside me on my first ever tea break in the snug.

'He said, and I quote, "Me and your mum are dating"!'

'No!'

'Yes! Dating!'

I'm out of my depth. I don't know what to say. I don't want to put my foot in it but probably will.

'And how do you feel about that?'

Alfie stares at me. Oh, there it is, a foot-in-mouth moment quite clear to spot.

'Have you not been listening to anything I've said about my parents?' asks Alfie, his brow furrowed, his blue eyes flashing in annoyance.

'Err yeah... just checking... You might have changed your mind following the father and son chat.'

'Holly, I haven't changed my mind. I think he's a fool to take her back.'

I nod. Seriously, I get it: no mind-changing.

'So, how's that leave things with you?'

'After we drove you back home, we sat up until gone one this morning... just going over and over the same stuff. He's totally hooked, line and sinker.'

'Anyway, now I wish I hadn't asked. Can we change the subject?' I ask.

Alfie gulps down his coffee, and stares into his mug.

'Had a good morning so far?' Alfie asks.

'It's been fine. I helped net a load of Blue spruce, labelled the last cut of Nordman firs and helped Zach try to locate the missing goat. Though I'm glad we didn't find him, given the weapons he's armed with. You?'

'Perfect, apart from getting a bit teary helping out with the Presents for Heaven collection point. I tried to hide it when an elderly man arrived and delivered a gift for "Elsie" only to find it contained an etching of a dozen red roses that he'd sat at home and drawn. How beautiful is that?'

I agree.

'I expected to be teary when I brought in my mum's present for my grandad, but I felt honoured to deliver it,' I add, recalling the gold ribbon and wrapping paper labelled: mantelpiece clock.

'You're filling up just hearing about the roses,' he says, nudging my knee.

'I know... but how lovely to care so deeply about someone that you'd spend time making something they'd love after they've gone.'

'Mmmm, fancy caring so little about someone that you walk out, divorce them and then ask to return when you can't find anything better in life. Go figure.'

'Alfie... don't.' I scowl. 'You're sounding bitter.'

'So would you if you'd experienced the year my dad and me have gone through. Seriously, the worst year of my life, so far... until you came along.'

'Go on, you're just saying that!'

He slowly shakes his head; his eyes grow wide.

'Hols, I'm really not.'

A silence lingers between us, we both look into the other's face and nothing needs to be said. Last night's moment of tenderness was far greater than if we'd actually gone all the way. I've heard my mum describe this as puppy love, at the most, a teenage crush... but there's more, much more to *us* than words can explain.

'Are you OK?' he asks, readying himself to return to work. 'You looked...'

'I'm great... just looking forward to spending Christmas time together without the interruption of school or homework.'

'Me too, though if my mum keeps popping around I'll probably be spending more time at yours.'

I smile. He'll be welcome any time, especially by my dad.

*

I spend the rest of the day helping the florist lady on her wreath stall, pitched over by the car park. She is literally selling mistletoe and making holly wreaths to order as customers wait. I take the cash, given that she's an independent trader not linked to the farm so customers won't pay at the cashier's cabin. I write down the details as regards size and colour of ribbon required and, bingo, her hands are super whizzy at producing a new wreath every few minutes. If the customers want a standard wreath or a small cross, then I show them the selection of pre-made ones available, which look fabulous to me for decorating a front door or a gravestone.

Either way, I'm kept busy and this beats working at the local chemist any day.

My mind keeps flickering back to last night with Alfie. Were we right not to continue after I suddenly felt all weird about doing it? I felt awful doing that to him, but everyone has always said you have to be honest, and if I can't be honest with Alfie, who can I be honest with?

'Are you OK, Holly?' asks Nina, approaching across the sales yard.

'Oh, yeah, fine, thanks. You?' She showed me the ropes first thing this morning, but I haven't seen much of her since. Alfie says she's a bit down at the minute about her dad passing away last Christmas. She's said nothing to me, but you can't help but sense that she's dealing with something big; she's always busy, always alone.

'So-so. I'll be glad when today's over and done with and we can all get back to normal.'

'Not till after the holidays, though,' I say.

'Ah, I'm not doing those this year. Giving it a miss and staying put in a log cabin over by the lake. That'll be my treat for the holidays.'

I instantly feel sorry for her. Fancy not being with family at Christmas.

'Not on your own, surely?'

'Oh, yeah, it's what I want. I asked Boss Fielding and he agreed that I can stay as long as I promise to go to the house should I feel lonely.'

I nod. Even so, spending Christmas Day alone seems like the saddest thing I've ever heard. For the second time today, I want to cry. First Alfie's story about the old gent and now Nina.

'And you?' she asks.

'With my parents and sisters, but we've got my cousin's wedding on Monday. Well, we're distant cousins really, but Isabella hasn't any sisters or daughters so she asked my sisters and me to be bridesmaids. We collected the bridesmaids' dresses yesterday so it feels real now.'

Nina nods. She now looks really interested and happier. I'll keep talking about the wedding; she must like weddings. It's the least I can do when someone is feeling down, or so my mum would say.

'Anyway, we had the day off school and—'

'And Luca? You know him well?'

'Not really. She's been with him for years – they've got two boys together – but we only ever see them at weddings or christenings, and then he only talks to my dad.'

Nina nods.

'So, the boys are his, then?'

'Oh, yeah, they've been together for years and years, he just didn't want to get married until now...'

Nina nods along. Her face doesn't seem as bright as a moment ago, but, hey, she's talking about people she doesn't know. You can't always feign interest, can you?

I spy a customer waving at me from the pre-made holly wreaths.

'I need to go and serve,' I say apologetically, pointing to the potential customer.

'Of course, yes... well, I hope you enjoy your day as a bridesmaid.'

I dash over to the lady as Nina returns to her usual spot on the sales yard.

*

Nina

It feels strange using a new key, having only known the feel of the cottage key. The cabin's gold key slides and turns within a sleek well-oiled lock, unlike the cottage one.

'I've allocated you the smallest cabin. I figured you wouldn't be needing anything larger,' was the boss's explanation for allocating me cabin number three.

He is right.

My intention is to hibernate for several days over Christmas, enjoy the lake, read a little and straighten my head ready for a new start come Boxing Day.

Inside I find everything I need. A one-roomed cabin, complete with a stable door split-section opening, a cosy double bed, small seating area around the wood burner, a kitchenette area before the cabin window and a small en-suite bathroom. And, a secure door lock so I can firmly get closure as regards Christmas festivities. And the wedding.

I trundle my suitcase up the three wooden steps and into my new home. A quick ten-minute dash-about empties my belongings from the suitcase. I carefully place the wooden box from under the stairs upon the coffee table. It doesn't seem right to place it on the floor, but nowhere seems appropriate.

After a difficult and long day on the sales yard this feels as if I'm a million miles away from Christmas Tree Farm and yet I am slap bang in the middle of it amongst the east side growing fields and the lake.

I hastily grab my coat. Before I prepare some food, I want to visit the lake and enjoy the tranquillity of nightfall upon the water.

*

Angie

'I don't see the problem, Alfie.'

'Well, I do!' He pouts, turning from me as I hold his suit jacket out for him to try on.

'Slip it on, check the fit and then take it off again. What's the issue?'

'You. That's the issue!'

'Me?' I point at my chest, to ensure that I've got his drift.

'You run out on us after New Year then think we can all play happy families when it comes to attending someone else's wedding... Slightly hypocritical, don't you think?'

I look around for Nick; a mere atom of support would be good here. He's nowhere to be found.

'Your father and I—'

'Oh, don't come that crap again about you trying to work through your pain and come out a stronger and happier couple at the end. You divorced the poor bastard—'

'Alfie!'

'You did, you put him and me through the mill to please yourself and run off with your fancy man, or should I say fancy men? I remember the old mum... the one before she skipped out on us.'

I stand open-mouthed. I can't believe I'm still holding his suit jacket out to him as if that is a feasible distraction, given his speech.

'I was just thinking that if we...' says Nick, walking into the lounge as we glare at each other, a million silent insults flying between us. 'What's wrong?'

We both speak at once to justify our own state of frustration.

'She just said—'

'He just said—'

Nick holds his hands up.

'Woo... I can't deal with both of you at once.'

'Mum's playing happy families and I'm not feeling it.'

'He's not prepared to fake it either,' I add.

'Absolutely, I agree,' says Nick. Alfie smirks. 'Don't give me that, son. My relationship with your mother is different from your relationship with her. We talked about this last night. Now, if we do get *this* back on track you are going to have to work it out. You might decide that—'

'Excuse me, are you actually saying not only do I rebuild my marriage, but I have to rebuild being a mother? Because I think you'll find that that bond has never been broken!'

'Yes, it was. You left. My mother left me for another man.'

'I did not leave for another man,' I snap. How have the bloody tables once again turned on me for being the

369

sodding bad guy? Five minutes ago, all I wanted was for Alfie to try the suit jacket on to make sure there are no dramas come the wedding, but oh, no, we have to start World War III instead.

'Angie... I told you the situation is delicate... Five minutes alone and this happens.'

'Nick, I was trying to ensure that the wedding goes well.'

'Maybe that's the problem – maybe we are being hasty in deciding to attend as a family. We're not there yet... and...' he says.

I don't believe I'm hearing this. Today of all days... What the hell am I supposed to say? Is he expecting me to say I won't go because it's his friend's daughter? Or should we all not go? And, most importantly, what about Christmas Day if *this* is going to cause an issue?

I thrust the jacket into Alfie's hand and grab my handbag from the edge of the sofa. Once I've collected my keys from the bottom stair, I pat Rolo on the head and dash from their house. Our house. My old house. The pair of them can suit their bloody selves. I've tried. I'll be fine over Christmas with my luxury hamper delivery. I've bent over backwards to fix us and I am not putting up with this, any more.

Sixteen

Holly

Sunday, 23 December

My mobile bleeps, waking me up just after midnight. Half asleep, I squint at the illuminated screen: a text from Demi.

> OMG! You'll never guess what's happened

*

Nina

I want to cry, as I have never cried before.

The frantic hammering on the cabin door frightens the life out of me. I jump from the bed and cautiously grab a hoodie to cover my pyjamas.

'Who is it?' I call out, standing behind the wooden door.

The hammering continues, drowning out my voice.

I carefully slide the bolt on the upper section of door and peer out.

'Thank God for that, Nina!' bellows Zach, out of breath. 'You need to get dressed. There's a fire on the south fields... you need to come quickly.'

'What?'

I stare at his stricken features. I haven't seen him as panicked as this since we were children.

'Nina, please don't start – just go and get dressed. The fire brigade are on their way, but we need to account for everyone.'

'One minute.'

I close and lock the upper stable door before getting dressed in last night's jeans.

Within minutes, we are leaving the cabin area and hurrying along the path towards the sales yard. Each time the spruce clear I can see the entire sky above the farm is lit up in an amber glow.

'Dad thinks the teenagers have had a party again and... it's gone wrong.'

'You don't say.'

Zach eyeballs me before continuing.

'He's hoping no one's caught or surrounded by the flames... but as Jackie said, how is he going to know that until the fire crew arrive and check?'

'And the Christmas trees?'

'They'll be burnt to the ground. If it spreads we could lose the lot.'

'Zach... they're the oldest trees on the farm, planted by your grandparents.'

He nods.

'And the wedding?'

'Exactly, another headache to fix. Come on, hurry up.'

We finally arrive at the huddle of people beside the snug.

'Nina!' cries Jackie. 'Can you believe it?'

I shake my head as we watch the approaching blue lights draw along the farm track. One, two and three bulky fire engines sweep into the sales yard and are swiftly directed towards the open gates leading to the south fields. Boss Fielding is frantically talking whilst pointing, in the direction of the tarmacked road leading into the Norway spruce growing area, as he speaks to a uniformed fire officer.

A cloudy hue drifts high above the scorching flames as they stretch upwards into the dark starry night.

'What can we do?' I ask, feeling helpless at the sight before me.

'Absolutely nothing,' mutters Bram, sitting on the wooden steps, his eyes to the sky.

'And Arthur... what if he's caught amongst it?' adds Zach, pacing back and forth.

'Don't. I can't begin to think about anyone or anything losing its life tonight,' says Jackie, as a heaving sob escapes from her chest.

'What about the Presents for Heaven?' I ask.

'They're all safely stored in the equipment barn so there's no fear there,' soothes Bram, from the cabin steps.

I feel physically empty. All emotion and thought has drained from my body. I feel useless, helpless and unable to contemplate the enormity of flame upon wood. Our beloved Christmas trees alight. By morning, we'll know to what extent: singed, burnt, dead.

*

I do the only thing I can: I make hot tea in the snug.

The fire crew report that the mature spruce couldn't be saved given the intensity and spread of the fire. Despite a deep covering of snow, some areas of the south side were densely planted so the fire spread above ground level from spruce to spruce. So, they managed it in a tactical manner by preventing the fire spreading to the farm's east and north growing fields. The tarmac roads that run along and between sections of the farm helped to provide a natural break barrier, but otherwise the officers had no choice but to organise a constant flow of water, dowse the flames and monitor the burning area.

No one has been found wandering amongst the spruce so Boss Fielding assumes the kids have bolted on seeing their handiwork. Perhaps they might have watched from afar, though they would never be able to appreciate all the damage they've caused.

There's been no sight of Arthur, which doesn't bear thinking about.

I lift each mug, complete with teabag, up to the water urn's spout and fill. I've organised sugar and milk on the counter top so the fire crew can help themselves.

'Any coffee?'

'Yeah, two seconds,' I say, over my shoulder, not caring to look at the speaker. As I turn back to the urn, his dark gaze sticks fast in my mind.

My stomach flips uncontrollably.

Luca?

I slowly turn, mug in hand, not daring to hope.

'Hi... yep, it's me again,' he chirps, his face smudged with smoke marks and his tumble of curls wet and plastered to his skin with sweat. His uniformed frame

375

seems wider and imposing on the other side of the counter top. 'I see barista has been added to your roles too.'

I nod.

I'm speechless. How is this happening?

He continues to chat but I can't answer; I'm on autopilot making his coffee.

I should feel ashamed, to be reacting like this to an attached guy. I've read about women like me; I abhor them. Chasing attached men, when there are plenty of fish in the sea. Aren't there enough single guys in the world?

'Cheers for the coffee,' he says, his smile radiating from his dark eyes.

'Pleasure.'

He joins his crew. I make more tea and chastise myself a little further.

*

Angie

I undo the large buckles on the wicker hamper that is meant for Christmas day and stare at the feast of calorific delights before me.

'Well, that's me sorted for Christmas,' I mutter, picking amongst the goodies.

Would it be wrong to start opening items before breakfast, when really there are two more days to go?

I've no one to answer to. Is the 23rd not classed as the beginning of Christmas?

I grab the tin of caramelised cashew nuts and plod back to bed, collecting my iPad as I go.

If Nick and Alfie can do their own thing, then so can I. I settle back under the duvet, open the tin of cashews and flick through Netflix for a suitable movie.

As rude as it seems, I have no intention of apologising for my absence at tomorrow's wedding. They can think on their feet and make up what trivial excuse they choose. I am done.

*

Nina

We traipse in a line through the spruce carrying wedding equipment towards the marquee, like the Magi bearing gifts. Underfoot the snow is compact and slippery, causing a succession of scary moments as staff gingerly tread the route towards the east side of the farm.

'I don't see why they can't load the trailer sky-high and have the tractor slowly tow it through the trees,' I say under my breath to Shazza as we linger at the back of the line.

'Jackie doesn't want tractor tyre marks or soot being left anywhere near the wedding scene after it was used last night,' explains Shazza. 'She reckons it'll ruin the natural appearance of the snow for the wedding party as they approach.'

'Couldn't the tyres be hosed down first? One decent journey and this lot would be delivered in no time,' I add, sulking as my arms ache after my third trek.

'Would you want huge tyre tracks running towards your dream winter wedding?'

I don't answer.

'Exactly,' shouts Shazza, over her shoulder. 'So get a bloody move on.'

Most Christmas Eves we focused on the spruce sales, maximising the effort to clear every last one, but this year we stayed open longer during this final week to accommodate the public as a means of helping ourselves juggle with the wedding preparations and the last-minute rush. And now, with the fire.

My mind fills with images from last night and the frantic attempts to dowse and save the Christmas trees. I visited earlier with Kitty, so know exactly how large an area the fire has destroyed.

'I thought the saddest sight was a bare-branched Christmas tree resting beside a dustbin,' said Kitty, as we stood on the tarmac this morning starring at the fire damage, 'but this... this is something else.'

I had to agree. In the cold light of day, the fire had been far greater than I'd imagined. The magical snow scene had gone, replaced by a thick layer of grey ash from which ugly blackened stumps rose at various heights for as far as the eye could see.

'What are they looking for?' I asked, pointing to the various people moving slowly through the debris.

'*Anything*. Boss Fielding has told them about the teenagers with their small bonfires and aerosol cans – they seem to think they can find evidence scattered amongst the ash. Shazza said her younger brother had been grounded last night so he wouldn't have been involved in last night's shenanigans.'

'Those responsible must be crapping themselves, right now. And Arthur?' I asked, dreading to hear more bad news.

'They managed to capture him at first light. The vets arrived earlier with a mild tranquilliser dart. Poor thing... he's got multiple burns from the string of firecrackers they'd attached to his horns but the vet said he's got a fair chance, but it'll take time. He's now settled alongside Gertrude, but have you seen the boss? He's none too clever – he's been at his desk all morning trying to sort things out.'

A sense of helplessness swells within my chest as we stand and stare in silence as the investigators drift amongst the burnt ruins.

'It'll be all hands on deck today to ensure the wedding isn't affected, but, hey, that's what we do here, isn't it?' said Kitty, leading the way back to the sales yard.

Shazza breaks my thoughts.

'Are you taking your spruce home tonight?' she asks, after my lengthy silence.

'No.'

'But, Nina, it's tradition,' mutters Shazza, shifting her hold on the large box of cloth napkins.

'Stop with the emotional blackmail. I can do as I please, thanks.'

Shazza turns around to stare at me over her shoulder. I feel uneasy; I didn't mean to be snappy.

I am about to launch into another internal monologue when our trek finally ends and the dense wall of spruce gently widens into a sweeping flatland, the new site for tomorrow's wedding ceremony. Beyond that, lies the lake surrounded by Blue spruce and the sloping embankment of Fraser firs.

Farm staff are as busy as bees piling equipment into specific areas – the ceremony pergola, the marquee or catering suite – ensuring that everything is available before creating a winter-wonderland wedding.

I don't want to help raise the marquee. You'd think it was an easy task, like pitching a child's Wendy house. Wrong... just bossy people need apply. So I deliver my box of condiments to the hired catering team, and quickly dart to the decoration team for a morning of floristry wire and oasis foam. I don't mind how long the garland has to be or the specific colour decoration of tied bows as long as I can be absorbed in one task to busy my mind.

'Are you joining us, Nina?' asks Jackie, piling fresh holly leaves into the centre of the circle of five chairs, beside which the pliers, red ribbon and ornamental robins lie ready and waiting.

'I am.'

Young Holly offers me a length of gauze meshing as I settle.

I have no intention of being all bright and cheery simply to fit in. I can't muster their happy tones given the sombre mood of the farm. I begin the laborious task of threading and securing pieces of prickly holly onto the garland's mesh. Realistically the entire meshing needs covering to provide a luscious and full garland; there'll be no skimping on the decoration under the watchful eye of Jackie, who is fastidious with her wedding planning.

Within ten minutes, the marquee guys are cursing and huffing at each other, all shouting for the same piece to be inserted into the right corner frame but no one is following the instructions.

Shazza and Kitty join us at the garland hub as the hired-catering posse count tables, chair ties and candelabras ready for a speedy transformation once the billowing canvas is a functioning marquee.

The garland group babble on about plans for the wedding, the colour scheme, Holly's connection to the bride's family and her excitement at being one of six bridesmaids, her youngest sister being excluded due to her age.

I continue to work in silence, listening out for any talk of Luca.

'How's it going with lover boy?' asks Shazza, a devilish glint in her eye. 'Planning any more dates?'

I ignore her.

'Nina,' whispers Kitty, nudging me.

I look up to view four expectant faces staring, their hands busily working.

'Oh, don't mind me. The twins might be my stepsons but I'm staying out of their love lives,' jokes Jackie, with a giggle.

Shazza raises her eyebrows.

'Spill the beans... and?'

'And nothing,' I say, my eyes firmly on my garland making.

'Hey, Jackie, can you see Nina as you in twenty years' time? Organising wedding parties, carol services and—'

Jackie gives a little cough. Holly simply watches from the sidelines.

I look up to catch Kitty glaring at Shazza.

Shazza changes tack.

'Sorry but the other night at the club… I assumed you were playing it cool regarding the twins but with the holidays you can spend more time—'

'Just stop! I believe you stated you wouldn't mind being Jackie around here in years to come, not me!' I snap, throwing down my section of garland. I stand and stride from the circle.

I need space. I need to breathe. I need to be away from these people and their constant chatter about men, love, life and being sodding happy all the time when deep down I feel like utter crap. Plus, I can't have what I want.

The cry of 'Nina!' fills the air as I quickly stride in the direction of the lake.

I want to be alone.

I know the catering and marquee teams will have all seen my hasty departure. One or two co-workers, such as Kitty, may well be wondering if they should follow me for moral support and a good cry.

It feels good to crunch virgin snow beneath my boots, as if making my own track is such a primitive action and so satisfying. I inhale the fresh air as I stride towards my lake. As I reach the water's edge, I calm. That's when I get it. I'm rattled, not just because of the anniversary, but because this bloody winter-wonderland wedding is secretly taking away someone I want. How am I expected to sit and make garlands for his wedding?

Why is life so complicated? So much daily energy is spent on correcting errors, getting around obstacles and being resilient. Surely, all this effort is better spent on the good things in life?

I know all these things and yet I don't know how to stop running away from life.

*

Holly

'Her dad passed away last Christmas Eve so she's not in the best place at the minute,' explains Shazza. 'Which is why I tried to jolly her up.' Her latter comment directed at the other two.

'Yeah and put your foot firmly in it,' says Kitty.

'So, Zach's back in with a chance, then?' says Shazza, a smirk dressing her lips.

'Seriously, Shazza… do you think she's in the right place to start seeing anyone right now? She needs to get her head straight before she even contemplates dating.'

'Our household can do without the twins being at war, given last night's troubles,' says Jackie.

'Hasn't she any siblings?' I ask.

Three heads simultaneously shake.

Wow, no one! As much as I complain about the abundance of bodies in our house, at least I can guarantee I will always have someone, be it a sister or parent.

'It was just her and him… and she took the brunt of his illness, mood swings, the lot, so it wasn't an easy living arrangement but, still, he was her dad,' explains Kitty.

'MS is tough due to the physical deterioration and pain being suffered, and yet the family try their best. Nina coped the best she could and for a long time too.'

'And her mother?' I ask.

'Long gone – she left years ago,' says Kitty.

I collect another handful of holly leaves and continue to work them into the floristry meshing as the silence lengthens. I'm waiting for someone to begin a cheerier conversation but they don't; everyone seems to be inside their own head space counting their own blessings.

*

'Have you said anything?' asks Alfie in the snug at break-time.

I shake my head.

'I daren't. That text message incriminates Demi and the police will demand names from her. She must be bricking it.'

'But I feel so guilty... Have you seen what they've done?'

I shake my head. Jackie has kept me busy from first thing carrying wedding stuff down to the marquee area.

'Totally gutted for as far as the eye can see. Seriously, not a single spruce left, just black stumps sticking up from the ground.'

'So, what are you suggesting – that we tell?'

Alfie looks at me, his blue eyes drilling mine. I know his answer and yet he can't bring himself to say it.

'I hate to be a grass, but I feel guilty for saying nothing. The family have been good to me over the last few shifts – I'd quite like to be kept on after Christmas for weekend work.'

'OK. When?'

'Now.'

'What about the wedding prep?'

'Boss Fielding hasn't been doing prep. He's been in his office for the entire morning. Jackie's in charge of the wedding.'

'What about Demi?'

Alfie shrugs.

'She'll have to answer their questions.'

*

'Whose mobile is this?' asks Boss Fielding, taking the item from his desk. His grey eyes flicker across the screen reading the brief message.

'Mine. Demi's my best friend.'

Alfie shifts in the seat beside me. He's as uncomfortable as me but it's the right thing to do.

'And she sent this at what time?'

'Twelve o'clock... the time appears at the side if you slide the message across,' I explain, my breath snagging in my throat.

His large fingers ease across the screen, before he slowly nods and looks up.

'And you pair?'

'We had nothing to do with *this*,' says Alfie, quickly. 'We feel guilty by association that we work here and teenagers we know have caused this.'

'But you've never joined them?'

We shake our heads.

'Never?'

'No. I was invited but I refused to join in. *They* aren't my type of friends,' I mutter, nerves flaring within my stomach as he stares at me. 'Seriously, we know nothing about last night, apart from the text.'

Boss Fielding sits back in his chair and eyes us both cautiously.

How can telling the truth about an incident actually feel so gut-wrenchingly difficult? You'd have thought he'd be pleased by our assistance; instead he sits staring for eons before he picks up the telephone receiver.

*

Angie

Nick hasn't called. I've watched three romcom movies back to back, consumed the entire tin of cashews, a jar of honeyed apricots and an entire box of marzipan fruits – I feel no better.

My mind is reeling. My gobby young pup thinks he knows everything after a two-minute crush on a classmate. And as for Nick, siding with him over me… surely that isn't right? I was only trying to help eliminate any last-minute issues as regards Alfie's suit not fitting and boom!

I snatch up my mobile, checking if Nick's texted me. Nothing.

Right, have it your way. Go to the wedding without me, parade yourself as the heroic single dad with the teenage son battling together to survive the family break – what do I care?

I press pause on Netflix, and stomp through to the kitchen. Eventually I find the corkscrew, grab a wine glass from the draining board and venture back to browse the wicker hamper for a delicious rosé.

'Merry Christmas!' I mutter as I uncork the bottle in the hallway before returning to bed. 'Even if I'm two days early!'

Seventeen

Nina

Monday, 24 December

Christmas Tree Farm finishes the year with a half-day closing, giving staff time to refresh and change for the wedding. I planned to spend my free time at the log cabin. Instead, I position myself behind a cluster of Fraser firs a safe distance from the wedding pergola swathed in garlands, and watch. The scene is beautiful. I can't imagine any bride being disappointed by the winter wonderland amongst our Christmas trees. I imagine she'll be dumbstruck as she arrives on her father's arm. I would be. The plush red carpet of the aisle cuts a distinct pathway through the pristine snow. The neat rows of decorated chairs are filled with dark suits interspersed with beautiful feathers and fur-like adornment. Several guests are still finding their seats despite the 1 p.m. ceremony. The string quartet is playing Bach and the soft sounds gently fill the air. The registrar lady keeps rearranging her documents and books upon the cloth-covered side table.

All morning, I kept myself busy on the sales yard, but very few people buy a spruce on Christmas Eve. I clock-watched all morning, my stomach churning while my head questioned why the universe would do this to me. I've had twenty-five years to experience a stomach flip and instead of the fairy tale being played out as Cupid clearly intended... the guy's getting married to someone else. Life isn't fair. And sadly, I've no other option than to accept fate's cruel ways.

I crane my neck to gain a better view of the front row to the right of the aisle. Two dark-haired men in tailored suits sit facing forward. I assume the best man is his brother; they look so alike from the back. I can't imagine what Luca's feeling right now. Nerves? Excitement? They don't turn about to view the settling guests. I suppose they've plenty of time to meet and greet after the ceremony.

The front row to the left of the aisle remains empty, presumably awaiting a row of colourful bridesmaids, clutching fresh bouquets.

My gaze returns to the groom. What should I do if part way through the ceremony, just as he begins his vows, he denounces his love for Isabella and confesses his undying love for the sales girl who sells Christmas trees? Oh, my God! I would die with embarrassment should he call me from my hiding place, take my hand

and... I look down at my jeans and jumper combo – what a bloody sight! I really must start taking more pride in my appearance.

'Turn around. Turn around,' I mutter, whilst staring at the nape of his neck. How come his sixth sense isn't so hot today? Does it only work when I don't want to be caught staring at him? *Bloody* typical. Obviously, wedding nerves have a direct effect upon telepathy.

What would I do if he did turn around? Wave? Smile? Or hide? Or lock eyes and hope that everything I feel is conveyed in a final look?

'What are you doing?'

I jump out of my skin as Kitty peers over my shoulder and whispers in my ear.

'Oh, nothing.'

'*Nothing?* Come on.'

'Don't tease,' I mutter, my eyes returning to the front row.

'Looks beautiful, doesn't it?'

I simply nod.

I don't want to be unkind – Kitty's always been good to me – but I'd much prefer to stand here alone and have my heart broken rather than have a witness endure my woeful tears once he utters, 'I do.'

'I just glimpsed the wedding party lining up to begin their procession. The bride looks amazing.'

Great! As if the blonde didn't look utterly amazing every day of her life, she'll look fabulously breathtaking on her big day. I check myself. I'm being so unfair. It isn't her fault that I met him after her, after an engagement, after two babies and after a wedding had been booked. That's the bottom line: simply bad timing, on my behalf. It's simple: you meet who you meet, when you meet them. And now, he has to forsake all others for her.

My heart grows heavy. I want to cry.

'Here they come,' whispers Kitty, pointing along the plush carpet to our right. Simultaneously, the string quartet switches from Bach to Pachelbel's 'Canon'. I don't wish to look at the bride, as beautiful as I'm sure she is. My eyes are fixed on her groom, who stands but doesn't stir to turn about. The guests stand and turn around to view the bridal procession.

Kitty's face is beaming at the approaching sight. I daren't look straight at the bride; my guilt will show on my face and she'll know, I'm sure. From the corner of my eye, I can see that she's dressed in a straight-fitting gown of white, carrying a huge bouquet in deep reds and emeralds, with a gathering of bridesmaids and pageboys sauntering behind. I'll recognise the two young boys from their grotto visit. Young Holly will surely look fabulous with her hair pinned up; her beaming teenage smile will say it all. I don't want to waste a moment looking at the bridal procession. My eyes are fixed on *him*. He must know she's nearing. In less than ten minutes, they'll be man and wife.

My stomach begins to flip. I want to be sick.

The bridal procession approaches us, turns and pauses to face the length of the aisle and... He's standing right before me! Luca literally walks into my line of vision from the right, walking at the bride's side, arms linked, dressed beautifully in a tailored suit.

His dark gaze catches mine, just for the briefest of exchanges, before he smiles, and turns to face the ceremony archway. That was risky. I blush.

Why break with tradition? I thought this wedding was planned to the minutest detail and yet the bride and groom walk the aisle together? Maybe fitting given the commitment of two children. They slowly walk towards the registrar, the elegant peacock-shaped train of her gown fanning out upon the red carpet. I stare at the front row – so, I'd been staring at the groom's men patiently waiting to support their buddy. No wonder they hadn't bothered to turn around and view the arriving guests.

'Doesn't she look amazing?' swoons Kitty, her hands clutched before her mouth in wonder. 'I love her flowing train.'

'Mmmm.' A gulp snags at my throat.

'What's wrong?'

'Nothing – the spicy smell of these firs has gone to the back of my throat,' I lie, unable to share my secret, not even with Kitty.

It takes him twenty-seven steps to reach the wedding pergola. The registrar greets them with a warm smile and a nod. The bridesmaids and pageboys file into the front row and take their places.

This will be an awkward manoeuvre as he now needs to be on her other side. Who messed up on planning this little detail? Will he step across her flowing train or walk around it to position himself on her right?

I can't take my eyes from his broad back. I know he shouldn't turn around, the entire wedding is watching, but if he could manage one last lingering moment between us... one last stomach flip... I promise, I'll let him go.

I watch as he releases her arm, takes her hand and raises it to his mouth, kisses it and gently releases.

He steps aside to the left and takes a seat. From the right the nearest groom's man offers a beaming smile as he takes a step nearer to the bride.

'What the hell?'

Kitty looks at me and then back at the couple standing before the decorated archway.

'What?' she asks.

'What's he doing?'

'Who?'

'Luca!'

'Duh, he's getting married.'

I stare at Kitty.

Confusion is bubbling behind her eyes.

'Yeah, Isabella and *Luca*... so what's he doing sitting down?' I babble.

'Nina, Luca's standing up... Luca's the groom.'

'Luca's the groom...' I repeat her words slowly as she watches me stare from the front row to the groom and back again. 'So, who's the guy that just sat down?'

'Her brother, I think.'

Her brother?

I want to be sick as my stomach begins to spin.

*

Holly

From the top table, I gaze across the marquee at the fabulous view before me, bedecked with candelabra and crystal droplet centrepieces. Seventy or more guests are seated at white linen tables, all here to celebrate one couple. This is the bee's knees. I thought the best part about being a bridesmaid would be having a posh frock and carrying fresh flowers but this, this is amazing. I keep glancing over to Isabella, but she's busy chatting with Luca or fussing over their sons. Once I'm shown to my seat, I quickly locate Alfie's table, number seven, which isn't too far from my position on the end of the top table, but far enough that we can't actually speak. Which might be a good thing, given how gorgeous he looks in his new suit. I watch as his tugs at his collar; he looks uncomfortable, like a trussed-up turkey. I know he didn't want to wear it, but his dad insisted that it was the right thing to do given the formality of the event. Their table of eight has an empty place setting; I assume that was for Angie – though Alfie said she wasn't attending. I feigned any knowledge of their tiff when Isabella asked me earlier. I'm not getting involved. Alfie and his dad seem fine just as they are.

Everywhere I look the garlands we made yesterday loop in soft curves; the deep red ribbons glint and shimmer in the light. I didn't imagine the marquee would look as beautiful as it does; maybe we could have this one day? One day...

My stomach flutters. Is this what Isabella feels for Luca? Or am I just feeling the beginnings of puppy love, as my mum calls it? Either way, it's not what I've felt before.

I look along the table, unsure of what I should be doing; everyone else is nibbling on bread and so I copy. My family are seated away from Alfie's on table three – we fill the table with eight bodies, some in chairs, others in high chairs.

Alfie catches my eye. I give a little wave. Am I supposed to be paying attention to others or just the bride? I'm under strict instruction from my mum to ignore Alfie until Isabella says I am free to enjoy myself, then I can dance with Alfie as much as I wish, as long as the wedding guest book is taken around on the hour, every hour to capture good luck messages.

I lean to the side as the young waiter collects my empty plate. It feels strange to have someone remove your empty plate from the dinner table. Within seconds another waiter appears and delivers a large oval plate, muttering, 'It's hot,' before walking off back to the mobile kitchens; on the plate sits a mound of beef and gravy. Is that it? I start to eat but notice no one else has picked up their cutlery. I stop. Do I continue or wait for someone else to join me? A large platter of potatoes appears at my ear, and a waitress offers me roast potatoes captured between a fork and large spoon. I ask for loads. Then loads of vegetables from the next waitress and, finally, more gravy.

I tuck in. What a feast!

That's when I see her.

*

Angie

'Excuse me, excuse me,' I whisper, sidestepping through the tables towards table number seven. I squeeze past each chair as the occupant pretends to move it forward an inch in a shuffle style, but they don't actually move. My stomach and thighs feel the edge of each chair as I make my way through the seated crowd. I dodge a waiter or two, and we do-si-do around each other before continuing.

I know where I'm heading. I studied the beautifully decorated calligraphy-written seating chart in the foyer of the marquee before making my entrance to the dining area. I don't want to cause a scene and avert anyone's attention to my late arrival.

I can see the rear of Nick's head as I near their table, Alfie is pulling at his collar and tie, just as I expected he would. Though his suit jacket fits perfectly. Fancy not taking it off as he sat down to eat, ensuring he is comfortable. Nick never gives the lad guidance, when it's necessary.

'I'm so sorry for my late arrival. I do believe this is *my* seat,' I say, calmly and casually, on finally arriving at table seven. A sea of startled faces look up from their roast beef and horseradish. Nick's mouth gapes. Alfie sighs deeply. The lady and three children simply stare and then she instantly produces a warm welcoming smile and the remaining male... My eyes lock onto his. Oh, my God! Never in a million years would I have imagined *that* face staring back at me.

'Angie!' says Nick.

'Mum!'

'Angie!' says Fabio.

'Angie?' asks the lady with the warm smile, which is rapidly dissolving into a quizzical stare. Her three little boys stare absently on hearing her startled tone.

'Hi, sorry I'm a little late,' is all I can muster as I quickly take my seat between Nick and the now scornful glare of the mother of three. I quickly attract the attention of the young waitress and explain my late arrival, trying to stall the three adults who are waiting to interrogate me, while my son ignores me. The three children sit nibbling at their fish-finger dinners.

'I didn't think you were coming?'

'Do you think this is fitting, Mum?'

'Angie? Is this *the* Angie?'

'Are you friends of the groom's side or the bride's?'

I don't answer any of them. Instead, I busy myself tearing open my wholemeal batch, locate the dish of perfect butter curls and slowly spread the thick creamy delight. If this is to be my afternoon from hell, I'll make sure I'm well fed and inebriated. Mid-mouthful, as they continue to stare, I reach for the white wine and pour myself a large glass. It would be rude not to under the circumstances.

'Eat up, now... your main courses are getting cold,' I say, as my heart rate continues to soar, while I calmly sip my wine. I hadn't bargained on this!

One by one they each collect their cutlery and resume eating.

This will be OK. I will be polite to each guest, rise above any accusations made by the wife and ignore any come-on from Fabio. In fact, Nick owes me an apology for his lack of support, before we continue our little tête-à-tête, so there'll be none too many pleasantries in his direction.

'Are you married?' asks Marcia, as her place-setting card informs me, as she leans around me to speak to Nick, who is struggling to communicate to Alfie to 'leave it'.

'No. Not now, but, yes, we were... once,' he replies, politely.

'Why... is that important?' I say, as the waitress delivers my hot plate. 'Thank you.'

Marcia stares, open-mouthed.

'You're Angie... the one that...' Marcia continues in Nick's direction. 'You know they had an affair, don't you?'

Alfie chokes on his dinner, grabs his napkin and blushes profusely.

Nick looks from me, to Fabio, and back to Marcia, whose warm and welcoming features are pinched and instantly pained.

'Angie?'

I give a nod.

'This is Fabio... the one I mentioned.'

Alfie is open-mouthed and staring, his fork suspended in his hand.

Wow, what a life lesson for a sixteen-year-old.

'Marcia?' interjects Fabio, trying to hush his wife's tones.

'Seriously, it's taken us five months to hold our marriage together and then, as brazen as you like, she pops up at your niece's wedding... Is this for real?'

I don't answer. I don't know who the question is aimed at but assume it isn't me.

'I can only apologise for—'

'Don't you dare, Nick. I was single, with no attachments, and as far as I was aware Fabio was single also, or that's what it said on his dating profile... so where did I mislead anyone? I didn't.' I turn to Marcia to continue. 'And the moment I knew he was married with a wife and three children I called it off... so please save your annoyance for him, not me. I was tricked as much as you were.' I feign an overly friendly tone, as not to upset the little ones as they munch their ketchup covered chips.

'Now, hang on a minute... I never said—' interrupts Fabio, his harsh whisper being killed with a death stare from Marcia.

'Would you like me to upload your current profile and show her?' I ask, bravely pulling my mobile from my handbag. 'Would you?'

Fabio sits back, his shoulders sag and his olive skin pales as his wife's pinched features turn into a venomous stare.

'Seriously, you can check out his current profile on SinglesFun.com,' I add, tucking my mobile back inside my clutch bag. 'Alfie, darling, could you pass me the gravy boat, please?'

I sit tall as Alfie looks to his father for instruction, before slowly offering the gravy boat across the table.

I keep my eyes glued to my plate and, for the first time ever at a wedding, pray that the speeches are lengthy with numerous hecklings from attending guests.

*

Nina

I stand alone in the darkness, staring out across the lake. The reflection of the night sky is picture perfect on the water: moonlight cascades upon the surface and a beautiful arc of untouched snow nestles in the distant backdrop.

The only disturbance is the muted tones of the wedding party a distance behind me, separated by a bank of spruce. I imagine the dance floor filled with elderly relatives, and little boys doing knee slides to ruin their trousers, having a great time amongst the celebration.

What would my dad say if he were here, now?

I watch the ripples skitter across the water and know that somewhere high above my head he is there, beyond the smoky clouds, watching me stand and stare across the lake. I'd prefer him to stand beside me, but I can accept a lengthier distance just knowing he is there.

Within seconds, my fat robin lands upon a nearby rock.

'I wondered where you were,' I whisper, as his tiny head bobs and twitches in my direction.

This is probably the closest he has ever landed to me. I'm tempted to reach out my hand. Inquisitive to see if he'd let me touch his deep red breast, but the fear of losing him restrains me.

I linger at the water's edge. Tonight, I'm not planning to skim stones but to honour dad's memory by doing the final job I need to do. As heartbreaking as it seems, alone in the dark, I know his anniversary is the right day.

I clasp the wooden box into my frame, my arms tightly wrapped around its polished edges. On Saturday, I'd spilt silent tears retrieving it from under the staircase at home, carefully packed it within my suitcase, and brought it along to the cabin. But now, I must say goodbye. Forever.

I gently remove the lid from the wooden box; the lip needs forcing before it gives and releases. A gentle billow of ash lifts, thanks to my heavy-handed jolt. Here, he'll be in heaven, surrounded by nature's beauty.

I haven't practised any lines. I don't know many prayers. I'm unsure of what I should say... only one memorised poem fills my mind.

Slowly, I recite the words.

'Do not stand at my grave and weep, I am not there, I do not sleep. I am a thousand winds that blow. I am the diamond glints on snow. I am the sunlight on ripened grain. I am the gentle autumn rain. When you awaken in the morning's hush, I am the swift uplifting rush of quiet birds in circled flight. I am the soft stars that shine at night. Do not stand at my grave and cry. I am not there... I did not die.'

I kiss the lip of the box before I kneel and gently upend the wooden casket, allowing the soft grey ash to slide onto the surface of the rippling water.

'You'll always be my diamond glints on snow,' I whisper.

Instantly, the tiny waves lift and separate the mass, slowly fanning the ripples of ash across the surface of the lake. I stand, replace the lid and watch as the watery cloud spreads further and further away from me.

*

'Nina!'

His voice brings me to, standing alone in the darkness at the edge of the lake, clasping the empty box. The grey watery cloud has disappeared, and so has my robin.

'I hope you're not contemplating a skinny dip at this time of year,' jokes the voice through the darkness. 'I won't be joining you if you do.'

I turn to see the silhouette of broad shoulders framed by the spruce trees as the moonlight illuminates his rhythmical stride.

Mr Stomach-flip?

He nears the water's edge, stands and stares out across the lake to the distant backdrop of firs. His presence portrays a significance and warmth that crackles in the air.

'Hi,' I mutter, unsure how long I've been standing here.

'I didn't mean to intrude but...' He peers at my features. 'Have you been crying?'

I don't answer; instead I clasp the wooden casket a little tighter to my body.

'Nina?' His voice is mellow yet firm. I can't ignore him.

'What's your name?'

'Bruno.'

Bruno? My mind repeats.

'Bruno Ferraro,' he adds, when I don't speak.

'I thought your surname was Romano,' I say, looking up into his surprised face.

'No, my brother-in-law is called Luca Romano... and today my sister became—'

'I get it,' I say, looking away across the water. What a fool. Luca Romano – wrong name, right bloke.

'Are you all right? I saw you earlier behind the spruce at the ceremony but haven't laid eyes on you since and —'

'I've had a free afternoon. I wasn't needed to staff your wedding... *their* wedding.'

'*Theirs*, not mine!'

'I saw the clipboard papers. I read the wedding details – you came on the visits with her and I thought... I thought you were the groom!' I blurt.

'Me, the groom? No way! Of course, I attended. He works away for weeks on end, she's my sister – I couldn't let her struggle with the two lads *and* plan a wedding alone, could I?'

'But I thought...'

'Well, you're quite mistaken,' he says, gently clasping my forearm and turning me towards him. 'Do you think I'd have returned several times to the farm... if I'd been about to get... if it wasn't to see *you*?'

'I thought you were just being kind, being a loyal son buying a Christmas tree or taking your lads to visit Santa.'

'My nephews, *actually*,' he corrects. 'And I was being kind to everyone, but mainly myself.'

'Nephews?'

He slowly nods. His body is close, almost touching but for the box clasped in my grasp.

'What's this?' He points to my hands.

'It's a long story... one I'd rather not explain, not tonight anyway.'

*

Angie

'What the hell did you expect me to do, stand up and walk out like a scarlet woman?' I ask, as my heels sink and snag upon the soft snowy ground. Darkness surrounds us, so I'm unware where I am heading.

'No, but have some bloody respect for the poor woman – she's pregnant, if you haven't noticed,' says Nick, hastily following me along the uneven pathway that leads from the marquee. I survived the formal reception by staying schtum but before long Nick requested a quiet word.

How the hell am I supposed to notice such details when Marcia is seated with a cloth napkin draped across her lap?

'To hell with the lot of you, I say. I try my best to rebuild what we had, you string me along thinking that we were on the mend, on the same page rekindling this relationship, and then bam! You let me down big time.' I gulp down the lump in my throat. 'Don't cry, don't cry' is the mantra circling my head.

'Angie, wait!'

I quicken my pace. If he wants to talk to me he'll have to catch me first. I kick it up a gear and stride quickly along the path, stumbling as I go, and come upon a large lake secluded from the marquee by mature spruce.

There's nowhere to run; the shoreline literally halts my stride. I have no idea if I'm standing on shale or mud, but stand I do, staring out across the water and taking a keen interest in the embankment on the far side – in which I have no real interest, but I know if I don't, I'll need to look at Nick. And looking at Nick right now is not an option. I am mad. I am sad and I am slightly drunk from two too many white wines, but even so I am not going to cry!

'Angie…' His voice is soft, tender and beside my ear. 'Please, just stop.'

I intensify my stare across the lake.

'We need to talk. I was as surprised about that fella as Alfie was… and the poor wife, well, what did you expect her to do, stand up and shake you warmly by the hand? She's five months pregnant, for crying out loud.'

I quickly calculate dates. Bastard!

We stand in silence. Nick staring at my profile, me studying the distant embankment, wondering how old the spruce might be.

'Are you not going to talk to me?' he finally asks.

I shrug. I know it's childish, but I want him to feel some of the frustration that I felt the other night. I spot a couple in the distance cuddling by the water's edge. Obviously happy, in love, sharing a moment together beneath the moonlight. When did we stop looking like them?

'OK, if that's what you want... there's nothing more to say. I asked for months if we could try again but you insisted it was no, we were over. I'd accepted that, Angie, honestly I had. I focused my attentions on Alfie and had accepted your decision. But when you phoned... ah, you don't know how happy that made me. These last few weeks have been great... as if we'd returned to the old us of our uni days when we actually—'

'So that's it, you're quitting?'

'*Quitting?* I have no choice if you're not going to communicate with me. I've left my teenage son sitting at a table watching over our drinks in order to follow you.'

I can hear the exasperation in his voice. Is this what I want? To call it quits and return to what I had a few weeks ago? No Nick? Very little contact with Alfie?

My stomach lurches. Is that hunger, my nerves or the alcohol?

'Angie... talk to me, please.'

I turn to face him. He looks tired beneath the gentle moonlight. His sad gaze searches my face, as if our answers are written upon my skin.

'Look, you chose to come back to me, Angie. You'll never know how happy that made me but now, this... this isn't what either of us want, is it?'

I shake my head.

My stomach lurches again.

That's it. He needs to know what I tried to explain to Alfie.

'Nick... do you remember the first time we met?'

He laughs.

'Of course, you were sitting on the grass enjoying the sunshine and I spotted you settled a few feet away and —'

'My stomach flipped,' I say, interrupting his memory. 'Not just a flutter or an excitement, but an almighty somersault reaction, which I'd never experienced before, and *that* moment, looking at you for the very first time, staring at me in the sunlight, I knew. I didn't know your name, where you came from... nothing, and yet instinctively I knew everything I needed to know.'

Nick smiles.

'It's that moment that brought me back to you, Nick. Remembering that one moment and knowing that no other man has ever stirred such a reaction in me... that's what brought me back to you.'

His hand reaches for my forearm and gently pulls me near.

'I can't pretend to have experienced that exact feeling, but I remember that moment as if it were yesterday.'

I need to be honest.

I lower my chin. I can't look at him as I deliver my next line.

'I lost track of that moment for many years, Nick. Somewhere between the school run and the grocery shops I forgot... until a few months ago when I realised

413

I'd lost the love of the only man that made my stomach flip.'

Tears spill over my lashes; my mantra hasn't worked.

'Oh, Angie.'

'I'm sorry... I took us for granted, and questioned what I was doing with my life and where I should be and what I was missing out on. When the reality was, I was always where I was meant to be, Nick, sharing my life with you.'

He pulls me close, so my forehead rests upon his chest; his arms wrap around my shoulders in a comforting hug as we stand in the moonlight.

As the tears flow I wonder if we look more like the couple in the distance.

*

Holly

'Holly, come on,' says Alfie, grabbing my hand and dragging me along as he runs ahead through the snow.

'What about your dad's drinks?'

'Forget that. He's been gone for thirty minutes – they are probably having a humdinger of a row somewhere in the car park. Now, hurry up.'

His fingers are tightly wrapped around mine. I can feel the urgency and excitement spilling from him into me like an electrical current.

'Where are we going?' I say, as he leads me away from the noisy marquee and its blaring DJ.

'I've got a key.'

'A key to what?'

'A cabin.'

'No!' I draw to a sudden halt, pulling him backwards, shocked that Alfie would be in possession of a key, but also that he'd masterminded such a plan, today of all days.

'How?'

Alfie taps the side of his nose.

'Secret.'

'Have you stolen it?'

He shakes his head.

'Bram lent it to me.'

'Bram?'

'Honestly he did… I didn't pinch it, if that's what you're thinking.'

'No, I'm just a little shocked, that's all.'

He pulls at my hand.

'So, are we standing here all night or do you want some privacy?'

We continue along the lake pathway towards the six log cabins.

'Be careful. I know Nina is staying in one of them. We'll be in trouble if she spots us.'

'I've got the key for number one. She's in the smallest one. Quick now.'

It feels wrong. Deceitful. Almost offensive, as we should be throwing some shapes on the dance floor at Isabella's wedding. But how fantastic to have a cabin to ourselves for a time. I haven't seen Alfie all day, given my role as bridesmaid. I thought we'd have had the opportunity to talk and have a laugh, but now as the night grows late, this is the first chance we've had to be together.

'This way.' Alfie leads the way up the wooden steps, fumbles at the lock and quickly pulls me through the large doorway. We don't wait to find the light switch; as soon as the door is closed we lean against it and make out. We can't get enough of each other, kissing, holding, touching, feeling. Our hands roam wildly over each other in a frantic manner, which would look quite comical if we could see each other's reaction.

'Do you want to move to the bed?' I ask, unsure if I should make the suggestion or not.

'Do you?' he replies. I can hear a quiver in his voice.

Yep, I really do.

'Did you bring…?' I whisper.

'Yeah.'

'Come on, then.' I begin to move into the room.

'Holly, are you sure…? You know you can say if—'

'Alfie. I'm sure.'

Fumbling in the dark, for fear of being caught, we tumble onto the double bed. His hands reach for the zip of my bridesmaid's dress as I tentatively loosen his belt buckle.

*

Nina

'Nina?'

I turn about from the wood burner, having stoked and fed the flames. Bruno stands in the doorway of the log cabin clasping two champagne glasses and a bottle.

'Hi.' My voice sounds weak.

'I found this going begging.' He indicates the bottle. 'I doubt anyone will miss it. Here.' He shuts the door with his foot and offers me the two glasses, while he uncorks the bottle.

I know what's happening. I can almost predict the conversation once we've drunk a glass or two.

'To us…' says Bruno, holding his glass aloft.

I repeat. I daren't not in case this warm fuzzy feeling that is gambolling around my stomach disappears for good and I am forced to return to reality.

The gentle glow of the fire radiates to light the cabin. I'm conscious that the single sofa is tiny, the other seats are hard-backed and the double bed, some ten feet away, would be a heavenly slumber if we'd known each other longer.

Bruno removes his suit jacket and settles upon the sofa, his long limbs spilling over the seat cushion.

'Come, sit,' he says, patting the sofa cushion beside him. 'I know it's the world's smallest sofa but there's room for two.'

I want to hold back, be coy until we get to know each other a little better, but why when being in his presence feels like the most natural thing in the world? In fact, do I trust myself, let alone him?

I sit down; twist around to face him, my glass resting on the back of the upholstery.

'How did you find me?' I ask, sipping my drink.

'I wondered where you'd escaped to... but a blonde waitress pointed me along the path towards the lake, when I asked after you.'

Good old Kitty, she was never far away from a good deed in helping others.

'A close friend?'

'Oh, yeah! She knows I go to the lake. It's my place...'

'To think?'

I nod, unsure how much I should say.

'I get that you're wary,' he says, his head lolling back and turning to face me. 'I don't blame you, especially if you thought that I was Luca and the whole bridal procession thing spooked you.'

I inhale. I will probably regret this moment forever but here goes.

'Have you ever met someone, a total stranger, and without them saying a word, you react as if by instinct...?'

'Like a stomach flip?' he asks.

'Oh, for a moment there I thought you were going to say something entirely different.'

His hand reaches to stroke my cheek.

'Nina, if you're feeling what I'm feeling, and I seriously hope you are... we've nothing to fear.'

I exhale. His words are like magic. Gone are the fears, the vulnerability, the scared child, the fearful woman. All that remains are two adults, with a mutual respect and, maybe, a future.

I stare up at him.

'Seriously, I came back to the farm on numerous occasions, purely to see you. My innards were jumping through hoops.'

'And my elf outfit... was it worth it?'

'The outfit maybe not... but the red underwear, *well*.'

'I had no choice. The boss sprang the job on me!'

'And now, do I get to talk to you about other things rather than Christmas trees?'

'Perhaps.'

I have nothing to be embarrassed about in admitting his effect upon me. I know he knows.

What if he rejects what I'm feeling? I don't know what I will do with myself. I don't know how to return to the woman of a few weeks ago, before I knew he existed in this world.

Bruno stares around the cabin; his eyes linger in the direction of the bed before his gaze returns to mine.

'Why are you staying here?'

It feels as if I've known him for a lifetime, like the twins, so I'm honest.

It takes me the next twenty minutes, another glass of champagne and some tissues to explain the last year. Throughout my explanation he nods, his eyes not leaving my features.

'And, the wooden box?'

'My dad's ashes.'

'Wow, what a task to undertake alone.'

I shrug.

His hand rises to gently stroke my cheek, as an eruption of tears cascades.

'I was mad at him for dying and leaving me on my own. I couldn't bring myself to scatter his ashes... I've kept them hoping we could continue to live how we'd always lived but...'

'Shhh now. Come here.'

His arms wrap around my shoulders, pulling me closer to his chest. Minutes pass as I listen to his heartbeat and wait for my tears to subside.

A lengthy silence follows.

'Given that it's Christmas, this cabin could do with some festive decoration,' says Bruno, resting his chin on my temple. 'Do you know anywhere near that we could buy a spruce from?'

With my head on his chest, I listen to his laugh from the inside – a deep rapturous sound full of life and vigour.

I jump up.

'Come on,' I say, pulling my coat back on. 'I have a plan.'

'Intriguing, but I forbid you to use a chainsaw having consumed two glasses of bubbly.'

*

Angie

'Where have you two been?' I ask angrily as the pair casually enter the marquee, holding hands. 'We've been looking everywhere for you.'

Alfie and Holly smirk before he answers, 'Walking by the lake, why?'

'Holly, your parents are ready to leave, so you need to say goodnight,' interrupts Nick, glancing from one to the other. All around us families are collecting their belongings and saying goodbyes to family and friends, promising to see them soon and to visit. The band are packing up and the DJ is dismantling his speaker set.

I watch as she quickly delivers Alfie a kiss, a hesitant glance occurs and she dashes off towards her family.

'Alfie?' I say as he tries to contain a smirk.

'Angie, leave it,' interrupts Nick, leading our son away from me.

'See you, Mum,' whispers Alfie, his smirk not masked.

'Alfie, your mum's coming home with us…' Nick's words linger as Alfie slowly turns to view my expression before turning away and sidestepping his father's arm. I hastily catch them up and link arms with Nick. It might not be the perfect day of memories I'd been hoping for, but my honesty beside the lake has paid off. Nick wants what I want… so tonight, we'll leave as a family and hope that with each new day, we'll attempt to unravel from the mess I began last January.

*

Nina

'Are you sure? It's hardly the largest Christmas tree I've ever seen,' says Bruno, standing back to inspect my choice.

'Three foot is a perfect size for the cabin,' I say. 'A Norway spruce with a beautiful traditional smell. Yes, in my opinion… it's perfect.' Despite my previous protests, this is what I want.

'Come on, then.' Bruno picks up the tiny tree, digs a tenner from his pocket before handing me the cash. 'As payment. I won't be accused of stealing.'

'We're not stealing. My boss always gifts each staff member a tree on Christmas Eve – I just didn't take him up on the offer earlier.'

'Even so,' says Bruno, marching from the sale yard back towards my cabin. 'Come on, slowcoach, we've got champagne to drink, which I borrowed from my sister's wedding.'

I trot after him, grabbing a bunch of mistletoe as I near the pallet.

*

'She looks a bit bare,' he says, viewing the tree positioned in the corner of the cabin as I pin mistletoe above the door.

'You won't find decorations at this time of night. The wreaths have sold out and...'

Bruno is up and out of the door, stomping down the wooden steps before I can finish my sentence.

He returns ten minutes later carrying his suit jacket in a bundle.

'Look what I've found,' he says, emptying his stash onto the floor before the wood burner.

I crouch down to watch him unbutton his jacket, revealing a pile of decorative robins.

'I unhooked them from the wedding garlands,' he explains, gently pinning the first fat robin onto a branch as I struggle to take in the effect his kindness has on me.

We pull the bedding from the mattress and make a comfortable nest upon the floor before the wood burner. From our position on the floor, a host of robins look down from their perches and offer comfort and calm. I wonder where my fat robin is, and hope he is settled in a warm nest amongst the Christmas trees.

'Come closer,' he whispers, raising his arm around my shoulder to draw me near. 'I really can't explain, but the minute I laid eyes on you I knew *this* was somewhere in our future.'

I don't interrupt him. Despite my original misunderstanding, I hoped that such an opportunity could occur and signal our beginning. There is a heartbeat between his words being said and his lips lowering towards mine. I simply raise my face to his, wrapping my arms around his back, and return his kiss.

*

'Nina.'

I jump as his voice awakens me. It takes just a second to recognise and remember where I am and in whose arms I'm lying. The wood burner has died, and our duvet nest upon the floor hasn't softened the wooden boards beneath my back, but I don't care because Bruno's face is before me.

'Hi,' I whisper as my mind floods with the memories of yesterday. 'Merry Christmas.'

His lips touch my forehead before he softly repeats the greeting.

'It's nearly morning... come on.' He pulls back our covers, allowing me to sit up before he can rise to his feet, pulling me up from the floor. Our clothes are creased; we put on shoes and smile inanely at each other. 'Quickly,' he says, reaching for my hand. His free hand grabs a woollen blanket as we dash from the cabin.

The glistening snow shines all around us. My feet can hardly keep up as his outstretched hand pulls me along, between the snow-sprinkled spruce and towards the lake. The woollen blanket billows and flies from his free hand, snagging and catching on nearby branches.

We arrive at the lake, where the blackened water is still and silent, a gentle mist gathering above the surface.

Today I feel different; for the first time I experience a true sense of calm.

Life seems to mimic a Christmas tree. It is nurtured, loved as it steadily grows, to be cut down when it's reached a most beautiful stage before it fades to brown, to be discarded and forgotten.

Bruno scours the area and walks a short distance away from the water's edge to the mature trees, beneath which sits little snow but a thick carpet of dried needles. He spreads the blanket upon the dry ground and settles his shoulders against the spruce's mature trunk, his legs outstretched and wide.

'Nina…' His hand beckons me, to sit between his thighs, my back resting against his torso, my head against his chest. I can hear his heart rate, steady and strong.

'What are we doing?' I ask as he pulls the edges of the blanket over our frame to cover our clothed bodies.

'*Shhhhh*, watch.'

I don't say another word, I simply watch. Before me a low spruce branch hangs in my line of vision, behind which the lake stretches wide, and beyond the far embankment the horizon slowly changes. Bruno's arms tighten about my body as a slither of light steadily grows with each minute. A gentle glow of orange colours the sunrise and a new day is born.

Epilogue

Nina

Saturday, 27th April 2019

Mr & Mrs M Pardoe
Request the pleasure of
Nina Salloway & Bruno Ferraro
at the marriage of their daughter
Kitty Louise
to
Mr Connor Austen
at Christmas Tree Farm, Baxterley village,
Warwickshire
on Saturday, 27th April 2019
at 2 p.m.
RSVP by 16 March 2019

The string quartet creates a beautiful ambience as Bach softly fills the air while the seated guests chatter.

'Nina, shall we?' Bruno gently takes my arm as we walk the length of the plush red carpet along the aisle towards our seats. I can't believe how beautiful the pink blossom covering the pergola looks in the spring sunshine amongst the emerald-green backdrop of the Christmas trees. This is perfect, just as Kitty wants. I swallow a knot of emotion that snags in my throat, knowing how delighted my dear friend will be. Tears are not welcome before the wedding ceremony.

Bruno waits while I settle myself, before taking his seat. Despite only four short months together, I know he's prepared for my happy wedding tears. He settles in his seat before taking my hand, and I watch as his long fingers interlock with mine. Much as our lives have interlocked over recent months. From Christmas Day, we've been inseparable.

'Nina.' I turn on receiving a small tap on my shoulder, to see Bram, suited and booted, sitting behind us.

'Oh, Bram, don't you scrub up well?' I giggle on seeing my friend. I smile a warm greeting to Selena, looking as elegant and polished as ever by his side, in a pale blue coat dress. Zach told me they've been getting serious of late, and I wish them well.

'Bruno,' says Bram, giving a sharp nod, instantly returned by Bruno.

'Abraham.'

The fellas are cautious around each other. They make an effort for my benefit but I doubt they will ever develop a fondness for each other. I feel an underlying vibe will always exist, in relation to the other. Maybe I shouldn't have been so honest, after all. I try to smooth the tension but, male egos being what they are, both are content with their polite interaction, nothing more. Zach is a different story. Bruno genuinely likes him, and frequently invites him to the cottage to watch the big match with a beer or two. Bruno turns to face the front, eyeing the pergola and registrar, while I scan the guests, seeking out my friends.

Zach walks the aisle alone, looking for a seat on our side.

'Zach!' I call and wave, to aid his task. A broad smile addresses his face as he settles at the end of our row beside Bruno.

'Nina,' says Zach, bending to give me a peck on the cheek. 'Bruno.' A swift handshake and back slap occurs between him and Bruno. A genuine gesture of friendship, which warms my heart.

'Haven't you brought a plus one?' I ask Zach, leaning about Bruno to speak.

'Shhhh! She's running a little late...' is his simple reply. I beam with delight. I know he's been seeing someone in recent weeks – I just hope she flipped his stomach, igniting his interest. Zach knows what he wants and is prepared to wait for her arrival.

'Oh, my God, I thought I was going to be late!' Shazza interrupts our conversation to squeeze in beside Zach.

Her left hand interlocks with his; Zach's smile reaches ear to ear.

'Shazza?' I say, trying to gain her attention. Her face is half obscured by a large tilted hat.

'Oh, Nina, you look lovely,' she coos, smiling at Bruno.

My eyes glisten as I mouth, 'Wow!' to Shazza.

'I know,' she silently mouths, her face beaming.

The string quartet switches music and the assembled guests stand to receive the bride. My eyes instantly fill with tears. I want to watch Kitty walk down the aisle, but my heightened emotions are going to get the better of me. I cling to Bruno's arm before turning to view Kitty's grand entrance.

She stands proud, her arm interlinked with her father's; her flowing white gown billows gently in the spring breeze, the backdrop of Christmas trees framing the image. Kitty's face is flushed beneath a white veil, her twinkling blue eyes fixed upon her groom-to-be at the top of the aisle. As she begins to walk, the image blurs and my tears steadily flow. Bruno hands me his pocket handkerchief.

*

Holly

'Ah,' escapes from my mouth as I grab Alfie's hand, and we watch Kitty begin her bridal walk along the aisle towards a smiling Connor. I can't believe that in the next ten minutes they'll be man and wife through the vows they pledge to each other.

How amazing is that?

Alfie squeezes my hand, as I frantically dab a tissue to my eyes, knowing that my mascara is running towards my chin. My first proper wedding attending as an invited guest and I cry like a baby. I hoped to portray the sophistication that Nina achieves on the arm of Bruno, but I fail miserably. Maybe that's what comes with maturity. I'm simply thrilled at the prospect of smiling brightly on the photographs given that my train-track braces were removed last week.

Life is slowly changing for the better. Right now Alfie and I are juggling GCSE study, with parents who constantly think we're up to no good behind their backs.

My parents are forever checking up on our relationship, asking if we're using protection and being careful. Ironic, given their recent baby news bomb. I wish they would stop worrying and be more like Nick and Angie. I suppose, like everything, only time will tell. I keep reminding my parents that Alfie makes my stomach flip and until that fades I don't wish to be with anyone else.

We bore the brunt of last Christmas as a duo. We've both made some good friends here at the farm, having been granted continued weekend work thanks to our honesty as regards the fire. We had much fun at New Year helping to distribute the Presents for Heaven donations. Alfie's mum managed to organise a huge trailer truck and driver from her boss at ASAP Parcel Delivery to assist with the project. Boss Fielding is hoping she'll repeat the offer this year, when the scheme is marketed throughout the Christmas season. Demi has finally forgiven me for naming her, but the mean girls are less forgiving – they continue to hamper my final school days. But what do I care? I'm happy with my lot and enjoying my time with Alfie. Come September we'll all go our separate ways based on our GCSE grades – I doubt I'll see the mean girls after that.

Kitty gently glides along the aisle, the jewelled detailing at her waist twinkling in the sunlight as the flowing skirt flicks forward with each step, passing our standing position, and automatically we turn to face the front, where Connor awaits her arrival.

*

Angie

I pull into the farm's car park and wait amidst the darkness of their sales yard. It looks empty and bare compared to our last visit when every inch was covered in heavy snow, pallets of emerald spruce and holly wreath sales. We sit back and wait, our eyes searching the darkness for the outline of two teenagers, no doubt intoxicated but pretending not to be.

'I hope they're on time as they promised, unlike the night of Isabella's wedding when they snuck off for some alone time,' I say.

'For teenage kicks.' Nick laughs from the passenger seat.

I chuckle. Who'd have thought we'd happily be playing taxi to the young ones, ensuring Holly arrives home safely before midnight? We're doing what we can, with Holly's mum expecting again; Holly's teenage life has been turned upside down at the prospect of a boy.

'So much has changed, hasn't it?' I say, reaching for Nick's hand.

'Certainly has, Angie – I couldn't imagine where we'd be if you hadn't called last Christmas asking for a date night.'

'I didn't ask… I suggested,' I correct him, though in my head the rerun stills sounds like a beg amidst his silent pondering.

Nick's right. My rental apartment is a distant memory. My belongings were returned to our family home by mid-February – I jumped at Nick's suggestion after we'd enjoyed such a fabulous family Christmas. Isabella's wedding didn't produce the picture-perfect memories I'd hoped for, thanks to Fabio and co.'s surprise appearance, but it certainly brought us Woodwards back together. Not as the old Angie and Nick but as the new improved version of who we once were – our divorce really was a blessing as regards our renewed relationship.

'Alfie's adjusted well, given his initial reaction,' I say.

'I think so. It'll take time but he's more accepting of the situation than he was.'

'Mmmm, I'm glad... for all our sakes,' I mutter, unsure how I'd have coped if he hadn't mellowed. 'Did I tell you that Jilly from work reckons her daughter's been working here for years and yet I never knew?'

'*Seriously?*'

'The girl with the freckles and mousy-brown hair, the helpful one who's always present when we visit each year... you know the one.'

'She's hardly a girl, Angie,' he says, adding, 'She's as strong as an ox.'

'I know. Well, Jilly's been in touch asking her if they can meet up... reconnect, as such.'

I suggested she takes it slowly and leaves the decisions up to her daughter. Our Alfie has taught me as much this year: he's no longer a child; he has his own mind. I have to respect his decisions from here on, which is much like Jilly and her Nina.

'Here they are.' Nick points into the distance as two shadowy figures loom through the nearest gate and cross the yard.

The car's rear door opens wide.

'Hi, Dad, Mum,' calls Alfie as he bounces along the back seat.

'Hi,' calls Holly, following suit and slamming the rear door.

'Have you had a nice day?' I ask, eager for wedding details.

'Great. The party is still in full swing but we're ready to go. It's been a long and tiring day,' explains Alfie, tugging at his seat belt.

'That's weddings for you.' I laugh.

'Though the effects can last a lifetime,' adds Nick, giving my hand a gentle squeeze before releasing it.

*

Nina

'Are you happy?' ask Bram as he gently leads me about the dance floor amidst coloured lights and the blare from the DJ.

'Do I look happy?' I ask, unable to comprehend his question knowing that Selena is watching us as she politely dances with Bruno a short distance away.

Bram leans back, observes my face and nods.

'Actually yes, you light up at the sight of that guy, which is why I bloody despise him.' Bram laughs.

'Ah, Bram... I can't help it – the heart wants what the heart wants.'

'Excuse me, may I?'

I turn to see Zach standing tall, tapping Bram on the shoulder.

'Seriously, little bro... you've come to interrupt us?'

'I have. I believe Selena would like a dance. As polite as Bruno is... she's not happy.'

We three sneak a peek towards Selena and my Bruno. He looks reasonably content; she is staring in our direction.

'Whoops, you're in someone's bad books,' I jibe, releasing Bram and switching my stance towards Zach.

'Selena, baby...' Bram hastily leaves to reclaim her smiles.

'So, how are we?' asks Zach as we move around the floor, bumping into other couples as we go.

'Fine, all fine.'

He gives me a knowing look.

'What?'

'I know you better than that,' he says. 'You're over the bloody moon to be with him, admit it.'

I blush, grateful that the coloured lights will hide my complexion.

'Is it that obvious?'

'Nina, anyone with eyes in their bloody head can see how loved up you are... but, hey, you deserve it. I wouldn't wish you anything but the best.'

'Oh, Zach!' I can't speak for the lump at my throat. I swallow frantically, until I'm able to speak. 'And you?'

He looks across to Shazza, who is busy chattering away to Jackie at the far end.

'Shazza's fun, she's endearing... and, yeah, we're taking it slow, but I'm happy.'

I nod; that is good to hear.

'Excuse me.' I don't need to turn about to know who this interruption is. Zach releases me without question into Bruno's strong arms. 'Thank you, Zach.'

'Ah, Selena gave you up freely, did she?' I jibe as I nestle into his chest.

'Something like that, or I could say she lost interest when she saw that my young lady was dancing with her fella. I couldn't abide the pouting, so I made my excuses,' he explains. 'Anyway, let's take a quick walk.'

He grabs my hand and hastily leads me from the dance floor, the elaborate marquee and out into the moonlight along the gravel path towards the lake.

*

I can feel my kitten heels squelching into the softened ground as we near the lapping water. My body finally comes to a standstill, having been half dragged in a running-cum-pacey-walking speed, thanks to Bruno's extended hand.

I stare out across the dark waters, where a cascade of moonlight dances upon the gentle ripples. Right here, right now feels special, as if he has something planned or something to say. I stare across the water towards the far embankment where the Fraser firs grow, suddenly too nervous to look at Bruno, to witness his expression for fear of misreading the moment, misreading his expression and being, well, disappointed and ruining what is a beautiful night.

Bruno says nothing. Glancing to my left, I can see he is also staring out across the dark lake, though why he's suddenly interested in the embankment of Fraser firs escapes me.

'When you were little did you ever make decisions based on outcomes?' he asks, suddenly peering down at me.

'Er, yeah.'

'Such as?'

'Such as if I managed to walk to the shop and back without losing count of my steps I would...' I stop as he laughs.

'Counting steps?'

'Hey, don't laugh.'

'Sorry, forgive me... anything else?'

I stare up at him. His olive skin looks darker, suggesting a brooding expression to his warm features.

'You?' I ask, unsure that I want to revisit my childhood and possibly misplace the current moment.

'I used to tell myself that if I scored a goal at football I could spend my pocket money on more trainers, or accessories for my bike.'

Boys are weird, if that's their equivalent to buying chocolate.

'So, here goes.'

I watch as Bruno bends, picks up a flat stone from the water's edge and skims it across the lake.

'One, two, three, four and five,' he mutters, counting each bounce. He shakes his head as the stone sinks beneath the lake.

'Is that the best you can do?' I ask, pulling a bemused face.

'Oh, is that a challenge? Are you some sort of expert, then?'

'Stand back… I'll show you how it's done.' I walk about the edge and search for my perfect stone. It feels smooth to the touch, flattish on both sides with a slight rise and depth towards one edge. *This* will fly.

I near the water's edge, stand side on and roll my shoulder. Bruno watches my every move.

'What are you going for?' he asks, breaking the silence.

A six? Go for it, girl.

'Maybe a six,' I say, nonchalantly raising my arm to launch my stone.

Bruno nods in a knowing manner.

I lower my arm.

'What?'

'Nothing.'

'No. What's with the nod.'

'Well, as I said… if the outcome's right I'll continue with my plan. Please carry on.'

'Your plan?'

Bruno looks out across the lake and nods towards the water.

'Please… continue.'

I watch him, carefully. What's going on?

'Seriously, go ahead,' he says, his eyes cast upon the water.

I raise my arm, sweep back and… throw sidewards.

One.

Two.

Three.

Four.

Five.

Six.

And seven.

I jump for joy, my excitement clearly apparent.

Bruno is silent behind me.

I turn from the water's edge and freeze.

In the darkness, at the water's edge, he is down on bended knee – one hand outstretched, his palm open and raised.

'Now, seriously, Nina, if you skim this rock in the same manner as that one – I will make you enter the lake and retrieve it... you understand?'

I can't speak. My eyes are fixed upon the tiny square box sitting in his open palm.

'Nina Salloway... with *this* rock, will you marry me?'

I'm sure my yell of 'yes' is heard clearly across fifty-five acres of Christmas Tree Farm. Within seconds I am jumping up and down on the spot like a child who's successfully skimmed her stone across the farm's tranquil lake.

We stand at the water's edge as Bruno gently pushes the diamond solitaire onto my third finger left hand.

'Bruno.'

'Mmmm.'

'What was your outcome plan? Did I have to achieve six bounces to secure a proposal?'

He slowly shakes his head and smiles.

'No. You just had to be the girl brave enough to act and respond to a stranger flipping your stomach… Following your instinct and being brave in life, even if it fails, is good enough for me.'

As Bruno's gentle kiss finds my upturned mouth, my tears overspill my lashes, and my stomach flips.

High above the lake, perching on a Blue spruce bough, sits a fat robin redbreast, its head twitching and its inquisitive beady eye watching the proceedings below, taking in the magic of Christmas Tree Farm.

Do Not Stand at My Grave and Weep

Do not stand at my grave and weep.
I am not there, I do not sleep.
I am a thousand winds that blow.
I am the diamond glints on snow.
I am the sunlight on ripened grain.
I am the gentle autumn rain.
When you awaken in the morning's hush
I am the swift uplifting rush
Of quiet birds in circled flight.
I am the soft stars that shine at night.
Do not stand at my grave and cry.
I am not there; I did not die.

Mary Elizabeth Frye

Acknowledgements

Thank you to Sarah Ritherdon and her team for working their magic on my manuscript. Without their dedication, my story would remain untold and unloved as a document upon a shelf.

Unreserved thanks to David Headley and his dedicated team at D H H Literary Agency – I couldn't ask for a more experienced and professional team to support my career.

Thank you to my writing friends within the Romantic Novelists' Association. You continue to be a great support and a wealth of laughter at every party and conference – I promise to repay the generosity and kindness received in recent years.

The Salloway family – thank you for the love and fond memories of happy visits, which we both treasure. Every year, Mary always had the most beautiful Christmas tree decorated with love – bless her x

Kathryn 'Kitty' Patrickson, Jackie Glendinning, Sharon Walker, Rebecca Hibbins, Steve Klym, Sean Phillips and Bexy Read from The George Eliot School – you guys have made my daily juggle of the day-job and the dream so much easier. I wanted to thank you in the only way I know how... forever in a book. P.S. Steve Klym, the year 11 pupils told me the 'drawing pin' joke.

Tim and Debbie Woodward, Graham Vann-Turner and Pid Pardoe – for your support and dedicated friendship to Lush. He deserves top quality friends given that his wife is often AWOL in Narnia. To all at Warwickshire Fire and Rescue who have followed my progress and purchased my books – it's been my pleasure to sign each and every book.

Thank you to the 'Polesworth Posse' for instantly answering my questions via social media regards 'stera', 'crashing ciggies' and reminding me of days gone by.

A large skinny mocha without sprinkles 'thank you' to the baristas at Costa Coffee in Atherstone for allowing me to linger at the corner table while I edited this book. Smiles, happy chatter and great service ensured that I returned each day.

To the 'Hollys' of this world, ignore the 'mean girls' – their unsavoury treatment towards others only moulds us into strong women from an early age. To the 'Ninas', may you experience your stomach flip and never settle for anything less. To the 'Angies', never doubt how precious that single moment was!

Robin redbreast – whether it be a coincidence, an urban myth or a sign of my faith, I really don't mind, but I'll provide the mealworms if you continue to appear and delight.

Mum, I think it can be safely said that I've finally converted you from a strict diet of autobiographies and memoirs into the realms of fiction, given that you've read my other books in a single day!

Heartfelt thanks to my husband, Leo, for your unwavering belief since day one that 'one day' would happen. Apologies for my constant stream of nonsense author questions regarding suitable names, haircuts and firefighting – I'll leave you in peace until my next novel idea takes flight.

And finally, to my wonderful readers... you continue to thrill me each day with your fabulous reviews and supportive emails. I am truly humbled that you make time in your busy lives to read my books.

Postscript: to Multiple Sclerosis, you stood in the corner and watched *our* struggle before leaving with my dad – thankfully, I'd collected a childhood full of memories. I'm still picking up the pieces :(*but* now, you are no longer a secret :)

HELLO FROM ARIA

We hope you enjoyed this book! Let us know, we'd love to hear from you.

We are Aria, a dynamic digital-first fiction imprint from award-winning independent publishers Head of Zeus. At heart, we're avid readers committed to publishing exactly the kind of books we love to read — from romance and sagas to crime, thrillers and historical adventures. Visit us online and discover a community of like-minded fiction fans!

We're also on the look out for tomorrow's superstar authors. So, if you're a budding writer looking for a publisher, we'd love to hear from you. You can submit your book online at ariafiction.com/we-want-read-your-book

You can find us at:
Email: aria@headofzeus.com
Website: www.ariafiction.com
Submissions: www.ariafiction.com/we-want-read-your-book
Facebook: @ariafiction
Twitter: @Aria_Fiction
Instagram: @ariafiction

Made in United States
Orlando, FL
09 October 2022

23179321R00246